Linda MacDonald was born and brought up in Cockermouth, Cumbria. She was educated at the local grammar school and later at Goldsmiths', University of London where she studied for a BA in psychology and then a PGCE in biology and science. She taught in a secondary school in Croydon for eleven years before taking some time out to write and paint. In 1990 she returned to teaching at a sixth form college in south-east London where she taught psychology. For over twenty-five years she was also a visiting tutor in the psychology department at Goldsmiths'. Linda lives in Beckenham and has now given up teaching to focus fully on writing.

Her first three published novels *Meeting Lydia, A Meeting of a Different Kind* and *The Alone Alternative* can all be read independently although together, they form a trilogy. *The Man in the Needlecord Jacket* continues the series but also stands alone in its own right.

BY THE SAME AUTHOR

Meeting Lydia

A Meeting of a Different Kind

The Alone Alternative

The Man in the
Needlecord Jacket

Linda MacDonald

Matador
9 Priory Business Park,
Wistow Road, Kibworth Beauchamp,
Leicestershire. LE8 0RX
Tel: 0116 279 2299
Email: books@troubador.co.uk
Web: www.troubador.co.uk/matador
Twitter: @matadorbooks

ISBN 978 1788037 112

British Library Cataloguing in Publication Data.
A catalogue record for this book is available from the British Library.

Printed and bound in the UK by TJ International, Padstow, Cornwall
Typeset in 10.5pt Aldine401 BT by Troubador Publishing Ltd, Leicester, UK

Matador is an imprint of Troubador Publishing Ltd

To
David and Lindsey
Andrew and Denise

Acknowledgements

When I completed *The Alone Alternative*, I believed I had finished with Marianne, Edward, their families and their lives. I thought it was all done and dusted. But then one of the characters stirred. She said, 'I'm not done yet. You haven't told my story. I want to be heard.' And at first I took no notice, but then it was as if she told me that she could be part of a new plot as well as the old one, with two new characters, one of whom also wanted to have a voice. Eventually I listened and *The Man in the Needlecord Jacket* is the result.

I should like to thank the following people: Lindsey MacDonald for her comments on the first draft; Brian Hurn for early editorial work and enduring support; Pat Hewitson and Heather MacQuarrie, my Beta readers, for their key plot advice, and Kit Domino for her painstaking editing. This time I have worked with a different team at Troubador, all of whom have been most helpful and efficient. In particular, special thanks are due to Chelsea Taylor, who has managed the production.

I would like to give a mention and thanks to the hidden faces on Twitter who have become fans of Lydia and who have taken the time to write reviews, offer encouragement and spread the word.

Prologue

July 2013

Sarah's Story

In early December last year, my life took an ominous turn. It was a time of grey skies and drizzle-filled days and when Coll came over to my place for a midweek supper. I had finished decorating the small Christmas tree, tidied leftover tinsel and trinkets into a carrier bag and was sitting at my dining table putting stamps on my cards ready for posting. He arrived with a local Exeter paper in his hand and he waved it at me with a flourish before plonking it down in front of me, scattering my neat pile of cards.

No *hello* or *how are you?* I could tell he was on one of his missions. I would have to listen before I spoke, and then perhaps feign enthusiasm for yet another wild scheme which would take a good half hour in the telling. His eyes were excited and there was a smear of green paint on the back of his left hand. It's interesting how one remembers trivial details surrounding major events.

He said, 'I want to find an outlet for my paintings and try to seize some of the Christmas present-buying market. There's a new restaurant opened this side of Pinhoe. I might ask there, if someone hasn't already beaten me to it. Look, it says "locally sourced produce".' And he jabbed a finger on the advert in question, demanding my scrutiny. 'The clientele might appreciate local art too. Can't get much more local than me. I'll go and have a meal there on Friday and see what it's like.'

I noticed he said '*I'll* go and have a meal.' Not '*we.*' He saw my narrowed eyes.

'You won't want to be hanging around while I talk pictures,' he said.

It would have been nice to have been asked. He was always inclined to do what he wanted without considering my feelings. A man of impulses. Highly annoying but also part of the attraction because when the impulses included me – which they did often at the start of our relationship – life was sublime.

'Good idea,' I said. I thought it was. I had no inkling that it was going to be the worst idea in the world.

Part 1
Coll

The Man in the Needlecord Jacket

Felicity – Early December 2012

My new restaurant has barely been open a week when I am hovering near the entrance lobby and a table for one is requested by an attractive middle-aged man. I assume he is on business, but as we are outside the centre of Exeter on the edge of a small village, this is unusual. Also, he is clad like a rock-star in faded denim and a dark grey needlecord jacket. Not the favoured garb of my clientele who are usually besuited or, that most broadly interpreted of phrases, smart-casual.

I show him to a small table by the window and give him a menu. He requests a glass of house white in a voice of liquid gold. In my mind, I begin to elaborate on the details as I do with many of my customers. It helps me to remember them in the future and so give them a more personalised service. He sounds as if he was privately educated, with perhaps an echo of Irish. I have a good ear for accents. Waitress Kylie takes his food order, fluttering a little in response to a comment.

As I flit back and forth in my front of house role, I can't help but sneak a look or two in his direction. I notice his iron grey hair and imagine that once it might have been a shiny black curtain sweeping his shoulders while he postured on stage with an electric guitar, adored by the young girls dancing, writhing, pouting and hoping to be lured backstage. He is lean. I like lean. Ted is lean.

An hour or so later, when he asks me for the bill, he says, 'I wonder if I might speak to the owner of this establishment?'

And he fixes me with an appreciative stare that acknowledges my existence and at once draws me in.

'You're speaking to her.' I am alarmed, thinking he may be a health and safety inspector in disguise. Or one of those most dreaded of customers, a food critic. I remember his menu choices and am relieved he picked two of our finest: the seared scallops with the pancetta, black pudding and cauliflower purée, and my signature dish, Mediterranean fish with tomato and prawn sauce. He didn't have dessert – which might explain his physique.

'Oh.' He lifts both eyebrows above cool grey eyes that complement his hair. I scan his face more closely and estimate his age at early fifties, a few years younger than me. He has good bone structure and a sexy mouth. I am aware of my brain processing finer points beyond those of most new customers.

'Is something not to your satisfaction?'

'On the contrary. Food's first rate. But I was wondering if you'd thought about hanging original paintings on the walls? I don't mean to sound critical, but they are crying out for some colour. I'm sure you have a plan. I know you have recently moved in.' He pauses and scans the room. A twinkle creeps into his eyes. 'I was thinking paintings by local artists. For sale, perhaps.' And he cocks his head slightly and gives me a big dazzling smile, displaying very slightly uneven teeth.

I glance momentarily at the three small prints on the wall of Canaletto's Venice. They are a temporary measure. It does look bare. There is a lot of white space that I intend to fill, but have not yet had time. I have been caught out in my haste to get the show running and address any problems before the Christmas rush. I can guess where this is leading.

'Do you have a local artist in mind?' I say, blank faced, but with a hint of tease. 'I have thought about it. But we've only been open a week. It's newly painted.'

'Merely a thought.' He doesn't push. He pays in cash, adds a generous tip, and then begins to walk away. I was expecting more; some salesman patter. I want to drag him back. I am curious. And then when he gets to the door, he turns and raises his arm, pointing to his temple like Columbo, as if he's thought of something.

'Perhaps I might return sometime to show you my work.'

I wonder if this strategy was planned. It has the look of a well-rehearsed manoeuvre; the cunning ploy of a fly on a hook, a fisherman's tactic to tempt a hungry trout from the shadows. In this instance, I bite immediately and he doesn't even have to reel me in. I suggest the following day which is Saturday. 'And come in the morning when I'll be able to give you my full attention.'

'Full attention.' He savours the words flirtatiously. 'That sounds a very pleasant prospect.'

We arrange a time. I forget to ask his name. Nor has he asked mine.

2

Coll

Sarah – Early December, 2012

My name is Sarah Bell. I'm fifty-one and I was widowed young when my husband of two years, Pete, foolishly followed a complete stranger's West Highland terrier onto a river of ice. We were in Scotland for Hogmanay, staying with his relatives near Loch Lomond. The ice cracked. The dog managed to get out, my husband didn't. It often happens that way. Those with heroic tendencies need to be reminded.

Pete and I were still very much in love at the time and I put him on a pedestal of wonderfulness that any other man would have found impossible to match. Afterwards, I led a lonely life, cautious about the notion of re-marrying; cautious about any relationship in case one thing led to another and opened the possibility of such a devastating loss happening again. I sometimes went out with men to please my friends and family. I wasn't short of offers. But all the time I was guarded. I built a wall around my heart and it stayed intact for nearly fourteen years, until I met Coll.

Coll is a thrill-seeker like Pete was, always hunting for the next rush of blood. But for Pete it was through outdoorsy things like rock-climbing and abseiling – and chasing dogs onto frozen ponds – whereas Coll pursues danger regarding matters of the heart. I must be drawn to the type. I should've stuck with my own kind: introverted-librarian. But then I would have missed all the fun.

At a rough guess it must be nine or ten years that we've been what you might call *lovers*. (I find it embarrassing to write such a word, even though I'm no prude.) In many ways, we are quite settled. We don't live together, but usually spend weekends at my house because I have more space, and then a midweek supper, also at mine because he says I can cook better than him. We plan ahead and are going to Venice during the Whit half term next year. We have even discussed combining resources and buying a property together in a nearby country village, or by the coast, perhaps in a couple of years when he intends to take early retirement. In the eyes of most of the people I know, we are a couple.

Coll has decided to go part-time from next September and is keen to pursue possibilities for some added income, hence the restaurant and the paintings. His longer-term goal is to develop his art such that when he retires, he'll have both an interest and a supplement to his pension.

He's named after the Scottish island, not Colin. That should be a clue as to the type of person he is: out of the ordinary; not run of the mill. I think his parents were eccentric arty-musicy types. They died before he met me. He doesn't talk about them much. When I ask him what they were like, he is dismissive and changes the subject. He is a former public school boy with a BA and MA in art, and a PGCE. My mum would have called him posh. Not that she was common, but after my dad died when I was thirteen, we struggled financially and lived simply in a small house on the outskirts of Manchester. I picked up quite an accent, but it's mellowed since I've lived all my adult life in Devon. If Coll and I had met as teenagers or even in our twenties, I would definitely have said he was out of my league. But age is a great leveller and he's been teaching at the local comp for long enough to have the edge knocked off his own accent and his upper-middle class attitudes.

When I told my best friend Laura – who works with me in the library at the University of Devon – that I wondered if I was good enough for him, she said, 'Sarah, what is it with you and your insecurity? You are one of the nicest people in the world. You're a saint. He's a lucky man.'

Laura is forty-three with a doting husband, two children and so far trouble-free parents. She reminds me of one of those capable women from a middle class TV drama who seem to be able to juggle a job with cooking, shopping, children, sex, painted nails and ever-changing hairstyles.

'I don't know how you put up with him,' says Laura, often, usually accompanied by a despairing shake of the head as I make excuses.

My doubts about not being good enough largely sprang from him having been married to a woman called Penelope who was most definitely posh: a Sloane Ranger of the eighties. In photos she looks like a gazelle – all legs and elegance, the opposite of me. She never had a proper job as far as I could tell, but lived off mummy and daddy until Coll came along. He referred to her as a vulture who had picked over the bones of their divorce until there was nothing left. She took with her more than a fair share of his money. He said she was unreasonable, but now I know him like I do, it could well have been that he was the unreasonable one. If he treated her the way he treats me, I don't blame her.

3

Exile

Felicity

In the haste of telling you about the visit of the man in the needlecord jacket, I was in such a fluster I forgot to tell you about me. Probably because it is the most man-excitement I have had in several weeks and it has fuddled my mind. Or maybe I am nervous of your reaction. If you get to know me better first, then perhaps you will be more forgiving. But I don't want to mislead you, so I am going to take a chance that you're not the judgemental type and will reserve opinion until you have all the facts at your disposal. I don't expect sympathy, but none of us is perfect and I would appreciate at least an attempt to see my viewpoint.

You see, I am that most vilified of creatures: the woman who betrayed her husband, the woman who left her children, a woman to scorn. If you've come across me before, I may not be your favourite person, although those of you who are skilled in seeing both sides and are generous of spirit may understand why I did what I did.

I was Edward Harvey's wife: a mother, restaurant owner, chef, allotmenteer, keeper of bees, hens, goats and sheep and much respected in my local village of Broadclyst in Devon. I am now Felicity Mayfield-Harvey, having attached my maiden name, and I have fallen from grace. I am not yet officially divorced, but proceedings are underway. I was married for thirty-odd years, but now I am an outcast of the family group, wandering the periphery like the meerkat who misbehaves, snatching moments of solace with those whom I love, and then scuttling off into the night to hide in my flat, often alone and mostly sad.

It sounds bonkers when I say it now, but I ran off to Italy with Gianni, my Italian chef. He was ten years younger than me. You wouldn't even blink at the age difference if I were a man, but for a woman, the younger man syndrome prompts questions about morality, sexuality – and sanity. It was mid 2011 when I left – only one and a half years ago – and I was fifty-four. My friend Olivia said, 'Darling, have you lost your mind? It won't last. What happens in a few years when you're through menopause, disinterested in sex, past your prime, sagging?' She isn't the most diplomatic of women.

'Botox,' I said feebly. 'Fillers, implants.'

'But you don't approve of those.'

I said, 'I'm technically past my prime now. And he says he likes mature women.'

'Women in the plural?' Olivia said. 'You don't want a womaniser at your age. And have you considered that he may be after your money?'

Since my mother died, some ten years ago, I've been pretty well-off. She left me almost a million. It sounds a lot, but once you start investing in property, it soon disappears. That's how I came to start up the first restaurant in Broadclyst. The Retreat. It was something I'd always wanted to do. Gianni had the flat upstairs, but it wasn't until my husband started working in London and only coming home at weekends that the affair started. I used to visit Gianni to discuss the week's menus. After a while it became more than that.

I told Olivia. She was the only one who knew. I had to tell someone.

I said, 'Gianni has reignited my interest in sex. I thought it was lost forever. I'm getting older. Who knows how much longer I will feel like this? I'm lonely when Ted's away and when he's home, we don't get on as well as we used to do.'

Olivia already knew about the tension between me and Ted, but she didn't approve of this turn of events with Gianni so I spared her further details. Her husband had been unfaithful and left her for another woman. She was never going to be on my side regarding this delicate question of fidelity.

When Ted was away, it was easy, but when he came back to work in his former job at the university in Exeter, it was more difficult to cover the tracks. When Gianni said his parents wanted to sell their little bistro in Siena, how about it? I took a chance. My marriage had been breaking down for several years, my children were growing up and leaving home, so at the time it felt like I had little to lose. As it happened, moneywise, Olivia wasn't far wrong. But that's for later.

Off I went with my handsome beau to live the Mediterranean idyll. But it didn't turn out quite the way I expected. I left my Italian dream after little more than a year and returned home to Broadclyst a few months ago, crestfallen, apologetic and hopeful of forgiveness. My illusions had been shattered and I was prepared to make an effort to repair my marriage; to try to rekindle the flame that had once burned so brightly.

Husband Ted is a head-in-the-clouds academic archaeologist, and I presumed he would have been up to his elbows in artefacts and research papers and hardly notice my absence. But the warm welcome I expected on return did not happen. Dear Ted was swanning around in the Isles of Scilly and, I discovered later, he was swanning with his new love, Marianne.

When Ted returned from the islands to be told by our daughter Harriet at Exeter airport of the news of my reappearance, he hastily despatched Marianne to a local B&B overnight and then back to London the following day. He doesn't realise I know this, but Broadclyst has a strong village community where news travels and there were several people who were delighted to tell me of the shenanigans behind my back. Retrospectively, I rather relished the thought of Marianne's discomfiture at hearing I was home, with every intention of staying. I also enjoyed hearing from Harriet of the contretemps in the village shop when Olivia put Marianne in her place and told her she would never match up to yours truly.

Ted found me surrounded by suitcases at the house and greeted me with thinly disguised horror. I was much more magnanimous when I later heard of his taking of a mistress. But I suppose he was well within his rights to be more than a tad miffed after my defection. He thought my reappearance was only temporary, to collect more of my belongings. When I put him right on that and said I had come home to stay and had been sleeping in our bed, he went berserk. I remember him dashing upstairs and throwing my stuff out of the room. It wasn't like him to be so demonstrative and uncool. I thought he might do himself a mischief in the process.

At the time he didn't mention Marianne, but I suppose his over-reaction was principally because of her. My jaw dropped when, later in the day, my crazy neighbour Jessica let it slip. Harriet and my son James had been diplomatic enough not to tell me.

'Marianne?' I said, my jaw almost hitting my collar bones. 'Fanclub Marianne?'

I know you won't have much sympathy for me. Serves her right, you will say. What goes round, comes round. Didn't she know it would all end in tears? You will say I brought it all on myself. After all, I was the one who ran away with Gianni: beautiful, charming and awakener of midlife desire; that elusive thing that slips and slides, and hides.

I had reasons. Excuses. I was bored. Ted had spent our entire married life going off doing exciting things and it was as if I had no other role than that of the housekeeper. Yes, I had an admin job at the university, but it didn't thrill me or challenge me.

Three of the children were teenagers and doing their own thing and Chris was on the threshold of the same.

When Mummy died and suddenly I had my own money, well, it was my turn to do what I wanted. I was forty-six; there was no time to waste. Ted kept telling me to think things through, discuss my projects with him. But it would have been like one of his university meetings and the upshot would have been 'not cost-effective and too risky'. He was comfortable with the way things were. Too much thinking and weighing up of the pros and cons and I would have been too scared. I don't analyse; I act. Always have.

Not like Ted's girlfriend … womanfriend … partner … whatever. Marianne Fanclub, the spanner. Without her, things might be very different and we might get back together. I told Harriet. Harriet was traumatised when I disappeared and is now ferociously (and I choose that word carefully) pro-Marianne.

She said, 'She is enthusiastic about Dad, but she doesn't fetch sticks.'

She thought I had called Marianne a spaniel. I laughed at the mistake. I could have called her that. It sounds as if she tries too hard to please. I haven't met her yet.

This people-as-animals thing started when I worked at the university and we were sent on a team-building exercise about self and other awareness. Since then, I imagine most people I meet as animals.

The course was run by a little butter-ball of a fellow called Phil. Odious man. He scratched the back of his neck frequently to reveal sweaty patches under the arms of his shirt. He began the session by saying to the gathered group: 'What type of animal are you most like and why? And what would you most like to be? Also, how do you see your colleagues?' The last bit was tricky, especially when he said we would be sharing our thoughts. Does one opt for truth or tact? After all, I have to work with these people while he won't ever see us again. Telling someone they remind you of a skunk or an anteater could cause future tension.

I hate these group revelatory courses. I always remember a social worker friend of mine saying that when she was training they did a session involving group hugs. I didn't like the sound of that at all. 'Group grope sessions,' I called them. I don't like my personal space invaded by strangers. I'm not a touchy-feely type, although I was with Gianni. Odd, that. As if his Mediterranean style rubbed off on me. Since I came back, I've returned to my bubble.

Anyway, I said I saw myself as a cheetah and was quite happy to be seen that way. 'Independent and powerful. Killer instinct,' I added. My colleagues came up with similarly feline alternatives for me, so clearly I have pretty good self-awareness and the course was a waste of time. Still, it was good to get away for the day.

Afterwards I catalogued everyone I knew as animals, starting with the family. Ted is a horse. A steady, reliable but extremely clever horse. A dressage champion, perhaps. I told him when we first met that he had a horse's eyes. My youngest son Chris is also a horse, but more of a Highland pony. He's a plodder although he is very talented at what he does. He left school and came with me to Italy to learn cheffing skills from Gianni and work with us in the bistro.

Chris will always be my baby even though he's now nearly twenty. And he looks so like Ted did when I first met him: the epitome of geekiness, but good-looking. He's got all the sensitivity and none of the defence mechanisms. Ted was sent away to school. It toughened him up, but did he lose something in the process? Who can be sure? I went to a private school as a day pupil but I wasn't enthusiastic about sending my children away. The thought of Chris aged nine being packed off with a trunk to one of those bastions of traditional education makes me shiver, even now. I wouldn't have minded so much if James and the girls had gone, but not my baby Chris. He was our mistake. 'Afterthought' – people like to say. 'No,' I say. 'Mistake. Too much red wine on the wedding anniversary.' People look embarrassed that I should be so blunt, but it's true. For some reason he became more precious because he very nearly wasn't.

Now, where was I? Eldest daughter Rachel is a cat like me, but a domestic cat. Harriet is a grey squirrel – swift as lightening, but doesn't always see things straight away. Dear old James, my eldest, is a gangly giraffe. He has an unusual quality and a formidable intellect. When I met Gianni, I thought 'fox' because he was enterprising in sourcing food. He's a fox all right. Wily. More anon.

I shouldn't have started this. It is hard to stop. I expect you will try it too, if you haven't already.

4

After That Most Fateful Visit

Sarah

On Friday night, Coll pops in to see me on his way back from the new restaurant. I've made an extra-special effort to look alluring in the hope that he'll stay. He doesn't always on Fridays because he's often very tired at the end of the teaching week.

As soon as I let him in, I notice a difference. But it's hard to define. Many people are multifaceted – especially Coll – so it's the addition of something new, something never seen before, that's the giveaway. That, and the suddenness of onset. He's excited to a level I haven't seen except when he's very drunk. And he isn't drunk because he only drinks one or two when he's driving.

'How long were you there?' I ask, trying not to sound suspicious as we settle on a chair and sofa in my cosy, homely, living room.

'A starter, a main and a brief chat after. Didn't talk for long. Once I knew she was willing to see my work, I thought I'd let it speak for itself.'

'Was the food good?'

'First rate.'

'Perhaps we could go together sometime. Give her some support – especially if she takes your paintings.' I have a motive for this: an opportunity to weigh up the opposition and also to alert her to my existence – something Coll is very good at forgetting to do.

He doesn't answer and I experience a tremor of anxiety. He says he isn't staying with me overnight because he's visiting the restaurant again the following morning with sample paintings. I'm disappointed.

'Got to move while she's warm,' he says. 'Do you think three or four to start with?'

He's always asking my opinion but rarely takes advice.

'Three will be sufficient to give her an idea. Take a range of prices and sizes. Are you coming here after?'

There's a moment's hesitation before he says, 'Y-yes.' A moment's hesitation in which my gut warns me of danger ahead.

Coll and I met at an art evening class in Exeter some twelve years ago. He was the teacher and I was one of fifteen or so assorted mature students of modest ability, at best searching for friendship and at worst companionship on one lonely evening per week during term times. In my experience of evening classes – and I attended a fair few after Pete died – the most one can reasonably hope for is the filling of the evening void. They attract the lost and dispossessed. During the short mid-session breaks, over green thick-rimmed cups of questionable tea and tasteless sugary biscuits, I shared a few words with my fellow students, trying to sift those with whom I might find friendship from those who were hopelessly lacking or simply weird.

Sometimes Coll joined us, sitting back in his chair listening to our repartee. Half way through the course, I was in heated debate about the merits of impressionism with a scraggy, bearded man who claimed it wasn't good art unless it was an accurate true-to-life representation.

'In that case, why are you here?' I said. 'Why not do photography?'

'Because I like to paint and want to learn techniques that may help me in my quest to reflect accurately what's there.'

'Isn't art about interpretation? Adding something more?'

I can't remember what followed but I was aware of Coll listening and holding back when I'm sure he had plenty to say on the matter.

When we returned to the second half of our session, Coll requested a word with me after class. In front of the others he said it was about a particular book that might be in our university library catalogue. He knew my day job was at the University of Devon because our first session involved an ice-breaker where we were asked to tell each other our name, our job (if we had one) and why we had chosen to come to an art class. But once the rest of the group had drifted away and I was left alone with him – feeling rather honoured to be singled out – he asked me if I would like to visit a local art exhibition with him at the weekend. He was very matter-of-fact about the invitation.

'I can see you have an "eye",' he said.

It didn't seem like a date, but I rather wished it had been. During our visit, as we walked from picture to picture and I tried to impress him with my knowledge of art history and different styles, there was no hint of flirting. He remained neutral in his emotional tone towards me, saving his enthusiasm for the art. I wondered if it was because he was my teacher, but even so, being

16

more or less the same age and on a ten-week course, it wouldn't have been exactly gross moral turpitude, whatever we'd done. Perhaps he didn't fancy me. I found that rather disappointing. I thought he was good-looking. Too good-looking to be interested in me.

Having no children, and deceased parents, I was pretty much baggage free apart from the inevitable trappings of midlife, both spiritual and material. I wasn't too set in my ways because I was always a free spirit – even if somewhat ground-dwelling as opposed to aerial. Since Pete died, I often spent weekends with friends in various parts of the UK, or with my sister Jane and her family in Dawlish. But I longed to do what couples do: lazy days, busy days, sharing the cooking and domestic burdens; shopping together; sleeping together – what Pete and I did for the briefest time.

After that outing, Coll waited until the course was over and then asked me if I'd like to go on a day trip to the Royal Academy in London. I didn't hesitate. He was good company. Talked a lot about himself and his recent marriage breakdown, but in an entertaining way. He didn't take himself too seriously and found the funny side in most situations. He was a skilled raconteur. I didn't have to make much effort and found myself swept along. After that, the trips became a regular weekend thing, often to galleries in London, but also to those in the West Country, nearer to Exeter where we both lived. The visits to my friends ceased and sister Jane and her family were relegated to evenings.

'I'm a bit squeezed for time with all this gallivanting,' I told her.

'We're only too pleased you have found yourself a man,' she said. The 'we' included her husband John.

'Oh, it's not like that,' I said.

'Oh really?' she said.

I remember her raising her eyebrows in two perfect arches. Very astute is Jane. She was on the right track. Twelve years on,

Coll is my boyfriend-partner – or whatever you call a man of mature years. It's difficult to be precise about the length of our intimacy because we drifted from friendship to relationship without any clear dividing line. Once the evening classes finished, the flirting began, but even then he drew away from anything physical. Too soon since his divorce, he said. I knew that feeling, so I didn't push, even though he was the first man since Pete to whom I was seriously attracted.

5

Coll

Felicity

Next morning the mystery man appears again as promised. This time I remember to introduce myself.

'Felicity,' I say, shaking his hand. It is cold to the touch. Cold, but dry. I can't bear men with damp hands.

'Col,' he says. Again I notice his jeans, this time with a grey anorak. He is muffled up against the cold, a black scarf looped trendily around his neck. I rather like his style. Understated sophistication. In his arms is a huge bubblewrapped package.

'"I don't mean to sound critical",' I say, quoting him as he steps inside, 'but you don't look like a Colin.' I'm getting my own back for the veiled comment last evening about my lack of restaurant decor.

If he were an animal, he would be a giraffe like my son James, or possibly a llama. One has to know people's personalities before one can be sure. It's unfair to base the selection purely on appearance. In that way I am generous with judgements. He has the cheekiness and curiosity of a llama.

18

He laughs and gives me a look that tells me he has noted my copycat use of his words from the previous night. I like a man who can tease and be teased back.

He says, 'You're not the first to say that. But the truth is I'm not a Colin. I'm simply Coll with two L's. It's an island in the Hebrides. My middle name is Tiree. But mostly I don't mention that.'

Is he serious? I can't be sure.

He continues, 'I was conceived up there on my parents' honeymoon. They were unconventional types; Dad was an artist and Mum, a musician.'

I lead him into the restaurant to one of the dark wooden tables that I have purposely not yet laid for service. Light streams in through the large windows. He sets down the package carefully, unzips his jacket to reveal a blue jumper and begins to free the tape on the wrapping.

I say, 'It's a good name for an artist.'

'I'm a teacher too.'

'So is my daughter, Harriet. I know a lot of people who teach in one form or another.'

'Then you'll understand the pressures better than most.'

'What's your subject?'

'Art.'

'I should have guessed.'

'Coll,' I say, savouring the word. 'There are worse islands to be named after, I suppose. Like Benbecula.'

'But Ben would be okay for short.'

'Or Mingulay?' I suggest.

'Ming would sound Chinese. Do you know the islands well?'

'Holiday before children came along.' And I remember with some nostalgia, when we drove our first car up the west coast of Scotland, staying in B&Bs and ferrying over to as many islands as we could. We laughed a lot that summer. Just Ted and me, starting out, full of dreams. 'Flodaigh,' I add.

'Now you're showing off,' Coll teases.

'North Uist.'

'Suitable for posy pop-star children.' He throws his hands up in defeat. 'You win. Let's to business.'

Inside one layer of bubblewrap there are four individually wrapped pictures, one large, one medium and two small. I am prepared to be disappointed. It will be difficult to say no – which will be a pity as I rather like this man. But as he reveals the first one, I am pleasantly surprised. It is a local landscape of impressionist style, competently executed and very sellable. He opens up all four on the table.

I nod appreciatively. 'My customers will like these. They're very Turnerish with perhaps a touch of Monet.'

'My wife used to say that.'

Wife. I am aware of disappointment, but note the words 'used to' and seek clarification.

'Not any more?' A leading question.

'Ex wife.'

'Ah. I'm one of those. Almost. So be careful what you say about the type.' I feel a tremor of something. I dismiss it.

'Almost?'

'Such a long story. I rarely talk about it with anyone. I keep thinking the past eighteen months have been a dream and it isn't happening.'

'Tell me.' He sounds genuinely interested.

'I hardly know you.' I feign offence at his presumption, but I am generally not fond of personal disclosures until I have known someone for a while.

He adds, 'We can swap stories of life after marital breakdown.' He twinkles and it is hard to tell whether or not he's serious. He has intrigued me with ambiguity.

'Not today. There isn't time. I have a few errands to do and then I have to help my son get ready for service. We are very busy tonight. The lead up to Christmas and all that.' I turn my attention back to the paintings, examining each one. 'I wasn't expecting to like them. I imagined they would be weird abstracts.'

'Oh ye of little faith. What makes you say that?'

'I don't know.' And I don't. 'I'm surprised I haven't seen your work before.'

'I've been teaching for thirty years. Never had time to do much painting for myself, but I'm planning to retire – in phases.'

'Ah.'

'I want to try painting again before I'm too old. See where it goes. I was thinking of having an exhibition, but showing them here could be even better. It's not so much about money, more about personal satisfaction and, hopefully, some sort of recognition.'

I can relate to this. 'That's exactly how I felt when I opened my first restaurant. Have you thought about giving your pictures away?'

Coll looks shocked.

I add, 'A marketing ploy. Apparently, Free Art is becoming quite the thing. All you do is leave a picture in a public place with "Take Me" – or some such – written on it.'

'I don't want to devalue it. Art is worth what people are willing to pay. And when I said it wasn't so much about the money, I didn't mean that the money didn't matter. But I do give to good causes: charity auctions, raffles and the like.'

'Free art doesn't devalue if you use it sparingly. It can create interest and possibly publicity.'

'I didn't bring my paintings here to be given away.' He sounds offended, but again I'm not sure whether this is a genuine reaction or part of the game we seem to be playing.

'I wasn't meaning here.'

'In that case I will give it some thought. Thank you.'

He says he has been looking for a suitable outlet and saw the advertisement about my new restaurant in a local paper. 'I know your previous establishment was very successful.'

'You have done your research.'

'It says so in your reviews. And I looked it up on TripAdvisor. I wanted the right place. I like your stance on locally sourced ethical produce and also on dietary requirements. Listing the ingredients on the menu and stating alternative options is helpful to those who are shy about asking.'

'I'm glad you approve.'

'My ex-wife had several intolerances.'

'Have you tried local shops – for your pictures?'

'They want too big a cut. I am guessing you would be reasonable.'

'What makes you say that?' I say, coyly.

Coll strides dramatically around the room and loudly proclaims, 'I'm decorating your walls, enhancing the ambience, creating additional interest.'

I feel hot. I can't help myself. This man has charm. 'They will go nicely with my bowls,' I say. 'I throw pots. Nothing special, but people like them.'

'Show me,' he says.

I dash upstairs and return with a selection of small pieces that I intend to put on shelves in the restaurant.

'Very pretty,' he says. 'Not only can she cook, but an artist as well. And how much is this one?'

'Twelve pounds usually, but it has a slight flaw. If you like it, you can have it – a gesture of goodwill to cement our business relationship.'

'Done,' he says.

I offer him a piece of cake and a cup of tea over which we discuss my hopes for the restaurant, the importance of matching the correct wine with food and, finally, terms for the hanging space. We decide twenty percent would be fair. Most will be priced between one and three hundred pounds. He says he will bring a dozen or so pictures the following afternoon.

'My daughter's partner can hang them for me,' I say.

'Why not let me? I'm good with a hammer-drill and rawlplugs. We won't leave anything to chance in an old building like this. Then we can discuss the placing of them as we go. They need to be positioned so that it's easy to fill any gaps.'

'Gaps? You are confident of sales?' My tone is teasing. I already know my friend Olivia will love them and she won't think twice about spending a few hundred pounds.

'We have to hope.' He pauses. He looks at me, disarmingly. 'And then perhaps you will tell me your long story.'

'Perhaps.' But somehow I know I will.

When he leaves, he hands me his card. *Coll T. Waterford. Artist.* There is an email address and a mobile phone number. No address or landline.

I Google him and find he has an unsophisticated web-page with little content. I can advise him about that. And then I stop and scold myself. Already I am trying to run his life. And I know better now. Since the Gianni episode.

But I find it quite pleasant thinking about him after he has gone.

6

Mrs Mayfield-Harvey

Sarah

Coll is jubilant when he returns the next day for lunch. At first I think it's because the woman at the restaurant is enthusiastic about his work. I read somewhere that a lot of artistic types get an adrenalin rush when overtly appreciated, and this applies especially to Coll who thrives on attention. *'Felicity'*, he calls her. *'Mrs Mayfield-Harvey.'* I've never trusted people with double-barrelled names although the *Mrs* is a small source of comfort until he says, 'She's in the processes of getting divorced.'

And he goes on and on about her as we munch our way through Sicilian prawns followed by *spaghetti alle vongole*. As the words gush forth, I can't believe he is able to appreciate fully my beautifully cooked Mediterranean meal. I may as well have served him cardboard. *Felicity … Felicity …* and what a wonderful set up it is at the restaurant and how her youngest son, Chris, is the *very talented* chef, but she also cooks and waitresses and orchestrates front-of-house.

'Dynamic,' he says. 'She's one of those women who *does*.'

The subtext I hear is that I am one of those women who doesn't. I'm a thinker more than a doer. At least that's what Coll says. He's oblivious of the amount of doing that goes into preparing a decent meal or working in the library.

'She knows her wines too,' he says. 'She made a couple of recommendations.' He produces a scribble on a torn piece of paper. 'You might get a bottle if you see one of these next time you're shopping. She gave me a piece of cake. She doesn't half make a good lemon drizzle. Best cake I've ever had.'

It was one of the many things that attracted me to Coll. He could name different cakes. My former husband lumped them all in the same category. A cake was merely a cake to him. I thought about my carrot cake and how Coll always relished it. How annoying to have it pipped by a lemon drizzle – especially as I have a touch of arthritis and try to avoid citrus.

The cake means he can't finish all of the pasta and he doesn't want any apple crumble that is browning nicely in the oven. Then he mentions that Felicity is going to sell her own ceramics in the restaurant, and from his bag he produces a little bowl.

'Isn't she clever? I thought you might like it.'

It's small and a sapphire blue with a pattern of green leaves. It's annoyingly pretty. 'Thank you.' I try to sound gracious, but I suspect he bought it to please Felicity rather than as a gift to me.

His present-buying tendencies over the years have been sparse, to say the least. I don't remember him giving me anything unless it was for a birthday or Christmas and even then, his gifts weren't always the most thoughtful. I remember the year he gave me a set of pans and wondered why I wasn't supremely grateful.

When he decides to have a post lunch snooze, I glare at the bowl. I've half a mind to hurl it at a wall but it will be useful for nuts and olives so a pity to destroy it.

Call it women's intuition. He refers to her by name more than once when he reappears from his nap. *'Felicity said ...'*

By this time it's getting dark and too late for the trip to Sidmouth that we had planned: a walk along the prom and then perhaps tea in one of the lovely cafés in the town.

He even says she is *'so nice'* and *'very sweet'*. I don't know how he can be sure after two brief meetings. Maybe they weren't so brief.

At supper he says, 'I wonder how old she is? She doesn't look more than fiftyish. But she said her eldest son was in his late twenties so unless she started young, she could be older than me. But it's possible she could be younger.'

Coll is fifty-two, a year older than me, and very sensitive about his advancing years. This restaurant woman's age seems important to him. He's showing a degree too much interest. I want to say *For God's sake will you shut up about Felicity*. But that would sound like I'm jealous. Instead, I listen patiently, say nothing and try to manage a smile.

I wouldn't be too bothered, but now I know she's willing to hang his pictures, he'll be returning the next day with more. And then if he sells any, he'll be back to collect money; back with replacements. And his work is sellable original art at affordable prices. My brain races down unhelpful pathways. I'm over-thinking.

At night, he doesn't make any romantic overtures like he usually does before we have sex (even though I can see through them now and know that it is all about conquest and having his way and nothing about pleasing me, even though it does – physically at least even if not emotionally). And afterwards, he turns over rather sharply and goes to sleep. In the morning, he drives home soon after breakfast because he says he wants to spend time sorting pictures with which *'to impress Mrs Mayfield-Harvey.'*

'I'm going to hang them for her,' he says. 'And I need to make sure I can find my drill. Do you happen to have any rawlplugs?'

I rummage through the drawer in which I keep a few basic tools. It's laughable that he's offered to hang the pictures. I've been asking him for three months to bring over his drill so that I can put up my new towel rail. I don't even expect him to do it for me although now I hear about this latest chivalrous offering, I may raise my expectations. But I say nothing. Instead, I give him what rawlplugs I can find.

While all this might seem quite innocent to anyone less suspicious than me, there are too many things that have alerted my radar. And the most tangible evidence that something is amiss is that he's stopped looking me in the eye. He's become distracted and inattentive in the space of two days.

I fell in love with Coll very early on, probably on that evening when he asked me to the first exhibition, although I didn't know it then. This seemingly unattainable lecturer caused me to lower my guard. It wasn't long before I was head over heels. How does one do that? Metaphorical somersaults of the head and the heart. It was magical and dizzying. I became alive again after years of going through the motions of a colourless existence. He challenged my torpor with theatrical visits, art exhibitions and overnight stays in swanky hotels.

As I got to know him better, I caught glimpses of a dark, depressive side to his nature which emerged every few months and caused him to withdraw. I blamed his divorce. I believed if we were together properly, I could make him fly into the light.

What a fool I was. I laid my dreams before him and he took advantage. No one told me that once power is relinquished, it can never be reclaimed without taking drastic action. And drastic action isn't my way.

He never *said* he loved me, but he was so attentive during that post-friendship first year, I was sure he did. It came as a shock when after several years he said, 'I don't love you, Sarah. I've never loved anyone except Penelope, and only then for a year or so.'

He'd been drinking. He often drinks more than he should. And every so often some little thing causes him to take offence and he metamorphoses into someone I don't recognise and has a rant about my limitations.

I thought he was in denial of his feelings: scared to risk being hurt again. And I do so love him. He is my Grand Passion if ever there was. That's the problem; my biggest ever mistake. I revealed my desire for him far too soon in our relationship and as a consequence, he assumes the top-dog role.

7

Felicity's Story

Felicity

Coll turns up in the late afternoon as arranged, bang on time and with more paintings and a hammer-drill. I've been looking forward to seeing him all morning and was very buoyant during our busy Sunday lunchtime service. The customers have left and Kylie is scuttling around clearing tables. When I told her Coll was coming and asked her if she would to do an extra couple of hours, she remarked that she thought him a 'bit of a flirt'. She's not wrong there.

Kylie is my eldest son James's ex from when he was at school. In those days she was a typical ditsy blonde but while I was in Italy, she knuckled down to developing some skills, stepped in as Front of House in my old restaurant, married an apple producer whom she helps part-time, and had a baby. She is now almost unrecognisable from the person she was. Not only is her hair a natural shade of brown and her dress more conservative, but she is startlingly perceptive regarding relationships.

I help Coll fetch the pictures from his Audi.

'And how's the Lady of the Pots?' he asks.

I quote, *'There she weaves by night and day a magic web with colours gay …'*

'Indeed you do,' Coll says, sounding surprised that I understood the origin of his comment. He adds, *'She has a lovely face, God in his mercy send her grace.'*

Oh, he's a flirt all right. I think I may be blushing.

'Tree's new,' Coll says, referring to the Norwegian spruce in the lobby.

'A gesture to the season,' I say. He's not to know that his turning up has cheered me sufficiently to make such a gesture, nor the cost of sourcing one of suitable size and shape and having it delivered early in the morning. The lobby is small and is already home to a hat stand and an umbrella holder. A tallish narrow tree is what I wanted and it took several phone calls to locate.

I've never considered hanging paintings to be an enjoyable activity, but being with Coll changes my view. He makes little quips, teasing me about my positional judgements. His eye contact is intense and burrows through to my soul. From anyone else it might be too familiar and intimate but from Coll it reminds me of my youth when I was less guarded and happy to accept attention from a range of admirers.

'Up a bit … Down a bit …' I say.

He purposely moves the picture too far in order to prolong the game.

He says, 'Are you too young to remember Anne Aston in *The Golden Shot*?'

I bask in the flattery. I'm not too young to remember, nor, it seems, is he. He starts to call me *Anne* and puts on a rough Devon accent with a lot of exaggerated *'Oo arr Annes'*. I'm in stitches by the time we finish, but the room looks great with the walls hung like a gallery.

I have asked Harriet's Rick to put up a few small shelves for my bowls. He said he'll come tomorrow when we're closed all day. Harriet's Rick is old enough to be her father and their getting together is a sore point. But he's a versatile handyman and I don't want to push my luck with Coll.

I wonder if I can persuade Coll to stay so we can chat some more and I can probe about his divorce. I am now finely tuned-in to the mention of the word as if wanting reassurance that it happens to the best of us and that life afterwards may still be enjoyed.

After we've finished hanging the paintings, I suggest we go up to my flat and have a cup of tea. I had already checked that Chris would be out as I don't like discussing the marriage in front of the children.

'If you can stretch to cake as well, I might consider it,' says Coll, gathering his tools and picking up his jacket.

'Cake it is.' And we make our way upstairs.

Once settled with mugs of tea and pieces of home-made gingerbread, he says, 'You promised to tell me your long story.'

I would prefer him to tell me his first.

'I don't recall promising anything,' I say. Yet I find I want to offload to this virtual stranger whom I sense will understand.

I tell him about me and Ted, and how happy we were for many years. And then I explain the awkward situation with Ted and Marianne Fanclub. I decide not to mention the episode with Gianni. Not yet, anyway. That's how I think of it now. 'An episode.' 'Affair' doesn't show me in the best light. He may jump to erroneous conclusions about the type of woman I am. I had been faithful to Ted all our married life till then and my relationship with Gianni was much more than an affair to me. It was supposed to be for the rest of our lives. What a deluded woman I was.

I launch in. 'Ted and I drifted apart as the children grew up. I focused on them; he focused on his work. He's an academic to his very bones.'

'What's his subject?'

'Archaeology.'

'To his very bones,' echoes Coll. 'I like that.'

I laugh. 'No pun intended. He likes animals and wildlife, but animal husbandry doesn't interest him at all and as for vegetables …'

'From where did Marianne Fanclub spring?'

'She's an ex-classmate who found him on Friends Reunited over ten years ago. They kept in touch by email.'

'An Internet Relationship,' muses Coll.

'My daughters – Harriet and Rachel – thought she must've had a crush on him when she was young and they called her Fanclub. It's stuck.'

'Did she have a crush?'

I hesitate. The existence of Marianne had never bothered me until I returned from Italy to find her in possession of my husband's heart. 'I don't know. It appears she does now.' My tone is a shade sarcastic. I don't try to hide the bitterness I feel. 'She had a husband until eighteen months ago and I never perceived her as a threat. I caught sight of one of her emails once and it was all boring blah about archaeology. That's why she and Ted get on, I guess.'

'And the husband? What happened to him?'

'He died. Heart attack.'

'Unfortunate,' says Coll.

'Sad. Very sad. Same age as me. Far too young. I haven't met her, but I spoke to her on the phone years ago when I needed a favour. It's another long story.' I pause, wondering whether to tell it and then deciding against it.

'When Ted was working for a few years at Stancliffe University in London, he lodged with Marianne and her husband during the week.'

'And you didn't mind?'

'I minded him being away so much. I didn't mind him lodging with them. I trusted him. And as far as I could gather, she was happily married. She was. It was her husband's idea apparently. Their only daughter had gone to uni and I think they felt bereft. I've no reason to think there was anything going on while Ted was there. In any case, he's useless when it comes to romance. He doesn't notice when women are interested in him – unless they are ridiculously obvious like some of his students used to be.'

'I have that problem,' says Coll with a hint of a twinkle.

'Her husband was a geology teacher and he and Ted got on brilliantly. He brought Ted part of the way home once when he was on one of his Jurassic Coast walks. We met briefly in a car park in Charmouth.'

I don't add that I thought he was Gorgeous with a capital G. When he got out of his car, he was wearing sunglasses and wouldn't have looked out of place in a celebrity magazine. Dazzling smile; longish hair; arty. Just my type before the Ted years. And instead of rushing to greet Ted, I couldn't take my eyes off the husband. Johnny was his name. Marianne and I could've done a swap. Interestingly, he was a similar physical type to Coll.

Coll says, 'What does this Marianne do?'

'Now? She's written a novel – supposedly inspired by finding Ted on the internet – and she does promotional talks in libraries, and to WIs and the like. She's also preparing an educational pack on sustainability – for the BBC – to link with a documentary with which Ted is involved.'

'Sounds a bit of a hotchpotch career.'

'She's retired. She was a psychology teacher.'

'Psychology? Mumbo-Jumbo,' says Coll with feeling.

'My thoughts exactly.'

'And have you read the novel?'

'I don't read much, but even if I did, I'm not sure if I would. I know bits about it from what Ted says. She based part of it on her experiences of bullying at prep school. And in the book, the character based on her does have a crush on the character based on Ted. I don't like the idea of reading it and finding him between the covers – as it were. I suppose you could say I'm not totally over our splitting up.'

'It takes a long time, especially as you're not yet divorced.'

I push on. 'I pursued him when we met, more or less orchestrated our relationship from the start and then when I stopped making an effort, it fell apart. It was quite sudden. After Mummy died and left me some financial independence, I began to reconsider my life.'

I don't add that the reconsideration involved the handsome Italian chef Gianni, and that the weekly discussions about menus involved lots of delicious bonking in the flat above the restaurant.

'You are the first person I've told all this to. I've no siblings and most of my best friends know Ted too. I can't tell the kids because I don't want them to take sides. Of course they have. Do you have children?'

'One. A boy. A man now. Jack. He's thirty-two, married with two kids. They emigrated to Australia after Penny and I divorced. We didn't get on and he sided with his mum. You're lucky if your kids are still on speaking terms with both of you. Makes life less difficult.'

'When did you split up?'

'About thirteen years ago.'

I wonder if he's had any romantic involvements between then and now. Probably, but I don't like to ask.

Instead, I say, 'There's a lot of it about. Midlife separation. We want something more than mediocrity in our declining years.'

'We look for love, again,' says Coll, wistfully.

'Is it possible?'

'For some.'

I am aware of tension in the air. He's staring at me intently. Devouring me with grey eyes. I feel the same beat that I felt in the early days of Gianni. Again I castigate myself for even thinking such a thing.

'I'll tell you my story another time,' says Coll. 'Let's talk about something cheery. Tell me what else you like to do, Felicity. In your spare time, when you're not churning out delicious food and making our stomachs happy.'

It is the way he said my name; it is the way he seems interested in me and not himself. Either he is a skilled lothario, or he is a genuinely nice guy. I want to find out.

We discover a mutual interest in theatre, especially Shakespeare.

'But I haven't been to see a play in ages,' I say, hinting.

'Then perhaps we can fix that sometime.'

I smile approval and then Coll rises and puts on his jacket. 'And now I must dash. I've taken up far too much of your precious time.'

'Do you live far away?' I ask, casually.

'On the other side of Exeter – but the school where I teach is on this side.'

I wait for him to suggest popping over after work; taking me out for a drink. But he doesn't. Perhaps I am deluding myself about his interest.

In the evening, after a few lunchtime leftovers to quell the hunger pangs, I drive over to Broadclyst to visit my friend Olivia. Since her divorce, she lives in a small, thatched, yellow ochre cottage, leased by the National Trust who run the Killerton Estate, and a trademark of the village. She is an angular toothy woman with masses of coiffed red hair, and always dressed up to the nines. I tell her about Coll. She has been internet dating on and off with limited success ever since her husband ran off. I suspect it is that which gives her a teenage attitude to relationships and an insatiable capacity to discuss them.

'You're in there,' Olivia says, flashing her super-whitened teeth. 'How do you do it?'

'I didn't do anything. In any case, I'm not sure if I can face going through the dating thing again.'

'Think bicycle,' says Olivia.

'Getting too old to be bothered.' I want the excitement, the feeling of being desired and the companionship of a man. But I am not sure that I want all the palaver that goes with it. Taking off one's clothes at my time of life comes with doubts. Yet in my mind, I am already removing some of Coll's.

It helps to distract me from constant thoughts about Ted but it isn't important. Not yet. Maybe not ever. It is in front of the cosy hearth at the Deer Orchard where I want to be.

8

Pretty

Sarah

I'm sitting next to Coll in my local pub having a pre-supper drink when he relates something of his picture-hanging visit. He's vague about specifics but lets it slip that he and Mrs Mayfield-Harvey 'Get on famously' and 'Come from similar backgrounds so understand the score'.

I'm not sure to what score he is referring, but it seems they swap divorce notes and both have grown-up children of which I've no experience. The ground under my feet seems less stable; the future less certain.

When I tell Laura at the library, she says I am over-reacting on flimsy evidence. I say I have a knot in my gut and that's enough. Laura doesn't know about stomach knots. She lives a life of emotional tranquillity that pervades her being.

'He's a clever customer. He knows how to wind you up,' she says.

I'm not as clever as Coll, but most of the time, we don't notice. I have my strengths. I have a wide knowledge of many things. It goes with the job, but it doesn't go deep. Coll is bordering on intellectual when it comes to music, art and literature. I muddle along in these fields unless it's the classics or Shakespeare where my knowledge is at least as good as his; I know the main works of other famous creatives but am flummoxed by the intricacy of most of the questions on *University Challenge*. It's one of the programmes we enjoy watching together – along with period drama, *Antiques Roadshow* and anything to do with art. We laugh a lot about people and the minutiae of life and we enjoy galleries and theatre. There's an amateur production of *Richard II* coming up soon in Exeter. I haven't mentioned it yet. I shall suggest he takes me but need to plan my strategy carefully. He likes to be the one to make the decisions.

'I bet she's attractive,' I say to Laura as we re-shelve books at the end of the day.

'You're attractive,' says Laura. 'Don't be so hard on yourself.'

I don't believe her. People say I've a pretty face. Pretty rather than attractive. Everything in the right place, no features too large or too small. Symmetrical. I remember a girl at school, Donna, saying, 'Pretty is false.' I took it to heart. She said it was better to be attractive. I said better to be pretty than neither. And she slapped me. I wasn't meaning her. In fact she *was* attractive. Squiffy teeth, but her smile had charm. Not like the characterless smiles of celebrities with more dental work than sense. The most attractive teeth don't sit in a regular curve like the Royal Crescent in Bath, but it seems this truism has yet to be discovered.

And my face is still pretty in a fifty-one kind of way. It is the rest of me that needs some work. I'm not fat, but I am on the curvy side. Coll says I'm sexy, but I think he would like me to be slimmer. He's always patting his not-quite six-pack and flexing his muscles. He uses the gym at his school, arriving early, working up a sweat, showering, and all before eight-thirty. He often says women turn 'square' in midlife and I have a fear of this. Once he mentioned liposuction at a particularly intimate moment. I was visibly upset. He said it was a tease; that I was 'far too sensitive'. Lack of love makes one sensitive and insecure. He's always making comments that make me feel inadequate. He says they're jokes; that people who are in long-term relationships can say things like this about each other. I think that maybe they can if they feel loved and cherished but not if their partner is always raving about the merits of other women.

He likes my face because it can adopt many guises depending on my hair and make-up. I change my hairstyle often, perhaps searching for one that he will fall in love with. I read once about a young woman whose partner was still in love with his dead spouse. She had thousands of pounds worth of cosmetic surgery to try to copy her look. I wouldn't go that far. I've seen photographs of Penelope. Nice, but nothing special. She had naturally wavy hair. I think he likes that. I wonder if Felicity's hair waves without the help of tongs? Mine is obstinately straight and unless I make an effort, the current hair-cut hangs like that of Richard lll.

'Ah, the Headmistressy look,' said Coll when I returned from the hairdresser. I know it was a veiled criticism, but until it grows a few inches, I'm stuck with it. I already know he doesn't like it too short and I draw the line at a perm.

You must think I'm stupid. I'm not. I've a degree in media

and marketing. I know it sounds like one of those Mickey Mouse degrees, but it wasn't. And I did get good A levels at a time when an A or even B grade meant something extra special. I know exactly what I do wrong and how my thinking is dysfunctional. I know, but I can't help it.

You may wonder why I stay with him. I often wonder myself.

9

Logistics

Felicity

I am glad I like the paintings. The arrangement promises future meetings with Coll and I could do with a new male friend in my life. I have tried to worm my way back into Ted's affections. Granted, it isn't so much that I want him, but I want my life back; my family life with spacious house and garden. It is claustrophobic in my flat and what garden there is has minimal potential. Space counts for a lot and at my age, how many of us are still enamoured of our spouses? I thought we could recapture some of our old magic if I made more effort. But Ted is so far immovable. I have betrayed him and he can't forgive me. Added to that is him being besotted with Marianne. I'm pretty hacked off about that. I thought it might wear off and that he would see it made sense not to go through the trauma of divorce. But his passion so far shows no signs of dimming despite my best efforts to be the charming woman he once found irresistible.

The family set up with regards to living arrangements is currently complicated. Ted continues to live in our house, the Deer Orchard, and apparently intends to do so at least until the financial aspects of our divorce are sorted. Daughter Harriet (teacher and grey squirrel) is part-time resident, spending week nights in her old bedroom and weekends with ancient boyfriend Rick, who lives at the other end of the village near the church. I call him ancient even though he is younger than me. But I'll tell you more of him later when he comes to put up the shelves.

Eldest son James (giraffe) moved back home with his partner Kate at the end of summer. (Kate is a resourceful monkey, but I haven't yet decided which species.) Both have landed jobs at Exeter University, he lecturing in marine biology and she as a part-time research assistant to one of the professors in the same department. Kate's dream is to do what I did – *sans* restaurant. In other words, she wants to grow veg, rear a few animals and sell produce locally. This is what she does for the other part of her job although chickens and my one remaining hive of bees are the only animals so far. I think her plans are a tad more ambitious than mine. She mentions goats and sheep – which I had – but also pigs. As the business (and family size) grows, she will reduce her hours at the university and the animal menagerie will expand. She also wants a farm shop and I think she fancies cheese making – from goats' milk and possibly sheep's too. We use a lot of goats' cheese in the restaurant so the sooner she starts this enterprise, the better.

James and Kate asked Ted and me if there was a way they could buy us out, but even though Kate has some money from her parents, and they are good candidates for a mortgage, they can't afford to buy both of us out at once. Keeping the home in the family is in everyone's interests, so we will try to make it happen. But Ted needs capital if he is going to set up a separate love-nest with Fanclub. And that, sadly for me, is their current plan. I don't really need capital urgently, but worry that if all James's resources go in Ted's direction, it may weaken my position with regards to my share. This is one of the stumbling blocks of the divorce.

When I arrived back in the UK at the end of August, I lived with Ted at the Deer Orchard for three months while the purchase of my new restaurant and flat went through. There were also a few refurbishments which were easier to do while I wasn't living on site. Ted visited Marianne in London every other weekend. He trotted off on the train and came back with that satiated look men have when they've been over-indulging in sex. Not that he used to over-indulge with me once the kids came along.

At the beginning of the month, I moved into my new premises on the edge of Pinhoe near Exeter and about five miles from Ted in Broadclyst. Chris is my chef and he officially lives in the second bedroom. However, he has quite a way with girls – no doubt benefitting from skills picked up when he was in Italy with me. Consequently, I don't see much of him on his nights off and hence my loneliness.

As soon as I moved out, cue Marianne Fanclub arriving at the Deer Orchard. She didn't take long before turning up with a case. And I am madly curious.

Ted has told me to keep away. That it would be unfair on Marianne to have to face me at this stage. Ridiculous of him to feel the need to protect her like that. She's a grown woman and will have to face me sometime. I shall go to the Deer Orchard in a day or two on the pretext of needing a few extra potatoes. I will time it when Ted is likely to be around. If Marianne sees the way Ted and I interact with each other, she might become jealous. Oh vicious thought as to where that might lead. But I can't help it. Part of me still hasn't given up hope. I fantasise about Marianne and Ted having a major row and him deciding that now he's evened the score with me, he and I might try again. He is still my husband and one hears of the separated getting back together.

Where there's hope, as they say.

Small World

Sarah

I'm struggling with a chicken on my kitchen worktop. A dead one. It's for a casserole. It's much cheaper to joint your own rather than pay supermarket prices for some extra butchery and plastic-packaged portions. Sometimes I can't be bothered, but Coll is a chicken junkie and because we eat at least the equivalent of one whole one per week, it's cost-effective in the long run. I have a vast chicken repertoire of three roasts, at least seven different casseroles, four pies, three curries, a spicy jerk and four Oriental stir-fries including a sweet-and-sour. Tonight it's a cross between one of Mary Berry's family casseroles and a *Coq au Vin*.

Now, where was I? Ah, yes … Why do I stay with Coll? I stay because we're good together most of the time and because ten years is a substantial investment to lose if I was to come away empty handed. I think the reason he thinks he's not in love with me is because I make it too easy for him and I keep promising myself I'll change. In the early days, I should have said 'No' more often – to dates and to sex. I should tease more. Make him guess; make him wonder; make him think that I've other options. I know what to do, but it's never been my natural way. And I probably do have other options so it wouldn't be a lie. But they're not the right type of options; that's the problem. I have a neighbour two doors down – widower, presentable, good handyman, and stalwart of the residents' association – who has made it known on several occasions that he would like to take me out.

He's called Dan. He used to work for the Environment Agency, but he's recently retired. Every few months, he says, 'You still seeing that artist fellow?' He doesn't approve of Coll. Thinks he doesn't pull his weight when it comes to helping me out on the domestic front. This is probably an accurate observation.

'If you should ever fancy a change,' he says. 'I know some good restaurants.'

I wonder if one of them is Felicity's. That would be funny. Turning up. Spying. But not fair on Dan.

I saw him with a woman once and I did feel a slight pang of jealousy – as if my safety net was being stolen. Turned out she was his sister.

And last week I was chatted up in the check-out queue at M&S.

But for good or ill, I love Coll. And I'm not good with change, including my job.

I started working in the university library when I was a student, and never left. It was Devon Polytechnic in those days. After a few years, my role became more senior and permanent so a move seemed pointless. I'm comfortable there. When I arrive each morning, it's like putting on a familiar cardigan rather than a new outfit. I don't like novelty and the stress that goes with it. I've enough stress in my personal life.

Laura gets cross with me sometimes. I'm always moaning to her about Coll. She said, 'Get out there and see what else's on offer. You'll never know if you don't try.'

I said, 'I do know and I did try. After Pete, before Coll, I did everything you suggest and nobody clicked.'

'And what about Dan, your neighbour? He sounds nice.'

'He is. But I won't give him false hope.'

There's an odd circumstance that I haven't yet told Coll. This Felicity woman used to work in admin at the university. I expect she'll tell him when he tells her about us. I've got a feeling he hasn't mentioned me yet – no doubt a deliberate omission. And the weird thing is, I know her husband. Sort of. He worked in our archaeology department until this week when the term ended. He was often in our library; probably more than any other member of the lecturing staff and always asking us to locate some research paper or other. We librarians refer to him privately as Dr Edward. When he went to work in London for a few years, he became Professor Edward. I think he's still an honorary professor at Stancliffe University, London, but we've always stuck with calling him Dr Edward.

He has something about him that even the younger members of the team are attracted by. Yesterday, he returned a massive pile of books and told me he was leaving. 'But I may be back to do the odd lecture, so don't lose me from your system, Sarah,' he said. He's a nice man with a kind face. Always courteous. A 'Please and Thank You type,' as my old mum would say. Remembers my name too. If Felicity was still his wife in the true sense, I could drop hints about Coll.

I never met her when she worked here and I didn't realise the connection at first, but when Coll said Felicity was Mrs Mayfield-Harvey and in the processes of getting a divorce, it rang a bell. I remembered all sorts of colourful rumours about her from a couple of years back. Laura said she'd left Dr Edward for her Italian chef and that they'd run away to Italy, taking her youngest son. The chef was apparently ten years younger and a real dish. A proper toyboy. It sounded like something off the telly. Poor Dr Edward. I don't know if Mrs Felicity has told Coll all this. He hasn't mentioned Italy, let alone an affair with a chef, and I don't want to be the one to disclose such potentially inflammatory information. In any case, you can't believe everything you hear. It would be very mean-spirited of me to try to rubbish her reputation and would probably backfire in a 'shooting the messenger' type of way.

Small world though.

11

Rick

Felicity

Harriet's Rick arrives to put up the shelves for my pots. He wouldn't have looked amiss among the Rolling Stones in their middle years; a wild man of rock. He grunts at me and doesn't smile. We are not on the best of terms since I came back and discovered the shenanigans with Harriet. I felt he had let me down. He was my gardener during my first venture into the food business, also making the multi-level hen house and converting some outbuildings into an office-come-workshop and a place for my kiln. He's very versatile, is Rick. The whole village knows him, and not always for reasons of household maintenance.

Although he isn't married and never has been, he has long had a dubious reputation with women, rarely staying with the same one for long and often running a second affair in the background. Wives flutter round him and husbands are wary. Added to that, he is more than twenty years older than my daughter: twice her age. He has known her since she was a young teenager, but thank God they only started seeing each other in the romantic sense when I went to Italy. By this time she was at least a grown woman, albeit a young one. It was all very secretive. They guessed correctly that Ted would have a fit. And I did too when I returned and the beans were spilled.

By this time, Ted had warmed to the idea. Rick is supposedly a reformed character, but I can't get past his cheek in courting my girl, and the age gap.

I remember storming round to his house near the church and hammering on his door. He appeared in the doorway with a small towel wrapped around his nether regions, hair dripping and droplets of water clinging to his skin. If he thought a sexy pose would take the wind out of my sails, it didn't. He was shocked that I was back, but unsurprised by my hostility. He stood back and folded his arms while I let rip. After I said my piece – which I am ashamed to say was full of colourful language loud enough to be heard by his neighbours – he raised an eyebrow, said, 'Is that it?' and closed the door, leaving me at a loss on the step.

Rick is the strong silent type so I suppose that balances Harriet's verbosity. But what they have in common remains a mystery to me. I'm thinking he is probably good in bed. He has had plenty of experience and older men tend to have a better understanding of women. And more patience.

Harriet pointed out that I was in no position to judge, but it grieves me to think of her at my age of fifty-six, looking after an old man. And that is assuming he is still alive. They are adamant they don't want children, but chances are by the time Harriet is free of him, it will be too late. That sounds harsh. It is a practical viewpoint. Harriet keeps mentioning Rod Stewart, but Rick isn't in the same financial league, so Rod isn't relevant.

Anyway, that is by the by. I have to try to be civil for Harriet's sake and offering him work does at least keep his finances buoyant. He has made a couple of white-painted, tiered corner units and a few small individual wall shelves for my pots. While he drills and hammers, I lie low upstairs, concocting the Christmas menus to discuss with Chris.

An hour or so later, there is a knock on the door of the flat.

Rick says, 'All good and ready for your bowls, Mrs H.'

He used to call me Felicity, but since our disagreement, I have become Mrs H.

I pay him in cash, then instead of turning and skulking away as is customary, he hovers.

'Me and Harriet were wondering if you'd like to come to us for Christmas. In the evening. We know you and Chris are doing a lunch here, but we thought if we ate at night, you could both join us and relax after your busy day.'

My immediate reaction is one of shock. 'That's very kind, but—' I'm about to think of an excuse when Rick interjects.

'And we hope Rachel will come too. We can just about fit five round the table if you don't mind a squash, and Harriet wants to have a go at cooking a turkey – with my supervision. You won't have to do a thing.'

Rachel lives and works in London and her trips home are very precious. It would be lovely to be with three of my kids on this special day. And if I say no, it will be churlish and do nothing to improve the situation between us. It is certainly preferable to sitting on my own with leftovers while Chris goes out on the town. I relax my demeanour. 'Okay, yes, if you don't mind. I'd like to very much.'

After Rick drives off in his van, I decide to go to the Deer Orchard with view to meeting Marianne. Now she has retired, she is not confined to visiting only during the school holidays so I have no idea how long she will be staying. Ted is also about to retire from his permanent lecturing job so come the New Year, the pair of them will be free to do what they want when they want. Wonder how long it will be before they get on each other's nerves? Weekends and holidays don't exactly prepare one fully for the 24/7 shock of living together. But I suppose when Ted was lodging, they did at least get used to what each other was like in a day-to-day warts an' all capacity.

Rachel says Marianne has sold her family home and now lives in a flat in Beckenham. Apparently, this is with view to freeing up some cash for an eventual co-purchase with Ted, possibly in Broadclyst. That makes it sound like a very serious commitment. Time is running out if I am to persuade him to have me back. And until last week – until I met Coll – that was my plan.

Now, there is a smidgen of doubt. But it is too early to say where that might go or what I can realistically expect. He has attracted my attention, but if I had to choose now between him and Ted, I would not hesitate to choose Ted because of the house and the family. I have had my midlife crisis with Gianni. I have dipped my toes – nay, feet – into a different partnership and realised it was a mistake. Better the devil you know. And Ted is no devil.

Surely there is still hope? I will have a better idea if I meet Marianne. The thought of them both living so close by on a permanent basis doesn't exactly fill me with joy. I suppose I could always start again in a new area, but why should I when three of my children are here?

I am not usually this negative and one hears of some ex-wives and new partners getting on rather well. Time to find out.

12

OWs

Sarah

The University of Devon hails from the era of grey concrete and rectangles but is blessed by surroundings modelled on those of Exeter University on the other side of the city, boasting undulating lawns and an abundance of trees. The library is part of a relatively new extension and although rectangular, it has a bright modern exterior of mostly reflective glass.

I'm cold. I'm not usually a cold person, even in winter. But today, even though the weather's not chilly, I've had to put on a thick jumper and a cardigan. The library is generally warm enough for summer tops all year round, but the Powers That Be are on an energy efficiency drive since getting slapped wrists from some environmental bigwigs who were called in to monitor our carbon footprint. As a result, the thermostats have been altered and we've been told to 'dress according to the season'.

Most of the students have left for the Christmas vacation and we are trying to restore order before we take a break too. It's a more relaxed working environment, but the lack of pressure gives me too much time to brood.

I must catch up on my reading. I love the classics and try to re-read my favourites every decade. Mostly it's like discovering them anew, depending on what's happened in my life. Hardy is my favourite. We did him at school; dissected the detail which is a different experience from reading purely for pleasure. But I also like to read new literature that pushes the boundaries of style. I'm happy as long as it's got a good story and leaves some imprint on memory. Not so keen on fluffy stuff, though. And despite the popularity, I can't be doing with murder mysteries, erotic fiction or anything outside the sphere of credibility.

Coll has stopped contacting me every day. This is another change of behaviour since he met Mrs Mayfield-Harvey. Morning, noon or evening, he always called. Sometimes only a few words to check I was okay, but every day, unfailingly, for at least the past three or four years. This was one of his positive qualities that helped me to believe he cared.

I tried phoning him yesterday. His mobile diverted me to his answer phone. I didn't leave a message. I didn't know what I wanted to say. It might sound like I was checking up on him and I don't want him to think that. I only ever call him if it's important. I learnt early in our relationship that if I call him, he's usually brisk and keen to carry on with whatever he's doing. If he's preparing lessons, I sometimes hear him turning the pages of a book, or the scratch of a biro, mid conversation. If he calls me, it's because he wants to and he's more inclined to chat. I'm therefore unfamiliar with his answer phone message. It sounded warm, sexy and alluring; the Irishness exaggerated. I felt foolish and tongue-tied and my face began to burn.

When I eventually caught him at home on his land line, I said to him, 'You've been quiet these past few days, are you okay?'

He said, 'End of term stuff. You know how it is.'

End of term stuff has never stopped him phoning before.

'I was hoping we could discuss our plans for Christmas,' I said.

'In the middle of something. Can't talk now,' he said. 'I'll call you.'

He hasn't.

Mrs Mayfield-Harvey isn't the first woman to attract Coll's attention since he and I have been going out. He gets bored easily and searches for situations that might bring someone new and fresh into his life. He falls into conversation at the drop of a hat and before you can blink, he's found a new best friend. Men and women, old and young and from all walks of life. He's gregarious and needs lots of stimulation and social stroking. Like a chameleon, he's able to adopt the tone of the company he keeps. He's very much sought after because he can talk about more than football. 'Artistic sensitivity,' he says. Men pour out their woes about their partners. Women find they can chat to him as they would to their friends. It's part of his attraction. He practises his charm like someone might practise the piano, honing his skills to ever higher levels. He tells me his dad was the same and brimful of Irish blarney. He reveres his late dad. Tries to copy his style and outdo his legendary flirting skills. I liken him to Damon Wildeve in Hardy's *The Return of the Native*. *'He wore the pantomimic expression of a ladykilling career.'* That's Coll all right.

He enjoys telling people about his paintings and how one day when he's free from trying to educate the unwilling youth, he will have exhibitions that will stun the world with their magnificence. He knows this is a load of codswallop but new acquaintances are impressed. He's very plausible. They believe him. I did too when I first met him. But after ten years and not an exhibition in sight, the story has worn thin for me. I pay lip-service. I nod and smile. I show interest. He's been so unproductive these past few years I was gobsmacked when he suggested showing his work in the restaurant. I thought it was a passing whim. Even when he went to investigate, I didn't think it would come to anything.

All of which leads me to believe that there's more to the restaurant than a few vacant walls. And so far he hasn't had to unearth his paints, dust off his pallet and lift a brush. Mostly he's giving Felicity pictures from way back. All he needs to do is have them framed. He says he wants to paint again when he retires, but I'll believe that when it happens.

So, as I was saying, there is often a new other woman hovering in the background for a few weeks until the novelty wears off. He takes them out, to the pub for a chat, or to the theatre. But he draws the line at anything romantic or sexual. I would draw the line here too. That would climb out of the grey area into unacceptable territory. And I'm not completely daft. Some would say taking them out anywhere was stepping over the line but he argues that they are friends and makes it difficult for me to object.

God knows what they think. If it was me – and once it was me – I would assume he was interested in a relationship and would be most taken aback to find this wasn't the case. I would feel duped; cheated. This is one of the reasons I won't accept any of neighbour Dan's restaurant invitations.

Coll says it's all in the thrill of the chase. He reckons it's a harmless pastime and that women are relieved to find a man who's not preoccupied with sex. If he knows he can, he doesn't want to. Laura thinks he's weird. She says it's very adolescent and he must've got stuck at some Freudian stage. She's been reading psychology books. She's thinking of training to be a Relate counsellor and practises her listening skills on me. I provide her with plenty of material. There's always something with

Coll. She calls these other women 'OWs', as if collecting them under an umbrella term diminishes their significance, sanitises their existence. She doesn't approve. I told her I thought Relate counsellors were supposed to keep their opinions to themselves.

Of course I mind. But there's a fine line between reasonable and unreasonable freedom. I don't want to cross it. I don't want to appear to restrict his behaviour or to be jealous and possessive. I talk to other men at work. There's nothing wrong in that. I sometimes have coffee with Newcastle John if the library's quiet and we can take a break together. And it's not unknown for us to go to the union bar if there's a reason to celebrate. He's called Newcastle John because I know three other Johns: Laura's husband John, Ginger John from next door and John the Storm, my sister's husband and a volunteer at the lifeboat station in Teignmouth.

It's Coll who gave them these identifying name tags because he knows a few Johns too: Fat John – who's actually thin now having given up drinking, Lenor John – whose wife is overly generous with fabric conditioner, Guitar John, and John-John. Coll's imagination knows no bounds! (He hates it when I'm sarcastic.) Mostly these are people from his local pub where he spends evenings when he's not with me. He says it's because his small flat depresses him. Privately, I think he has a drink problem. It's also a place where he bumps into women who may become OWs.

But the OWs from the pub are unlikely to be his type and they come and go and don't cause me undue anxiety. His behaviour towards me doesn't usually change. Not like now.

I've told Newcastle John about Coll. He's married with kids and thinks Coll pushes the boundaries.

'My wife wouldn't have it,' he said. 'Not if you're committed to someone.'

'That's the problem,' I said. 'Coll isn't fully committed to me. We've talked about a future, but there are no plans in place.'

'Very convenient,' said Newcastle John. 'Perhaps you should be less committed to him.'

Wise words, but if you are, you are. Simple as that.

13

Marianne Fanclub

Felicity

The Deer Orchard is our large rambling family home: a former farmhouse with some converted outbuildings, a sizable garden – now almost entirely under vegetable cultivation – an orchard with apple, plum, pear and olive trees, and a paddock. It is off one of the roads on the edge of Broadclyst village and borders a farm belonging to the Molwings. Before Italy, I rented an additional field from them for some sheep. It was across the lane at the bottom of the paddock and perfect for keeping a watchful eye. Once Kate is more settled, she will probably do the same.

In the evenings, I often used to go and lean on a fence post at the bottom of the paddock and watch the sheep. They seemed to be without a worry in the world, only ever showing stress if their lambs were missing. It was there where I accused Ted of always putting his work before me. He denied it of course. I said it was time he learnt to compromise and he looked at me as if he didn't know what I was talking about. This was before Gianni, but it was another sign of disenchantment.

As I turn my car from the road onto the gravel drive, I look with some satisfaction at the wind turbine rotating in the far corner of the orchard. It was originally my idea to have it installed and, although it is enormous and was extravagant at the time, it has now paid for itself and vindicated my decision by providing plenty of surplus electricity to sell back to the grid. It caused many arguments between Ted and me, largely because I didn't tell him about it and had it erected while he was on a lecture tour on the Isles of Scilly. When he saw it, he was livid. Rachel believes that it was the wind turbine that prompted him to accept the job offer in London. *The spider that swallowed the fly* … If he hadn't taken the job, I probably wouldn't have had an affair with Gianni and the marriage may not have spiralled to the point of irretrievable breakdown. So you could say that the predicament I'm in now is all down to a wind turbine – or at least my decision to get it without asking Ted.

But deep down I doubt we'd be happy. There were too many tensions regarding bedroom matters and too little commitment on his part in supporting my ambitions. If I were to be given another chance, I would have to be more affectionate and stop resenting his lack of involvement in my enterprises. Huge compromises on my part, but might be worth it to get back to the family home.

I park up close to the back of the house. Ted's Volvo is still there so I'm hoping he and Marianne are both in. They might even invite me for lunch if I adopt a conciliatory and unthreatening face. I suppose I should knock, yet it feels all wrong. It is still my house. I still have a key. Ted wouldn't have had the nerve to ask for it back when I moved into to the flat. I could have phoned, but I will pretend I was passing. I tap gently, aware of the cost of my stupidity with Gianni.

Marianne opens the door and that act in itself annoys me. *As if she owns the place!* I will offload onto Olivia later. She is more attractive than I imagined. I have deliberately avoided looking her up on the internet and had visions of a studious type – not unlike Ted – although I don't know why, given her hunky husband. I had thought glasses, no make-up, hair scraped back in a bun and frumpy shoes. It pleased me to think this when I was feeling down. But she looks quite stylish and glossy and sports well-fitting jeans and a rather sumptuous cerise cowl-neck sweater which I immediately covet.

'I'm Felicity,' I say, offering a hand, forcing a half-smile.

'Oh!'

I expect she has seen me in photos, but my turning up has certainly given her a shock. She blinks and does a double take before grasping my hand firmly. 'Are you here to see Kate?'

I lie, 'I need more potatoes.'

'Kate will be back soon.'

'I can always help myself. I know where they are.'

'Of course,' Marianne says, but she looks uncertain, as if I might have a thieving agenda.

She invites me in.

'Edward's upstairs,' she says. 'Working on some paper.'

Typical. Nothing new there. He's always working on some paper. It annoys me that she calls him *Edward*. It's the name she knew him by when they first met as nine year olds, sharing a classroom in a boys' prep school in Cumbria. Yes, I did say *boys'* prep school, but girls were allowed as day pupils and Marianne was one of those. Harriet told me she was the only girl in the class when Ted first came across her. That can't be good, but I don't have room in my heart for pity.

'Would you like a tea or coffee?' she asks.

'Tea would be fine, thanks.'

Marianne reels off a list of herbal options, plus caffeinated and decaf in green, white and breakfast varieties. I'm impressed. She's expanded Ted's selection. If all else fails, we can talk teas. She makes a pot of decaffeinated white tea and we settle on stools by the breakfast bar. She asks me how I am settling in to the new premises. I immediately imagine her as a deer: big eyes, well-meaning, easily startled.

'Early days, but encouraging.' I don't want to admit to my feelings of isolation and loneliness after sharing the family home again for three months. I elaborate with positives about the continued support from old customers, the spreading word of new customers and the advantages of being nearer the city centre.

I hear footsteps coming down our creaky stairs. Ted appears. Dear old Ted, hair a little greyer, looking a little tired, still in great shape for his age. Somehow he has become more attractive now someone else wants him.

He says, 'I thought I heard your voice.'

He's cross, I can tell. He will guess I have come to be nosy. I can't resist touching him on the arm as he walks past. After checking it is decaffeinated, he pours a cup of tea from our pot and hovers without sitting down.

I ask him about potatoes.

He says, 'I think Kate was going to dig some more when she comes back.'

'I can do that,' I say.

'I'll come with you,' he says.

I suspect he wants to have Firm Words about my turning up, but I don't object because the potato patch is behind the runner bean wigwams which although not entwined with produce at this time of year, provide enough cover to fuel Marianne's imagination should she be watching us through the window.

'Now?' I ask.

'Now,' says Ted. 'The tea can wait till we get back.'

He busies himself with wellingtons and drags on his anorak and then we take a walk in silence to the outbuildings from where he takes a large garden fork and a sack. He's rather sexy when he's brisk and businesslike. No wonder his students used to fall for him in the early days.

I attempt some humour to break the ice. 'You rarely offered to dig anything up for me when I lived here.'

He ignores the comment. 'Why have you come, Felicity, when I expressly asked you to keep away for Marianne's first visit?'

He has switched into pompous mode, a rarely seen trait until we started disagreeing about my restaurant venture. Still sexy though. I see a challenge to try to soften his demeanour.

'It's not strictly speaking her first visit though, is it?'

'First visit since summer – since you came back.'

'Sorry. I know it's a bit awkward but I need potatoes … and she would have had to meet me sometime.'

He gives me a look and cuts behind the bean-poles. He looks helplessly at the potato patch as if uncertain where to plunge the fork. I consider offering to do it myself, but I'm not feeling generous today. He has an iffy back and if he tweaks it too much, it might put paid to any plans Marianne might have for nookie. I suggest which potato tops he might lift and give him a hand in collecting the spoils.

When we return to the house, Marianne is sitting where we left her, looking slightly anxious. Over the tea, I talk to Ted about daughter Rachel and our concerns that she is focusing too much on her career at the expense of relationships. She is in her late twenties and has yet to have a serious boyfriend.

'Sorry to bore you with family stuff,' I say to Marianne.

I'm not sorry at all. It is a deliberate attempt to remind Ted that I won't be excluded.

Marianne offers a tentative thought that we shouldn't worry about Rachel and there is nothing wrong in being single.

I give her a look that says *Don't Interfere* and she withdraws into her shell. I receive no luncheon invitation and I am not much wiser when I depart with five kilos of Maris Piper.

14

Life of Sarah

Sarah

My little terraced house is on the eastern side of Exeter, not far from the main road to Honiton. It's a characterless semi, a build of red bricks and newly installed white PVC windows. Downstairs there is a small cosy living room, and a back room that Pete and I knocked through into the cramped kitchen. Modern estate agent parlance might describe it as a kitchen-diner, but it hardly lives up to its name and most of the time I eat in the living room in front of the telly with one of those lap trays with squidgy undersides balanced on my knees. They're a great invention for solitary dwellers but when Coll and I are in a lazy mood and both eating supper from such trays, I sometimes look at him and think we're not a million miles from being an elderly couple with rugs. Upstairs, it officially has three bedrooms but the third is so tiny I use it for storage. The bathroom is big enough to swing only a very small cat and the garden is almost non-existent – a yard with walls on all sides and an overhanging chestnut tree (under a preservation order) that blocks the light. I do what I can with pots and have a few thriving ferns, perennial bulbs and other shade dwellers including a small patch of temperamental lily of the valley which is a delight when it decides to flower. But I struggle with summer herbs and floral annuals.

Pete and I bought the house soon after we were married. Prior to that, we were in his rented flat. We could only afford small at the time and intended to upgrade as our incomes and (hopefully) family size grew. After he went, it was always going to be big enough for me, even if uninspiring. Initially, I stayed to try to preserve what memories I had of him. But after so many years, there's no trace of him left and I stay because I can't be bothered with the faff of moving – especially if Coll and I manage our long talked of combining of resources and eventual upsizing. If it wasn't for him, I might move to the coast when I retire.

Coll is on the west side of the city. We straddle the river Exe about two miles apart. I'm nearer his school and you would think it would make sense for him to move in or stay more often. But I think he prefers to be out of range so I'm unlikely to come across him when he's up to no good with the OWs. He has his own turf, as they say, and I suspect this is why he's dragging his feet about sharing a future.

I'm also nearer Felicity's restaurant than Coll. Even if I won't go there for a meal with Dan, I could go with Laura. But it would serve no purpose other than to add visual fuel to my over-active imagination. And I'm still hoping I'm being paranoid and that she will turn out to be at least no more significant than the other OWs.

Laura says, 'It's not unusual for men to delay commitment. Sometimes they need a push. A pending baby sometimes provides the necessary impetus, but you're well past that. Men like Coll commit because they want a family and not necessarily because they want to share their life with one particular other.'

'Thanks,' I say, demoralised. If this is true, I may have a long wait.

I don't so much regret not having children as I regret not finding a replacement for Pete while I was still young enough to do the daft things that young couples do. We were still in the rosy-glow stage when he died. I watch the dating twenty-somethings on the telly, running after each other through fields and on beaches and then falling in a heap of breathlessness and windblown hair and kisses and wish I'd done more of that while I could. Now the old knees aren't what they were and Coll isn't one for overt displays of affection. 'Too intimate,' he says. I ponder this often. How is it not 'too intimate' to sleep in my bed and enter my body?

Laura says, 'Sex and love are not the same thing. Sex doesn't necessarily equate with intimacy, especially for men. Look at prostitutes.' She says I should search for someone who will treat me better.

It's not that easy when you get to my age. If I was going to look elsewhere, I should've done so sooner when I had more options than Dan-the-Neighbour and the odd opportunist in the supermarket. Although the online dating world has opened up possibilities for many, I'm too shy to do that meet-up thing when you don't know someone and lurk with intent at a pre-arranged place wearing a crazy hat or clutching a rose. I've seen too many TV shows where the guy (or girl) brings a mate to check the look of the person and then report back. If he or she doesn't measure up, they do a runner. I couldn't stand the humiliation. And even if you get past the introductions, the thought of all those first impressions and only an hour or two to prove that you're worth seeing again makes me quake. I'm too lacking in confidence and fearful of what they might think of me.

Before Coll, I did go out with the occasional man, but they were people I knew already and I always kept things casual. If they showed too much interest, I backed off. With Coll, he was the one who kept backing off, so I didn't have to. That's how he kept the relationship going long enough for me to realise I was in love. And I thought he felt the same; just that neither of us said.

I had been physically alone for ages – and so had Coll. 'No one since Penny,' he said. I believed him. I still do. He has a puritanical streak when it comes to sex. He took a couple of years to get physical with me. I began to think he was gay. But he said it was important that it mattered, and until he met me, it wouldn't have. That's how I know he won't go too far with the OWs and that I *am* sort of special. It's reassuring, in a way.

By the time he decided that I mattered (a fact that I seemingly misinterpreted as love), we had both been in the sexual wilderness for so long that our early couplings had all the ineptitude and urgency of teenagers. We laughed a lot. You have to. And we learned. It was another of our compatibilities. I blush to say this, but it still is, despite everything. Except when he's in one of his distancing moods, like now. At times like this, I use sex as a way to try to get close to him, but he responds with all the clinical coolness of a professional transaction without the monetary reward. Perhaps Laura is right about the prostitute analogy. It's an uncomfortable thought.

Coll admits he's frightened of committing again. Like most men, he's protective of his freedom. He says he needs space for his painting and that's his main reason for not moving in with me. I still think it's because of the OWs. But every few months or so when he thinks I may be losing interest, he lures me back with speculation of a future together 'when he retires'.

And so on my evenings alone, I fantasise.

15

Coll's Story

Felicity

I love walking down into the restaurant in the mornings and seeing Coll's paintings adorning my white walls. They put me in a good mood with their vibrant colours and aesthetically pleasing style. There are seascapes, sunsets and blossom-filled orchards. Within four days of hanging, I have sold seven of them. Seven! Olivia went into raptures as expected and bought a pair for her living room.

'Aren't they divine?' she cooed. 'If he's as adorable, I can see why you like him.'

'They're very commercial,' I said. 'He knows what people want. He says he's past being pretentious and trying to push boundaries. He just wants to make people happy.'

An elderly couple from Pinhoe buy three small ones and a further two go in individual sales. The walls are already looking bare. I know it won't always be like this, but with Christmas almost upon us, they are attracting a lot of attention from those looking for special presents. One gentleman asked if Coll does commissions.

I text him and he calls me and says he is 'ultra delighted' and that he will pop over in the evening, after work, to collect money and deliver a few more. We don't open on Thursdays.

I am cheered by the success and the way it gives my restaurant something different from the usual. I've already taken a couple of bookings for next week because of them; people from Silverton and Broadclyst wanting to check them out.

I have also sold several of my pots. The paintings cause people to take time to stand and look and then notice that there are items for sale on shelves below or beside. Even if their budget doesn't stretch to one of Coll's works, they have no trouble in affording one of my bowls.

Rick has done a good job with the display shelves. Since the invite for Christmas, I am trying to feel more positive about him and Harriet. He doesn't realise that I was rather struck on him before Gianni made overtures towards me. It was all girlish fancying, nothing more and nothing different from most of the women in Broadclyst. I would never have taken him up on any offer he might have put my way, but when I heard he had developed a relationship with Harriet, I found it difficult to swallow for more than the reasons I have already stated.

Harriet said, 'You shouldn't have left us. It wouldn't have happened if you'd still been here.' She was waving her arms about in a typically theatrical Harriet fashion, furious that I had dared to be critical. But as a mother, I can't help it. A twenty-two year age gap is almost a generation. I fear for her future but I want to make amends with her. Maybe I do feel guilty about running off, especially as things didn't work out. This Christmas meal may be an opportunity to repair the rift.

My elevated mood causes me to drive down the road to buy another small Christmas tree for the flat. I spend the rest of the morning festooning it with gold baubles and tinsel.

'I thought we weren't bothering with a tree up here,' says my son Chris as we meet for lunch and a chat to ensure we know what we have to do for the following day. 'We've already got the one downstairs and lights in the trees in the car park.'

'We weren't, but I thought it would help us to feel Christmassy.' My real motive is in case Coll pays a visit upstairs.

'It wouldn't be anything to do with this artist bloke, would it?' He gives me a quizzical stare.

'What makes you say that?'

'You've been in a good mood since he appeared on the scene and I heard you gushing to Olivia over the pictures. But I thought you were trying to get Dad back.'

'Have you been listening to our conversations?'

'You're not exactly discreet and Olivia has a foghorn voice.'

Chris has been very understanding over the Gianni business, witnessing it all imploding under hot Mediterranean skies among the olive trees. He looked up to Gianni as his mentor so it was doubly difficult for him when I decided to call it a day. Gianni said he could stay, and he did for a few weeks, but once my new restaurant looked like being a reality, and knowing I needed a chef, his loyalty to me brought him home.

He looks so like Ted, it makes my heart ache. Have I already said that? It must be age. Repeating myself. When we went to Italy, Chris's glasses were almost invisible, but now he has bought some of those fashionable black-rimmed ones – almost like the ones Ted wore as a child – and they spring out from his face, making a statement. I am not too keen, but that is another sign of my age. He has had his hair cut too since we came back. Out there it was the norm to have longer hair, but here, most of his mates are shorn and he says it is easier to manage, being a chef.

'I met Marianne,' I say.

'And?'

'She's all right, I think.'

61

Chris hasn't met her yet and has been avoiding visiting the Deer Orchard while she is there.

'As long as Dad's happy,' Chris says, pointedly.

'Y-yes,' I hesitate. 'But it may not last. You never know.'

'And Coll Waterford? What's that all about?'

'Insurance policy. Distraction. I hardly know him, Chris, and you need to stop eavesdropping.'

'Poor old Mum,' he says.

I give him a weak smile. I know he understands how I feel, but he is fond of Ted too, and now he is almost twenty, all he wants is for us to get on with our lives so he can get on with his and not have to worry. He is kind-hearted and generous of spirit and even though he is never going to have a business brain, or be as professionally go-getting as my other children, I love him to bits. All I hope is that he will find a woman who can do accounts, deal with customers and organise his work schedule. Then I can take a step back and ease into retirement. But for the time being it's good to have him around.

Later, Coll arrives armed with paintings. He returns twice to the boot of his car to fetch a further two bubblewrapped packages.

'Enough to fill the gaps and a few extra,' he says. 'Because you are proving to be an excellent saleswoman, Felicity. Much better than me.'

'They are selling themselves,' I say, taking one of the packages and leading him through to the restaurant. 'I can take no credit other than providing walls.' This isn't strictly true. I had flagged up the existence of paintings for sale to any customers I already knew. And with the restaurant so recently opened, there were a lot of friends and acquaintances from the village popping along to show support. It only takes one person to start noisily appreciating and other diners turn round to see what all the fuss is about.

He shows me the replacements and we slot them into the spaces: cornfields with poppies, woodland with bluebells, autumnal riverbanks and what look like scenes of the Scottish

Highlands. There is a lot of standing back to admire from both him and me. He is not exactly modest.

I decide to be brave. 'Would you like to come up for a cup of tea?'

'You wouldn't happen to have a bottle of wine on the go?' he asks, cheekily.

It is the way he says it, I can't help but find it charming.

We adjourn upstairs to my small living room. It's five-thirty. Too late for afternoon tea and too early for supper.

'Like the tree,' he says.

Purchase justified!

I say, 'Are you hungry? I can offer you cake or leftover chicken from yesterday's service.'

He accepts the chicken. 'If that's okay. It'll save me cooking when I get home.'

I decide to join him and put the food in the microwave. It is another opportunity to impress him with our menu.

Once we are settled at the table, I say to him, 'Your turn; your story.'

He hesitates and for a moment I detect reticence. 'Ah Felicity, do you really want to know?'

'I do.'

He takes a couple of forkfuls of the chicken and rice mixture (a Persian recipe with a fragrant sauce) and makes appreciative noises. 'This is wonderful. I don't remember it from your menu.'

'Once a week we introduce a dish from around the world. It encourages regulars to keep coming back, knowing there will be something different to try.'

'Great idea. What will it be next week? I may drop by.'

'Italian. Chris's choice.' I fear he is using stalling tactics. 'Your story,' I say, again.

'My story is one of getting married too young and then growing up to find that the person I was with wasn't the person for me,' Coll says.

'Not unusual.'

'I was doing a degree in art and met Penny at a gallery show. She liked my work. She was a socialite and had contacts. She had visions of organising exhibitions in trendy London venues where she planned to introduce me to her moneyed world and woo them with promises of my potential. They would invest and I would become famous. It sounded easy. She would then bask in my glory.'

'The innocence of the young.'

'And the belief. Where does that go, Felicity?'

'We lose confidence as we age,' I say. 'We understand the consequences of failure. When we're young, it matters less. We have time to try again.'

He narrows his eyes. 'I know many teenagers who lack confidence – and many older people who are very self-assured. I am in my teaching, but not in my art. There are no clear cut rules.'

He is probably right. My children are all confident. So is Ted. So am I. But I am less so than I was. 'Maybe it depends from where you start: the confident lose it as they age, while those lacking, acquire it.'

'Penny believed,' Coll says. 'In the beginning. She saw something in my work that excited her. In retrospect, I think it was me that excited her – I know that sounds arrogant, but she said she had never met anyone like me.'

I can understand why she said that. He is unusual. The kind of man about whom one talks long after they are gone.

'She used enthusiasm for my work as a way of playing up to my need for reassurance. It had the desired effect. But it's made me suspicious ever since.' He looks meaningfully at me.

I laugh. 'No need to be suspicious of me. The sales speak for themselves. You don't need me to massage your ego.'

I wonder if Coll's self-deprecating comments are genuine, or designed to elicit flattery. It is not the first time and it contradicts his air of confidence.

'She was considered "suitable" by my family. Classy. They thought she would be good for my career and they invited her to stay.'

'Where were you living at the time?'

'In London. We started out in Ireland, but came over here when I was about seven. Dad was becoming known as a musician and Mum was selling paintings for ridiculous sums.'

It made complete sense to me that Coll was the product of creatives.

'Should I have heard of either of them?' I say.

'Doubt it. Their success was short-lived, but made them enough money for Dad to start a business. He was resourceful and had tons of charm.'

So that's where Coll gets it from, I muse. And the slightly Irish twang.

'And the business?'

'A wine importer. Luxury wines, not your average plonk. They sent me away to school and led extravagant lives. I think they wanted me out of the way so they could party unhindered. Penny was of their world: champagne and expensive holidays. I realised I didn't quite fit in. I know that sounds odd, but I never felt I belonged to my parents. I even went through a phase of thinking I was adopted. In the end I decided to do a PGCE and train to be a teacher where being a socialite is of no benefit whatsoever. On the contrary.'

'This all explains why you are so difficult to pigeonhole. Why you are such an enigma.'

'Is that what I am?'

I can tell that he knows he is and enjoys the intrigue.

'By this time Penny and I were already engaged. She wasn't pleased by the turnaround in my career decision, but I was too young to realise that she saw teaching as a low status profession, even though it earned me more money and security than my art most likely ever would.'

I thought the same when Harriet decided to train, but I keep this to myself.

Coll says, 'She was naive; I was naive; and because we were in love, we carried on with the relationship. In those days sex and socialising took precedence over a more settled way of life. So we didn't notice our incompatibility for the long term. Even though it was never exactly right, it was never exactly wrong, either. We had problems, but so do all couples.'

'It's hard to split after a big investment of time. Usually there needs to be something serious – like someone else.' I need to be careful here or I will find myself telling him about Gianni.

For a moment he is thoughtful. It is as if he is going to say something random and then changes his mind back to the track. 'Things got worse before the wedding. But we focused far too much on what our families would say if we split up. It was all about not losing face for our respective mothers.'

'Kids are less considerate of parental feelings nowadays, but maybe that's a good thing. They do what they want,' I say, thinking of Harriet and Rick.

'Afterwards, it was a classic case of believing having children would solve all our problems. Which it never does. I know that now. We had Jack. She doted on him. I felt pushed out.'

'What you say sounds similar to what happened to us. Except much later on. It wasn't because of the children. Ted says he felt pushed out when I started the business.'

We carry on chatting about how his marriage finally broke down. He says it was about twelve years ago that they divorced, after both their sets of parents had died. It is difficult enough staying together for the sake of the children, but doing so for the parents – I am not sure I approve of that. Whose life is it after all?

I grill him about the divorce details and he seems happy to share. Penny got a good deal and left him with only enough cash to buy a two-bedroom flat.

'Women always come off best these days,' he says.

'I'll bear that in mind. With Ted in the family home and me stuck here, it doesn't feel like that to me.'

'Ah, but you've a long way to go, Felicity. A good lawyer will see you right.'

I'm surprised he didn't fight his corner better. I also wonder what happened to his parents' wealth.

By this time we have finished the chicken and eaten a piece of cake. Coll has drunk a glass of wine but refuses more because he is driving. I clear the plates. He seems disinclined to leave so I offer coffee, which he accepts and over which we talk about my children and his virtually estranged son and I tell him about my concerns for Harriet. He is a good listener as well as a good talker and the evening wears on effortlessly. Chris comes in, puts his head round the door, is introduced to Coll and then says he is going to bed. Only then does Coll get up to leave. It is about ten. He apologises for taking up so much of my evening.

'If I had anything better to do, I would tell you,' I say, meaning it. 'I've enjoyed the chat.'

'I haven't forgotten what you said about the theatre,' he says as he leaves. But although he thanks me for the supper, he doesn't even try to kiss me on the cheek. In a way, I am glad, because I worry about the complication this may bring. But on the other hand, I am a jilted woman, a soon to be divorced woman and I want to be desired.

16

Sarah's Fantasy

Sarah

My fantasy goes something like this:

If Coll and I combine resources, we'll be able to afford more space and a bigger garden, maybe even an outside studio so Coll can pursue his art in peace. Men need sheds, or the equivalent. Pete told me that. Sheds for cave-time; a primitive need passed on from the generations of long ago. I don't understand why this need has perpetuated into the modern day when it causes so much stress in relationships. Perhaps in a few thousand years, men will yatter on like women and women will be the ones needing to escape to caves.

Anyway, what I've learnt is that when men are in cave mode, they don't like to be bothered. Pete used our spare bedroom as an office and den, but he didn't make a big thing of it. Coll will definitely need space – and the more, the better. He seems to be in cave mode more than he's out of it, especially at the moment. Pete told me that men come out of their caves of their own accord and on no account should they be forced into unwilling interactions. And they think women are complicated! I'm not saying that we don't need space, but our need is not governed by so many rules.

You may wonder what happened to my painting – or *art*, as I like to think of it. Once Coll and I got together, it somehow fizzled out. He stopped encouraging me. I think he felt guilty because he wasn't painting. He didn't want me to outshine him while he was pontificating to all and sundry about his own pictures at imagined exhibitions. I remember him saying, 'Sarah, your appreciation of art is top notch – that's why we get on – but you'll never be more than a journeyman painter.' Journeyman painter! What a cheek! It was true, though. Even I knew that. But the words hurt sufficiently to dampen my enthusiasm to continue even at the hobbyist's level. Mrs Felicity's bowl reminds me that I've invested so much time in Coll's pursuits, I've lost some of my own. I shall rectify this if we move somewhere. When I retire, I'll need to do something other than read.

I've always wanted a conservatory and enough space to grow a few flowers and herbs. I think I've a natural aptitude for gardening although at present it's only demonstrable via the perennials out the back and my small collection of indoor plants.

I've a rubber plant that's so tall it contorts in a right-angled turn on the ceiling and is fast making its way towards the central light fitting. I also have ubiquitous spider plants alternating with tradescantia on my living room window sill. Coll hates them. He thinks they clutter up an already small space. If I had a garden, I could exercise my passion out of his domain.

I would also like two or three hens and a couple of cats. I've often imagined us breakfasting on a patio with summer sunshine gently warming the morning air and songbirds twittering sweetly from a nearby hedge. The cats are stretched out lazily on the lawn and the hens scrat about the borders making comforting hen noises and acting as pest controllers. Or it might be a balmy evening under darkening skies, sipping wine and pretending to be in foreign lands.

And a thatch would be nice. A thatched cottage in somewhere like Broadclyst with old oak beams, a log burning stove in an original fireplace, tons of quirks and character, but modernised with a proper kitchen-diner, a walk-in shower that is separate from the bath, and a master bedroom with an en-suite – and a decent-sized garden for the shed-come-studio. A downstairs loo would be useful … and a utility room. My dream cottage also has a huge wisteria around the door and over the window-tops, like one I saw in Silverton.

Or we could go to the coast and have a bright modern dwelling with sea views and bracing air. Is it too much to ask? Between us, we could afford this fantasy. It's nothing special for two people in their fifties who have worked all their lives.

If we were together, instead of me waiting for phone calls from Coll and him controlling when we meet, he would be here, coming and going, pottering, painting, cooking (I hope), looking out for me and I for him. We would discuss what we do instead of him making all the decisions before he phones me, always expecting me to fit in with his plans and never him considering mine.

I dream of security and normal things that other couples share and that I had once for the briefest time before it was snatched away in a moment of madness.

17

Texting

Felicity

After Coll's disclosures, the see-saw of intimacy exchanges is balanced. There is something reassuring about our shared traumas of relationship breakdown and parental loss. And it is good to have an impartial man with whom to disclose.

I meet Olivia for lunch at the New Inn in Broadclyst. It is a cosy pub and eatery not far away from the Deer Orchard and I secretly hope that Ted or one of the children will be there. It was always a regular haunt of ours before I set up my own restaurant.

Olivia is all teeth and coiffed red hair as usual and is in one of her gushing moods having been to an over 50s speed dating evening in Exeter. She's picked up three new potential suitors and has them lined up for dates next week.

'You would have loved it,' she says.

I wouldn't.

'Such a hoot. We could've compared notes. Two of the men were completely ghastly. Purple-faced drinkers. Slimy types.'

I listen patiently until she has acquainted me with nearly every one of the fifteen or so seven-minute dates.

She says, 'The woman who ran the evening said she was allowing seven minutes per date because of our age. She said we had more life lived and more to share than could possibly be revealed in five minutes.'

'Not so much speed dating, then. More like snail dating.'

'Snail dating,' muses Olivia. 'That name could catch on.'

When at last she sits back to draw breath, I find she is keen to hear the latest about Coll, and says I am being too cautious when I tell her I don't think I want to pursue a full relationship.

She says, 'Neither of us has much time left before the hormones go AWOL.'

I say, 'I left most of mine in Italy.'

'Then you better get them sent over sharpish,' she says.

And we laugh.

What happens next are texts between Coll and me over a period of three days.

From Coll: *Thanks for supper. No wonder you have returning customers.*

From me: *You're welcome. And thank you.*

From Coll: *Thanks also for listening to my story. It was good to talk.*

From me: *Good to know there is life on the other side.*

From Coll: *Life on the other side is more pleasurable with a like-minded companion.*

From me: *I wonder where you might find one of those? ;)*

From Coll: *I wonder too. ;)*

From me: *Touché.*

From Coll: *Antony and Cleopatra on at small local theatre between Christmas and New Year. Interested?*

From me: *Interested!*

From Coll: *Will make enquiries. Is there a good evening for you?*

From me: *Monday or Thursday. No restaurant service.*

From Coll: *Tickets for Thursday 27th. 7.30 start. Pick you up at 6.45?*

From me:	*That's kind, but I'll make my own way. Where shall I meet you?*
From Coll:	*In the bar of the Cider Press theatre. Accessed up a narrow staircase. Shall we say 7ish?*
From me:	*In diary. 27th at 7. Look forward to it!*
From Coll:	*And I. x*

I look suspiciously at the x. I heap it with so many pleasurable connotations that it collapses with the weight.

There is method in my refusing a lift. Much as it would be nice to be picked up, if I have my own transport, I will have control and can make my own way home when I choose. If he were to bring me home, I would have to invite him in. And what if he said 'yes', what then? It is one thing to have him visit with paintings – and even to come upstairs for a chat or a snack after – but it is quite another for him to enter my space after a date.

Date … Is that what it is? I am not totally sure. Nor am I sure what I want it to be.

18

Texts

Sarah

Coll deigns to spend a weekend with me. But he's still in a weird mood and has started checking his phone like a maniac. And when it pings with a tell-tale message, his eyes dart from side to side like he's thinking how he can break off from our conversation to take a peek. He may as well not be here for all the attention I'm getting.

He's acting like he's obsessed. With something. Or someone.

One hears of people so dependent on their phones that they go into withdrawal and have panic attacks if they become separated. But Coll's not usually like that. We are from the pre-mobile generation who travelled the motorways and country roads in our unreliable cars when we were twenty because that's the way it was and we didn't know any different. Our parents didn't expect to hear from us unless there was a problem – and even then it wasn't always easy to find a phone. There was none of this constant checking on whereabouts. It was assumed you were going where you said and unless anything dire had happened, there would be no contact until you reappeared.

I ask him why he's been so unavailable this past week or two. He says he's been seeing Anne. Anne is a work colleague in her forties, a teacher in the Art Department. He's known her for ages so she probably doesn't qualify as an OW. Makes me uneasy though because over the past year or so, he's started arranging to meet her out of school. His excuses always begin with, 'She's in a state.' Anne always has man problems. Don't we all. And she's always 'in a state'. Hers require lengthy discussion, usually over a drink in some pub. Coll is particularly adept in advising on such matters – except when such matters relate to him.

I can hardly object. He's worked with her for years. She's an old friend of sorts. But I met her once at a school do and she didn't strike me as the *State* type. She was very assertive and confident. Still, men can have a funny effect on the strongest of women. Recently her states seem to be more frequent. I'm none too pleased. But Coll looks at me as if I'm being possessive and jealous. I am, but I hate him thinking that. Times have changed. Women seem to have men friends and vice versa – even when they're committed to someone else. It wasn't like that in my parents' day. If my dad had had a woman friend that he went out with in the evenings, even infrequently, my mum would have gone spare. I don't want to be unreasonable. Not if this is how

73

people are in the new millennium. It's just that I'm not totally sure that it is how things are. I'm constantly uneasy.

So maybe all these texts are from Anne. But then why doesn't he say like he usually does? *It's Anne, she's in a state.* If we're sitting side by side when it pings, he angles the phone slightly away from me as he reads the message and taps a reply. I try so very hard to seem disinterested, but my heart starts pounding and I can feel the stress in my stomach. Today, I ask him who it is.

'I have to have some secrets,' he says, mysteriously.

That makes it even worse. It means it's probably not Anne. I wonder why he doesn't wait until I'm not around. It's as if he deliberately wants to annoy me.

I wouldn't dream of snooping, but I can't help but remember his face after his first visit to see Felicity about his paintings. I have a nagging feeling that these texts might be something to do with her. *Mrs Felicity Mayfield-Harvey.* Even her pretentious-sounding name is starting to annoy me. And if they are texting, what are they texting about? There's only so much text mileage in picture sales.

Ask him? No, I can't do that. He'd say I was checking up. If we're ever going to live together, there has to be trust. And I'd hate it if he did the same to me. But then I don't give him reason to be suspicious. I'm an open book.

He rushes to the loo. He takes his phone. He's there for ages. Either he's up to something or has a serious digestive problem. When he returns, his mood is light. But he doesn't look me in the eye. He's stopped looking at me like he used to do. I feel him slipping away and I am powerless to stop him. It's as if I'm the one in the quicksand and he's walking away without even throwing me a rope.

19

A Trivial Pursuit

Felicity

I hear on the Harvey Grapevine (Rachel via Harriet) that Marianne Fanclub has scooted back to her flat in Beckenham for a few days. I must seize the opportunity to fit in a few visits to the Deer Orchard in the hope that some will allow unplanned meetings with Ted and a chance for some casual interaction, conducive to improving our relationship. Arranged chats only happen about the divorce and they are stressful.

It would seem I can't let go. Weird, that. I thought I had while I was staying at the house, but now I am alone I am experiencing a heartache I hadn't envisaged. It is not for Gianni. I am over him; the ratty fox! It is for the love I had with Ted before everything went wrong, way back during our middle years, long before my mother died. I have too much time to think now I am isolated in the flat above the restaurant. Destructive thoughts about the future; romanticising the past. Not like me. I am usually very *here and now*.

I leap into the car ten minutes before the time Ted usually stops for a mid-morning break. I wish I were nearer.

Orchestrating an incidental meeting reminds me of our first encounter during our student days. It was in the refectory at UCL. I had been watching him in the library for weeks, impressed by his work ethic and intrigued by his apparent lack of a social life. My friends thought he was such a geek and laughed when I said I thought he was actually quite good looking if you took off his glasses and roughened him up a bit. It was the late 1970s and compared to most students, he was very conservative. He wouldn't have been out of place on *University Challenge*.

I was in the final year of my biology degree, hunting for distraction having split up with my third serious college boyfriend who turned out to be another Jack-the-Lad. I caught him in bed with some floosy who shared our student residence. Bastards, both. Anyway, thrice bitten, I decided I needed some stability and that I had been going for the wrong type; the long-haired Bohemians who played guitars into the night and were usually high on something. Cool dudes. Sometimes I joined in with the something, but it wasn't the real me and it was time to move on.

Anyway, I became a super-sleuth, finding out from one of the librarians that this studious geek with the glasses was called Edward Harvey and was a post-graduate in the Archaeology Department studying for a PhD. That explained why he seemed more mature than most. I was the same age, having taken a gap year after school. Further subtle questioning of the librarian yielded the information that as far as she knew, he wasn't attached. I was conscious of the possibility of a meek little woman at home to whom he returned in the evenings after a day of research, but I doubted it.

I started stalking him and discovered he took a break in the refectory at the same time and alone at the same table most mornings. A man of habit. Some would say boring, but I was looking for stability and someone to father my children. One day I engineered a situation whereby I and my friends sat in his vicinity. I wore a sexy top and jeans, made sure my hair looked its best, and much to the amusement of said friends, I went over to talk to him.

I knew I would create an impact. I found it easy to attract men in those days. I was also lucky to have the looks that went with the times and I had matured early and spent my schooldays honing my dating skills.

Poor old Ted. When I think how forward I was, and how I flirted. But it worked. He didn't stand a chance. Once he started turning puce, I knew I had scored a hit. And he had a brain, so when he had got over his nerves, we engaged in a witty exchange which led to me asking him out. We met again in the union bar and I found we had lots to talk about. I started planning our future. Unlike most men, he seemed perfectly happy to be controlled. In any case, I was very subtle and he was always buried in research, so he probably didn't notice. And it wasn't long before I moved in with him. I can't remember who first suggested marriage, but it might have been me. He wasn't my first love, nor my Great Love, but I knew he wouldn't let me down.

And he didn't. He stuck with me until I became impossible.

Looking back, it was a combination of menopause, Mummy's money and the feeling of life having slipped by while I was raising the children and Ted was making his name climbing professional ladders. He hadn't changed much and I had become bored with the familiar – including sex. This didn't please Ted, so what with that and my restaurant plans, we always seemed to be arguing. When Rick and Gianni entered my world and started paying me attention, I realised I hadn't lost my ability to attract men – even younger ones – and became restless. Classic midlife crisis I suppose. One thing led to another and I ended up leaving the family and going to Italy.

On this chilly December day, it feels like a world away; another life; a big mistake.

When I returned in August, I planned to try to make a go of our relationship again. I remember thinking on the plane of what I would say to him, how apologetic I would be and how forgiving he would be. Eventually. I expected some harsh words, displays of hurt, sulking. But I hadn't factored Marianne Fanclub into the plan and although I don't blame him, I believed our long marriage, much of it very happy, should have been sufficient for him to give me another chance.

The more he has resisted, the more I find I want him back. I tell myself that perhaps he has doubts since Marianne's stay at the house. It is probably the longest time they have spent together since her husband died. I suspect she is more demanding of attention than I ever was and he won't like that. But I have no evidence other than that her social and family worlds are smaller than mine.

When I suggested this to Harriet, she said, 'Mum, Marianne is a writer. She spends as much time as Dad does closeted away constructing prose. She's not a bit like you imagine.'

Ted is in the kitchen when I arrive. He says hello, but not with any enthusiasm. I tell him I have come to collect produce for the evening service. He asks if Kate knows. I hate that I am expected to tell everybody of my comings and goings as if I were a stranger.

I say, 'I wonder if we could have a chat?'

He raises an eyebrow. I expect he thinks it's about the divorce.

'A chat? What do you want to chat about?'

It's as if I have asked for something outrageous. I say, 'It's odd being stuck in Pinhoe ... I miss you a bit.'

He laughs nervously.

I put the kettle on and help myself to a teabag. I think I probably shouldn't, but with Marianne out of the way, it hardly seems a crime. He is looking particularly sexy this morning: ruffled hair, a chunky black jumper and jeans.

Ted hovers, deflated. 'I thought you were here to collect veg?'

I try again. 'I am interested in what's going on in your life. The kids don't tell me anything. How is your TV project going? When can we expect to see it aired?'

He tells me it's going well and due to air at the end of January. I let him speak uninterrupted and make him a mug of tea, choosing his usual decaf and adding the barest splash of milk. Gradually, he relaxes, the tense expression leaves his face and he begins to look me in the eye. We move to the stools by the breakfast bar, sitting on opposite sides clutching mugs.

And then I make a mistake. 'What does Marianne thinks of *our* house?' Bitterness escapes in my emphasis of 'our'.

'Felicity ... Don't.'

'Sorry. But seriously, does she like it? Did she have a good time here?'

'She has been here before,' he says. 'While you were in Italy.'

I know this and it didn't matter then. It matters now. Very much. I say, 'How did we end up like this? I mean *us* of all couples?'

'You know how,' he says.

And I do. 'I wish ...' I say, reaching across to touch his hand.

He pulls away. 'It's too late, Felicity.'

'Is it? Absolutely? Completely?'

'Absolutely and completely.'

'No point discussing?'

'We've been through it all several times. I'm sorry. There's nothing here.' And he touches his heart in a way that makes my own deflate in sadness, even though there is not much love left in there either.

After that, the tension returns and Ted makes it clear that he needs to get back to his work. I drink my tea, collect the veg and return home.

Too late. Nothing here. Those words echo for the rest of the day and into the night. After service I retire upstairs and console myself with a bottle of wine. This isn't like me either. Chris has gone to stay over at his latest girlfriend's and I begin to brood. I try to convince myself there is nothing that cannot be changed. That if I am patient, his relationship with Marianne will falter and I will be there heroically to pick him up.

I am having one of those periods of life where I am scared and uncertain about the future. It is a new feeling for me. I have discovered I am uneasy on my own in the winter months when the skies are grey.

Another glass of wine and I start thinking about Coll. I may have to wait a while for Ted to be available again, but Coll could be an interim measure if I play my cards right. He fits the template of my early boyfriends: an ex-hippy, creative, enigmatic. As a type, they are often difficult to live with and not always reliable, but as a distraction and temporary measure, we might keep each other company, have some fun. And almost as I am thinking this, my phone vibrates and I discover he has sent another text.

Have just had a couple of snow scenes framed. Perfect for the season. Will drop off Thurs after work if that's ok.

No 'x' this time. We women notice these things. Especially those of us who were courted with many Italian x's. But my mood lifts immediately. I wait until morning before I reply. I read in a magazine that four hours is the minimum time one should leave between texts if one is interested in a man. Unless an earlier response is essential. So if he is playing games with x's, I will play with time.

Interested? Am I?

20

Distancing

Sarah

Coll's been very quiet this past week. Gone are the regular updates about work. When he speaks to me, he says he's busy with a new painting.

That's a surprise. He hasn't painted at home for so long, I'm amazed the paint hasn't solidified in the tubes. He says he wants to finish as quickly as possible to take advantage of any pre-Christmas rush of purchases at the restaurant.

I might have guessed *she* would have had something to do with it. *Felicity …*

'I can't see you this weekend,' he said. 'All my stuff's here and I'm running out of time.'

It's difficult to make demands against that type of logic. And my sister advised me to lie low when he's in one of his distancing moods. Jane thinks he's got commitment phobia and is a control freak. She's probably right. In both cases she says that backing off is likely to be more successful than pushing him into something he doesn't want to do. It's all very well Jane saying that when she's happily married to a man who will do anything to please her. John the Storm is one of those selfless guys who put other people first.

When Coll visits on Wednesday the following week, he's preoccupied and cool – even cold. He doesn't try to engage me in our usual wordplay conversation about current affairs, or entertain me with quips. Instead, he says, 'I may not be able to see you as often.'

We are enjoying spare ribs with barbeque sauce, baked potato and salad.

'What? Why?' I ask, immediately losing my appetite.

'My painting requires me to spend more time at home.'

If that's all it is, then no matter. As long as it's a temporary state. But I fear it's so much more. I seek clarification. I say, 'All the more reason to consider our future options, especially as you're going part-time next year. We could find a place with a workshop or studio.' And as soon as I've said it, I wish I could suck the words back, erase them or negate them. I should not mention *Future Options* with Coll unless he mentions them first.

There's a long pause during which I can hear the cogs turn in his brain.

'I don't know what's happening. I don't know what I'm doing,' he says, looking beyond my left shoulder. He always says this when he needs space. It's all about him.

I panic. 'And what about Christmas?'

'Too much pressure, Sarah.' His tone is sharp.

'But I need to plan meals, gather provisions.' He's been coming to me for the past ten years or so. If he's got other ideas, I don't want to be stuck on my own at the last minute with a turkey and masses of trimmings.

'I'll call you,' he says.

My stomach tightens. I feel like hitting him. 'And this weekend?'

'I don't know, Sarah. I can't think at the moment. I've a lot on. End of term, like I said. Painting. This opportunity is important to me.'

'I have to plan. Meals don't magic themselves into existence.'

'You are such hard work sometimes, Sarah.'

Tears are close. This is so unfair. Me hard work? When he's like this, I appreciate how inconsistent messages can drive people insane. Laura told me about some dogs that were conditioned by a psychologist to respond to ellipses and not to circles – or it could have been the other way around. But then the circles gradually became more elliptical and the ellipses more circular and the dogs went crackers. 'Neurotic,' was the word she used. Anxious to the point of madness. That's what it's sometimes like with Coll.

During a quiet moment in the library, Newcastle John says, 'I think you should confront him. Have it out. Ask him what's going on.'

I told John because I had to tell someone and Laura is off sick.

'I'm scared of the answer.'

'Better to know. It's Christmas. You can't expect to wait forever for him to decide. My wife made her lists two weeks ago. She sat me down and we went through everything together. It's what people do.'

82

If only Coll was more like Newcastle John.

Our boss says John and I have been selected to represent the library at the leaving do of the Dean of Historical and Social Sciences, Dick Fieldbrace, who has been here even longer than me. I appreciate the gesture, but would rather not have to make the effort. I could ask someone else, but John says my longevity of service entitles me to attend and that I'm the best person for the role. It's nice to know I'm good at something.

'You know Dick Fieldbrace much better than I do,' he adds. 'And the distraction will do you good.'

I relent – and immediately go into meltdown about what I'm going to wear.

21

Pots and Plots

Felicity

Coll turns up and I take him through to the restaurant. The tables are already laid for the following lunchtime so we use the desk area behind the counter by the till. It is a bit cramped, but it will do. I catch a waft of aftershave and wonder if it is for my benefit.

He unwraps two beautiful impressionistic snow scenes of medium size and in attractive silver distressed frames. They are very Monet. They could be of any wintry English village, but through the snowflakes I recognise Broadclyst church with its double lych gate and twin yew trees either side. One picture depicts a few sheep faintly visible in the field opposite, while the other is from a different angle, emphasizing the Somerset tower. This is close to where Harriet resides with Rick. I wonder if they would like one as a Christmas present?

'Lovely,' I say, pointing to the one with the sheep.

'I painted them years ago, but I've only just had them framed.'

'What's your best price?' I adopt the negotiating terminology of a TV bargain hunter. If I spend too much money on one of my children, I have to balance it with the others and the one-seventy price tag is a little too steep even after a twenty percent reduction.

'For you?' says Coll. 'Hundred, cash.'

This is generous. I pay him from the till and write myself a note. Thinking that his coming on a Thursday might be because he knows I don't have service to worry about, I invite him upstairs for a cup of tea or a glass of wine.

'Sorry, can't stop today,' he says. 'Got to rush. Have to keep painting while in the mood. If I do a little every evening … And there's stuff for school. Busy, busy.'

I am disappointed. Despite our date with *Antony and Cleopatra*, I begin to doubt his interest in me.

Then off he shoots without even a backward glance.

However, I don't have time to dwell on what's going on. No sooner has Coll left when Harriet appears on a rare visit on her way home from work. I quickly hide the new pictures and am relieved she didn't bump into Coll on her way in. That could have been awkward.

'All right, Mum?' she asks. 'You look a little flushed.'

'A tad hot,' I say, even though it isn't.

Harriet wanders around the restaurant admiring the paintings, vindicating my hasty decision to buy 'Broadclyst Church with Sheep in Snow'.

'Nice if you've got the cash, but your stuff is more my price range,' Harriet says. 'Bowls make perfect presents for friends.'

I still haven't got used to her more conservative style of dress. She has toned down her wild ways since she started teaching. Gone are the piercings and she has even stopped dying

84

her almost black hair even darker. She has a softer look and I like it. She is also less abrasive in manner, though still not slow to say what she thinks.

'I haven't many left,' I say. 'They have been flying off the shelves. I should have made more while I was still at the Deer Orchard.'

'It's not too late,' she says. 'Bowls or shallow dishes. Small ones would be great. It'll save me so much time if I can buy from you. And it keeps the money in the family – and I know you like that.'

She is referring to the fact that I get prickly when my children go to eat out at other restaurants.

'Okay,' I say and we discuss how many she would like.

She says, 'I'm glad you've accepted our invitation for Christmas. Rick's over the moon.'

I doubt that.

I find Coll's enthusiasm and drive have inspired my creativity and before I go to bed, I make some sketches for my ceramics. I have an idea for a new pattern. I like using images from the natural world; probably a hangover from my biology days. My last collection was *Leaves*. This time I'm thinking *Seaweed*. The greenish brown tones will sit well against an aqua wash. I can develop it further into *Shells,* maybe even *Corals* or *Anemones*. Perhaps a *Rockpool* collection in the New Year. But I need some blanks first.

Next day, I head out into the weed-covered garden at the back of the property. It is very bare apart from a few fallen leaves tight against the fence. I have plans for minor cultivation in the spring but it isn't big enough for more than a few herbs and perhaps some flowers for table decorations. I might even ask Rick to do it for me if the Christmas visit goes well. Some pinks, perhaps. And if we put in some trellis on the edge of the car park, sweet peas would be nice.

At the end of the garden is a small shed where I keep my clay and potter's wheel. It's not as comfortable a workshop as is my bespoke

85

outbuilding at the Deer Orchard, but it will do for now. I still can't believe I am stuck here. Part of me still thinks it is a temporary move and that any further alterations will be an unnecessary extravagance.

I spend all morning in there and once I get into it, I enjoy the rhythmic repetition and the sensual feel of wet clay oozing through my fingers. When I have amassed two dozen small bowls on the wheel, I use plaster moulds to shape thirty small, shallow oval dishes of various sizes. Then I break off another small piece of clay and, using a template from a drawing taken from the internet, I fashion it into an irregular shape that few would recognise and at this stage has no obvious purpose. However, I have an idea. A plan that makes my lips twitch into a smile when I think of the reaction it may provoke in Coll. Next is the drying process which I will start here, but then finish in my kiln room tomorrow at the Deer Orchard.

I call Kylie to see if she can help out the following day. It is likely to be busy and if she brings her friend Jules, they can help Chris with the prep and cover the evening service between them. Ted would tell me not to be so extravagant paying staff when I could do the job myself. But needs must.

The evening service is quiet and passes uneventfully and once upstairs with a glass of wine, I find Coll floating into my thoughts. I'm miffed by his cursory visit and lack of attention. I want to know why he was so brisk and cool. When I call Olivia and explain how he rushed off, she says, 'Oh, he's one of those.'

'One of what?'

'A player.'

This online dating thing has given her a window into the world of men that she never saw through before. I have been out of the loop (can't count Gianni) for long enough to have forgotten the strategies of the game players. But it makes sense.

Olivia says, 'I bet he'll be all over you next time you meet.'

That remains to be seen.

Next day, after lunch, I pop my partially dried ceramics carefully into the boot of the car and head off to the Deer Orchard. There is no sign of anyone when I arrive, so I lay my pieces of shaped clay on shelves in the kiln room. Then I offer to help Kate with her garden duties. She has a huge surplus of winter veg and I suggest putting a sign by the road advertising the fact at times when she is not at work.

'Word will soon get round the village. It saves people a trip to the farmers' markets further afield and is cheaper than the shop.'

She agrees and I help her bag produce and make notices.

Afterwards, I hang around the kitchen on the pretext of wanting to speak to Ted when he comes back from the university. Kate makes me a cup of tea and suggests I stay for supper.

'Do you miss being here?' she asks.

'How did you guess?'

'Because you keep coming back when you don't have to. Because you're paying someone to do your work at Neptune while you help me unpaid.'

'Am I that obvious?'

'It must be difficult.'

'It is. Especially when Marianne is here. But it is my own fault.'

Kate misses nothing. She is very bright and has finely tuned person skills. She has never been slow at speaking her mind, either.

'It will be easier if Ted and Marianne have their own place.' I can hear the hint in her voice. She wants me to push on with the divorce. They all do.

'Do you think it will last? Ted and Marianne?'

'Yes. Sorry, but yes.'

I can hear Ted's car on the gravel outside. In seconds he is in the kitchen, rubbing his hands together, trying to get warm.

'I'm glad you're here,' he says.

For a moment I think he is pleased to see me. But no. He takes a white envelope from a pile of mail on the breakfast bar. 'This came here for you.'

I open it. It is an invitation.

'Dick?' says Ted. 'I received one too. Thoughtful of them to send ours separately.'

'Is it?' To me it is another unpleasant reminder of my solitary state. 'It's this Tuesday! That doesn't give me much time to arrange staffing.'

Dick Fieldbrace is the retiring Dean of Studies from Ted's faculty at the university. Scottish, tweedy, dour, steady. A small, strong Highland bull of a man. He had red hair when I first knew him. Last time I saw him it was mellowing to a shade of sand.

Ted says, 'I didn't think you'd want to go. With the restaurant …'

'I knew him quite well, once,' I say with a touch of sarcasm. 'If you remember, he and Janet came to us a couple of times for dinner. When we lived in Exeter. When you were starting out.' I remember those times fondly. Before the children were born when Ted was a bright young archaeologist, keen to make a name for himself. Dick was his head of department in those days. It was only later he became Dean.

'Are you going?' asks Ted.

'If Kylie can cover yet again, then yes. Perhaps we could go together,' I offer tentatively. 'I could drive then you could have a drink.'

'I will already be there,' says Ted.

'Then let me fetch you home. James can drop you off the next day to pick up your car.'

'I still have a lot of stuff to sort from my office.'

'So?'

'So I may do some more sorting after the do.'

'I could help, you know. I'd be happy to.'

88

'Marianne offered.'

'Marianne isn't here.'

'I'm not sure.'

I can tell he is wondering how Marianne would feel if she knew we were holed-up together in his office for an hour or two. 'She won't know if you don't tell her.'

'That's not how it works with us.'

'You need help; I'm offering. Then you'll have more time for getting ready for Christmas when she returns. You can decide over supper. Kate's asked me to stay.'

'Has she indeed.'

His displeasure is evident and later when I am in the sitting room and he is in the kitchen with Kate, I catch the odd stern whisper from Ted and think I hear him say, *'Run it by me first.'*

Over supper, most of the time Ted looks at me suspiciously while I interact with James and Kate about plans for the next planting of vegetables and deliberately drink too much in the hope of eliciting an invitation to stop overnight.

It works.

'Oh that would be great, Kate. Then in the morning I can put my pots straight in the kiln for firing. Save me a journey.'

Ted gives me a sharp look. He can see through me, but I make it impossible for him to object. I want to find out how Marianne deals with the news that I stayed while she was away.

I am banished to what was Chris's room, where I camped out for the three months between my return from Italy and moving into the flat. I say 'banished' because after supper I started flirting with Ted, giving him coy looks and teasing him about his popularity among the students. Eventually he snapped and said, *'Stop making a fool of yourself, Felicity. Go to bed.'* I vaguely remember having a rant about being kicked out of my own home by a London tart. Perhaps that was why he looked so angry. I didn't mean it, the tart bit, but I enjoyed saying it.

So here I am with half of the 2010 Manchester United football team grinning down at me from the walls, plus an odd collection of pop stars from Chris's adolescence. It was not what I had in mind.

What I had in mind was an unrealistic fantasy. I thought if we both drank enough, something might happen to rekindle the long-dead embers of Ted's passion for me. When I am a bit drunk, I forget we are separated and I want to touch him. If only I had wanted to when we were still together. How strange the workings of the human mind.

Being here brings a lump to my throat. All my babies grown. I find myself welling up. I am not usually so sentimental. On the shelves are models of dinosaurs from when Chris was eight and Ted was hoping he might follow him into archaeology. But the craze was short-lived, soon to be replaced by his interest in growing things which later evolved into cooking. I must get him to come and clear it; keep what he wants and dispose of the rest. It is not a shrine. He is not dead. I start to weep.

By the time I get up in the morning, it is late and I have a headache. I am calm and embarrassed. Thankfully Ted, James and Kate have made early starts for their respective seats of learning. I make a coffee and sit at the kitchen table surveying my former domain. I must have been behaving badly for Ted to explode. After the coffee, I write a note of apology and thanks, stack the kiln with the dried pots, collect the veg, check I have locked up properly and drive home.

Ted has reluctantly agreed to my driving him back from Dick's do and getting a lift with James the following day as I suggested. Kylie has texted me to say she can stand in, so all I have to do is transform into a diva and hope my glad rags are a reminder of the times we had when we were younger. It is a forlorn hope. I know it is, yet I have to try.

22

A Bit of a Do

Sarah

The 'Do' for Dick Fieldbrace is being held in the senior common room which is located on the first floor of the original part of the university. It has a high ceiling and chandeliers and is usually frequented by the older members of staff who try to escape the over-enthusiastic students who badger them all day long whether in lecture theatre or office.

The great and the good of the University of Devon are gathered: most from the Faculty of Social and Historical Sciences and assorted odd-bods like me and Newcastle John representing the different departments and administrative areas. Dick has been a well-respected Dean for many years. Selfless yet shrewd. He's already surrounded by people waiting to speak to him, to bid him farewell. Their good wishes will be heartfelt and genuine.

There's a long table at one end of the room covered with a white tablecloth on which are glasses of wine and fruit juice. I'm driving so I opt for orange juice. Young women and men circulate with trays of canapés, no doubt a more economical option than laying out the food buffet style and finding it all disappears in seconds as the gannets see a free supper and swoop, loading their paper plates high with goodies. I take a passing sausage roll and a couple of spicy morsels from a thin Asian waitress dressed in black.

Dr Edward arrives with a woman beside him. I wonder if it's his new woman friend, the existence of whom has been rumoured for several months.

'Whoo, that's interesting,' says Newcastle John. 'Dr Edward with his estranged wife. I wonder if they're back together.'

My heart flutters. I make a nonspecific noise and John gives me a funny look.

'I don't think so,' I say. My short-sighted eyes squint to gather details. So this is her. *Felicity*. I'm transfixed. She's tall and quite slim wearing a smart black jersey dress with a tomato-red waterfall cardigan and ankle boots; a striking combination. She still has something of a waist despite having had four kids. Coll's liposuction comment comes to mind again, yet I'm in almost as decent shape as she. Her hair is piled on top of her head in the modern deliberately tousled style with escaping tendrils. A simple gold necklace hangs round her neck and she has small reflective studs in her ears. I bet they're diamonds. Everything about her is classy. I feel a frump by comparison. She spots someone she knows and makes a bee-line, exchanges a few words and then moves on to someone else. I can tell she's an experienced networker and she knows a lot of people here. Poised, confident and attractive for a woman of our sort of age. I shrink into the carpet.

'What do you think of her?' I ask Newcastle John.

'She's all right, I suppose. Wouldn't kick her out of bed. But she's not as pretty as you,' he adds, thoughtfully.

'Charmer,' I say. I don't believe him.

'Honestly. Truly, honestly,' he says. 'And she's a bit fierce.'

'Have you met her before?'

'When she used to work here. Ages ago. Would you like an introduction?'

I'm suddenly scared, diminished, irrelevant. 'Oh no,' I say.

But what if I said, *'Yes'*? My heart pounds at the thought. Anxiety grips my throat. I feel faint. I swallow a mouthful of juice. The scenario plays in my head.

'I believe my partner's paintings are on display in your restaurant.'

'Your partner?'

'Yes.'

'Coll?'

'Yes.'

'He never said he had a partner.'

There are a couple of options here. The polite and dignified one: *'Didn't he?'* Perhaps a puzzled, *'Ohh …'* And then shrug it off; wait to see what she says, if anything. Or there's the 'cat among pigeons' response, undignified and potentially embarrassing.

'Well, he wouldn't, would he? Not when he's obsessed with trying to woo you.'

'Woo me? Coll?'

She might laugh, dismiss it. She would pretend she doesn't know, feign innocence of his attentions, look down her nose at me and accuse me, as Coll does, of being paranoid. She would appear to be unmoved, but deep down she would be angry at Coll's deception. She may confront him; take him by surprise when he goes to collect money.

'You never said you had a girlfriend.'

'Oh, you mean Sarah? Didn't I mention her?'

'No, you did not.'

She would give him a suspicious look. She has the air of a woman who wouldn't stand any nonsense. Not like me. Coll would be ready with an excuse to diminish my significance and absolve him from any obligation to have put her in the picture before.

'She's someone I've known for a long time but you don't need to worry about her. We're not committed. She's not important.'

'I'm not important,' I say out loud.

'What?' says John.

'Nothing.' My mind is elsewhere, wondering if I should take the plunge while I have the chance. It's a perfect opportunity. A legitimate opportunity. I didn't seek her out. She was here, in my territory. Surely Coll couldn't blame me for introducing myself?

But he would. Dignified or undignified, he would find a reason to blame me and create a scene.

She's still moving from person to person, smiling, laughing, hugging and air kissing a few old friends and colleagues, heading in my direction.

If I make her aware of my existence, it would give her an inkling as to his nature. Surely if she knew the half of what he's like, she'd back off.

I don't sell him well, do I? If I was to offer him at an auction, I doubt there would be many takers. But then again, he's good looking for his age, and he can charm the pants off women. And we women are susceptible to charm. If Felicity's up for a bit of fun and company, she's not going to be discouraged by an irrelevant girlfriend in the background. And if she falls for him like I did, why would she want to let him go?

'Are you all right, Sarah?' says Newcastle John.

'I shouldn't have come.'

Still I stand transfixed, watching her. She turns and catches my eye. I look away. It's now or never. She's only a few feet away from me.

But I suffer brain-freeze. I can't risk it. Sweat is oozing out of me at the thought of a confrontation and my heart pounds like it might escape my chest. I am having the hottest of hot flushes and must look a complete sight.

The moment passes and she moves on.

23

Behaving Badly

Felicity

After sneaking away from Dick's do early, I persuade Ted to let me help him in his office and we spend an hour and a half sorting through files and folders and disposing of mounds of unwanted paper. Black bin liners swell as they are filled with rubbish and recyclable materials. For a while it reminds me of when we moved house. We slot into our old roles, intuitively knowing what to keep and what to ditch. Then Ted spoils it and brings me back to earth with a jolt.

'Marianne's told me not to bring anything back unless it's absolutely essential,' he says. 'We may not have much space when we move.'

I swallow before I reply. 'She's right. And you'll have a job downsizing the clutter at home too.'

After that we focus on the task and mostly we don't speak.

On the way back from Dick's do, Ted says, 'Marianne's coming back in a couple of days. I trust you will keep away. I don't want any more scenes.'

Clearly the diva look hasn't worked its magic.

'That's charming considering I have just been your office clearance manager and taxi service.'

It is the first time we have been alone together in a car for ages. Our physical proximity is like old times: Ted and me; a couple. Our emotional distance is anything but. Ted is bristling with self-righteousness.

'I didn't ask you to – you offered. But I am asking you to keep a low profile over Christmas.'

'The kiln—'

'Damn the kiln,' he snaps. Then he lowers his voice and tries a more reasoned approach. 'I know ... I know you have to do what you have to do. But you can be discrete. Please. Come and go as you need to. You don't have to make your presence known at the house.'

'We could all have a drink together. Get to know each other better.'

'It's too soon. I mean it, Felicity. It's our first Christmas and I don't want you to spoil it. Kate and James will visit you at yours.

95

And Harriet says she and Rick have invited you over for a meal on Christmas Day. Rachel too. You'll probably see more of the family than I will.'

'But that's not the same as us being all together.'

He says, 'Like last year, you mean, when you were in Italy?' There is bitterness in his tone.

I have no answer to this.

But despite what he says, I am not going to keep a low profile. I want to continue to test Marianne's nerve. If she really loves Ted then nothing I do will make any difference. If she is playing with him, then my interference may shake her commitment. If that is the case, she doesn't deserve him.

When I turn up unannounced three days later to collect my pots from their second firing, there is no one home but Marianne, and although my intention is to heed Ted's words and make my way straight to the kiln room, she spies me through the window, waves, opens the back door and invites me in.

'Just for a moment,' I say, stepping in and closing the door against the cold. 'I won't keep you.' I can see she is busy and I loiter, making small-talk so I can watch what she is doing.

She is preparing a meal: a casserole of some description. Some chicken pieces are sizzling in a pan and she has a mound of vegetables on my lovely central work station. She waves a knife at me and says she's, 'Doing a Delia.' I wouldn't say that, quite. Ted says she cooks, but she's not in the same league as me. I can tell by her expression and her nervous laughter that she worries she doesn't match up. I pass the time talking about the weather while she peels and chops, looking flustered. I have to say, she has good chopping skills; almost as good as mine. She keeps rushing to the hob to check the meat in the pan. I wonder what she would say if I offered to help. Probably think I was finding fault. She is well-mannered enough to ask if I would like to stay to eat, but I refuse. She has enough trouble catering for four. Don't know how she would manage if she had to do what I do for a room full of paying customers. I expect she will be glad when she and Ted have their own place. If it ever comes to that.

But despite her uneasiness, she is keen to keep me talking and in the end I agree to a cup of tea. I make it myself and then perch on one of the stools by the breakfast bar. If Ted asks, I can say she forced it upon me and I didn't like to refuse. I wish she wouldn't be so charming and nice to me. I don't deserve it. Underneath, I can tell she is uneasy; that she thinks I might still be a threat.

Ted will not have told her that I stayed over last week when she was back in Beckenham and Kate and James invited me for supper. But I make sure she knows by a casual reference. I say, 'When I stayed over last Sunday.' My voice trips out the words as if she must surely know. There is no trace of Bitch in my tone. I see her eyes flicker with uncertainty and the knife she is using hovers in mid air for a moment. Who knows whether she will berate Ted afterwards. I know she is the jealous type.

Once the casserole is in the oven, she asks if she can see my bowls and I take her out to the kiln room where she is full of praise. She says, 'You're so lucky being able to create such beautiful things.'

And she sounds as if she genuinely means it and I feel a bit of a heel. The truth is, she is the lucky one and I resent her.

On the morning of Christmas Eve, I am back at the Deer Orchard cutting some stalks of sprouts from the garden when Harriet beckons me into the greenhouse. Rick is still in charge of garden maintenance and is doing his thing with a spade and wheelbarrow, looking hunky, every bit the lover of Lady Chatterley. He nods at me and I nod back. The humidity in the greenhouse envelopes me with deep layers of organic smells and again I feel that tug of nostalgia for when I started out on my smallholding enterprise. My tiny greenhouse at Neptune is a joke by comparison.

Harriet says, 'Mum, I wish you'd stop trying to upset Marianne. It's not fair.'

Someone's been telling tales. Or maybe Harriet has overheard the fallout between Marianne and Ted after she discovered I had stayed over. Harriet's defence of Fanclub amuses me. Rachel said it was Harriet who brought Ted and Marianne together, inviting her to a party, ostensibly to protect Ted from the amorous advances of my friend and neighbour Jessica Hennessy who had set her cap at him.

My mind has wandered. It does that. I click back to the present. 'Who says I'm upsetting her?'

'I do,' Harriet says. 'You've got her all wrong, Mum. She's funny. She makes Dad laugh. I think you scare her.'

'Why should she be scared of me?'

'There's a lot more "us" than there is of her. Dad only had to win Holly round. There's four of us – plus two partners if you count Rick and Kate – and then there's you and the Broadclyst collective. Her husband's dead. Not only are you alive, but you're here.'

'Then she needs to toughen up.'

'That's unfair. And Rachel is openly hostile.'

Good old Rachel.

'She doesn't need you stirring,' Harriet says.

'I don't stir.'

'You flirt with Dad.'

'He's still my husband.'

'Only in name. And that's the point, isn't it? All these divorce delays are making her feel insecure.'

'You know this?'

'I overheard her talking to Dad.'

'A good relationship isn't built on insecurity.'

'Do you want Dad back? Is that it?'

I take time before I answer. My reasons for wanting Ted back are unchanged; still as much about the family and the house as they are about him, despite the odd wistful flip of the heart.

'It's my old life here I miss.'

'Exactly, so you are acting like a well-fed cat playing with a mouse.'

'And I wouldn't like to see him make a mistake.'

'The mistake would be to go backwards and settle for a dull companionship when he has the chance of passion.'

'Ouch.' I am hurt by this. Hurt by the truth. Dull is what our relationship had become before I went away.

'Sorry, Mum.'

Harriet is only twenty-four but she has good moral sense. Of all my children, she has been the most surprising. A rebel as a teenager and now a local pillar of society.

She is correct about the divorce delays. We are progressing at tortoise pace. The finances are proving challenging. A lot of my money is still tied up in the restaurant in Italy and I am insistent that Gianni must find another buyer for my portion – about seventy percent – but he hasn't yet. *'I need time, Felicity,'* he says. *'I not rush into partnership again with someone who let me down.'* It is crazy that he feels he is the wronged one.

I foolishly told Ted, when I left, that he could have the Deer Orchard. But I am named on the deeds as part owner and disinclined to honour my original rash promise now I am alone. Ted said if I want half the house, then he will claim a portion of my inheritance. *Quid pro quo.* He likes throwing the odd Latin phrase my way because I once criticised him for being pretentious. He only does it to annoy me. I said claiming any of my inheritance is not fair because it is my family's money. He said that I have lived for over twenty years on his and his family's money. After that I threw a wobbly and cited my contributions to the household. And so it goes on, all the while our solicitors benefitting from our inflexibility.

Indeed, our solicitors are becoming very well acquainted. Olivia said she saw them having dinner together in a restaurant in Exeter. I wonder if the purpose was to try to find an amicable solution to the Harvey impasse, or if they had more salacious matters in mind.

24

Liability

Sarah

I regret not saying my piece to Mrs Felicity. I had my chance. I blew it. A few choice words and I could have put the kibosh on Coll's little dalliance. Afterwards, I was in quite a tiz and I beat myself up for a good twenty-four hours. *Why? … Why? …*

It's what I do.

Seeing her has not helped. Especially as she was looking so tall and slim, swish and competent. I haven't worn high-heeled shoes outside of the house since I ended up on my face in Budleigh Salterton three years ago. I swear it was a paving stone. Coll said it was me being clumsy. I pointed to the stone, slightly raised. Coll said there were dozens of raised paving stones but you didn't see people prostrate on the ground every five minutes. 'Other people,' he said, 'trip but rebalance themselves.' I said that's what I used to do. I tried to argue the case of menopausal women being inclined to fall over, but he said he'd never heard anything so ridiculous and I was 'a liability'. This does not help one's confidence. Indeed, it ends up as a self-fulfilling prophesy. He says he worries that I might 'disappear' from his side any moment when we're out.

It wasn't the first time. There was an incident when we went to Tresco for a mini break. It was one of his extravagant gestures and it was the most beautiful place I'd ever been. It started out as my suggestion. Dr Edward goes to the Isles of Scilly to do archaeological research. I was trying to locate a paper for him in the library and he said I ought to go.

'Don't leave it till you're old, Sarah. The more energy you have the better – and you'll probably want to go more than once. People do.'

I told Coll, knowing that he would go off and do some research online. If he liked what he saw, he'd suggest it to me as if it was his idea.

Three months later, he said to me, 'Fancy the Isles of Scilly, Sarah? Tresco? The Island Hotel won't be functioning in its present form for much longer. According to the website, it's going to be turned into an "Apart-hotel" – whatever that is. I think we deserve a bit of an indulgence just once, don't you?'

I jumped at the chance.

'It might inspire me to paint again,' he said.

It was typical that he had found some reason why he wanted to go. He couldn't bring himself to do it just for me.

When we arrived, I gasped. Our room was so luxurious. I had never been in such a place. French windows opened onto a rustic wooden balcony with table and chairs and steps leading directly down to the ornamental gardens, decked out with tables and parasols. We overlooked a sea of turquoise hues in which were tiny rocky islands scattered like jewels. We could have been in the Pacific Ocean and not twenty-eight miles off the end of Cornwall. It was Whit half term in 2010 and for the three days we were there it was as hot as high summer. It was heaven, it was perfect. Except it wasn't.

We hired bikes. Neither of us had cycled since we were kids, but they say you never forget, so we took the plunge. After all, there are no cars on Tresco, only buggies and transport vehicles, so it seemed pretty safe.

I was peddling away merrily on one of the coastal paths, enjoying the sea breezes and the beautiful scenery, when my sun-hat blew off. I grabbed at the hat, lost my balance and ended up steering into the hedge. I wasn't hurt – apart from my pride – but that night Coll drank most of a bottle of red wine and went on and on about possible dire consequences of falling off a bike on a remote island and about air ambulances and inconvenience and how the holiday would have been ruined.

As it was, he ruined it by being so critical. He couldn't see the funny side. I did. You have to laugh at yourself when you're like me. Anyway, having started ranting about the bike incident, he raked over all my other imperfections. He told me he still didn't love me. And he told me with such force, I believed him.

'Then why are you with me?' I asked.

He didn't answer. That night, instead of passionate love-making in our island paradise hotel, he turned his back on me. I lay awake brooding for hours while he snored beside me, sleeping off his over indulgence in wine.

The morning after the bike incident, we cycled to the quay on the other side of the island at New Grimsby, left the bikes on the grassy bank and picked our way down onto the almost deserted beach overlooking the island of Bryher. It was empty but for a mother and toddler playing languidly at the far end with a plastic spade.

The sun shone out of wide blue skies, baking the silver sand and we sat among the stones, a few feet apart – and promptly had another argument.

I was expecting him to apologise for the previous night, but he hadn't finished.

That was when he first called me a liability.

'You make me nervous, Sarah. It's stressful being outside with you.'

Like it was my fault! I don't do it on purpose. These things happen. I am careful, but since the old hot flushes started, I seem to have become unstable.

Words flew back and forth. I can't remember the details now but it wasn't pleasant.

The woman and her child didn't stay long. Afterwards I was embarrassed.

On the way back to our accommodation, Coll rode way ahead of me, standing on the pedals up the hill while I struggled on foot, pushing the bike past the pub and the church, freewheeling down the other side. He never looked back. I didn't catch up with him till he was replacing the bike in the racks at the hotel. In the afternoon he went off on his own for a swim and I sat on the balcony reading and feeling very alone.

On the journey home on the plane to Exeter, I pretended I was asleep, all the while agonising over whether to end our relationship.

Back home, we went to the pub for an evening meal and it was almost like everything was back to normal. But for me, it wasn't. Even the next day, when I returned home from work and found flowers on the doorstep and a note of apology, I did no more than waver. I was thinking through what I might say; picking my time; plucking up courage; wanting to be sure.

But then I got sick. I had a bad dose of gastric flu which took all the stuffing out of me. I'd never had such bad gut ache in my life and I was wobbly for a good week afterwards. I couldn't deal with that and finishing with Coll in the same time frame – especially as he was massively supportive and looked after me for the duration. I expect it was his guilty conscience. By the time I recovered and felt strong enough to do battle, the moment was lost and it was too late.

Since then there's been no more bike riding and no more major rows. He knew he'd gone too far. We've grown closer, talked of the future, become more settled. Until now. Until he met Mrs Felicity.

And now I wear flat shoes or sandals whenever I'm outside and only a small elevation for special occasions. Not particularly sexy, but better that than ending up in A&E with Coll saying, 'I told you so' and 'Liability.' I try to make up for it with push up bras and cleavage. Felicity has both: cleavage and three inch heels, and seeing her gracefully strutting made me dislike her even more.

I think it is best not to tell Coll I've seen her. Not that I've seen much of him since he started painting again. He's continued to be very elusive; the odd meal and no overnight sleepovers. He says we'll catch up over Christmas.

25

Gifts

Felicity

It turns out Olivia is right about Coll.

During the cold, grey afternoon of Christmas Eve, he turns up with another painting – a small one of Marker's Cottage, the ancient cob house and visitors' attraction in Broadclyst village. He's cunning, I'll give him that. He knows my clientele will swoop on it. It is his loose style that brings fresh eyes to the familiar and the much photographed. I say to him, 'You'll get commissions from people wanting paintings of their houses.'

'I know a little restaurant that would make a very pretty picture. Or even the lady owner, herself.'

He is back to his flirting. I am relieved.

'Do you do portraits?'

'Not often. But I might be persuaded if you would sit for me.'

'Too busy, just now,' I say, not wanting to commit, though the thought of it makes my spine tingle. For a second I wonder if he would want me clothed or unclothed. When I was at uni, one of my Jack-the-Lad boyfriends was an artist. His name was

Kevin Ossett and once he painted me nude. Sitting for him was a very sensual experience. He had me draped on a chaise longue with a billowy scarf only partially hiding my nether regions and my long hair tumbling in a cliché of waves across my breasts. After most sessions he would silently remove his own clothes and have sex with me. Sometimes he was even nude while he painted. Looking back he may have had a fetish, but at the time it was exotic and exciting.

We had pet names for each other. He called me Felicity-Wicity and I called him Kevinsy-Wevinsy. How silly, but we were nineteen, thought we were madly in love and that it would be forever. It lasted for most of my first year. Then I discovered he was painting a girl called Christina, also in the nude – including 'afters' – and that was that. He never finished my painting and I don't know what happened to it. I never told Ted. Occasionally I worried that it would turn up in some exhibition, that I would be recognised by someone I know and that it would cause me problems. Now I am older, separated, self-employed and with grown up kids, I don't suppose it could harm me. It might even be good for business. *Restaurateur in Nude Scandal!* I would enjoy seeing Ted have a fit.

Coll comes up for a cup of tea and enthuses about how having his pictures here has inspired him to paint again and how great it is to have someone like me admiring his work.

'Like me?'

'You know what you're talking about.'

I ask him what he is doing for Christmas and he is vague. Says something about catching up with friends and family, though what friends and what family he doesn't elaborate. From what he has told me so far, his family are either dead or estranged. I find it a little unsettling when a person doesn't seem to be connected to others. There is no one to validate the stories. This is how people get into trouble with internet relationships and end up fleeced of their life savings or, worse, under a patio or behind a bath panel.

At least I know Coll has a respectable job in the locality – though come to think of it, he has never mentioned the name of the school.

I tell Coll about Harriet and Rick inviting me over and he allows me free rein to explain my concerns for Harriet's future.

He says, 'Practicalities and common sense don't go hand in hand with love.'

I should know this after Gianni. I do know this. And Coll has given me a perfect prompt for telling him my Italian story. But still I hold back.

I say, 'Perhaps I don't want to be accused of not saying anything – further on, if things go wrong.'

'There are no rules when it comes to age.' He gives me one of his penetrating glances, so deep I almost flinch.

Then, while we are on the subject of Christmas, I give him his surprise.

'It's not a present,' I say. 'Just something small. Inconsequential. I don't want anything in return.'

'Pretty wrapping,' he says. 'As is your dress, Felicity. Going somewhere special?'

Such smooth-talking charm. I see through it. I give him a look that says I know it is all blarney. But I can't help but enjoy his flirting.

Before he leaves, he asks if he might use the bathroom. I think nothing of it, but after he has gone, when I next use the loo, I discover a small grey furry seal on top of the cistern. It is so cute, I can't help but smile. I haven't been given a cuddly toy for decades. He must have smuggled it in, hidden in one of the pockets of his trademark needlecord jacket. All evening I contemplate its significance.

Olivia says it's 'a sign'. 'You don't give thoughtful little gifts like that unless you have an agenda. Same as yours.'

Do I have an agenda? I mull this over while Chris, Kylie and I do most of the prep for Christmas Lunch. Soon we are up to our elbows in sliced parsnips, potatoes, sprouts and swede. Then while Kylie busies herself with stuffings and Chris assembles the pigs in blankets, I make French-style fruit pies as an alternative to Christmas pudding.

Rachel turns up unannounced later in the evening. Rachel is almost two years younger than James and looks like I did at twenty-five with long wavy hair almost to her waist. But her temperament is more like Edward's and she used to be Daddy's Girl until the Fanclub business. I think she is jealous. She has tried to approve like Harriet, but it is an effort. Meanwhile, I have cashed in on her disapproval and our common enemy has brought us closer.

We hug on the doorstep. I detect a new perfume. Outside, the rain is falling and a cold blast of air envelopes us. I hurry to usher her in.

'I've brought your present,' she says, mysteriously. 'Not something I could put in the post.'

She is looking and sounding very metropolitan these days. A new black coat and boots; an expensive-looking chunky scarf; more high gloss make-up and up-to-the-minute styling. Working in London has changed her.

'Are you staying?' I wonder if Chris will be able to vacate his room at such short notice.

Rachel looks embarrassed. 'At home, yes. I'm on my way there now but I thought I'd see you first.'

Home. She is referring to the Deer Orchard.

'Harriet says I can have her room as she's at Rick's for a few days.'

My heart squeezes. I remember what Harriet said about Rachel still being *openly hostile* and wonder how that one will pan out.

'You do know Marianne is there?'

'Yes. But it's okay. It's only a couple of days. I have to leave the day after Boxing Day. It's not as if I haven't met her before

107

when Dad had his accident. She won't be aware that I disapprove – unless Dad's said something – which I'm sure he hasn't. In any case, I want to spend some time with Dad. I'll see you again when we eat with Harriet in the evening, won't I? She said you were coming.'

'I hope you know what you're doing, Rachel.'

'Aw, Mum!' She gives me another hug. 'Your present's in the car. I hope it's okay. I took a risk. I talked to Chris and he thought it was a good idea.'

I wondered why she hadn't removed her coat. She disappears into the dimly lit car park and returns with a closed basket from which I can already hear plaintive mewing.

I am immediately excited and thrilled. I can't wait to see what's inside. Rachel hands me the basket and then dashes back to the car. 'Wait before you open,' she says over her shoulder. Soon she is back with a further large box, wrapped in Christmas paper. 'Stuff they'll need,' she says.

'They?'

'Two.'

Another hug around the box and the basket.

We go up to the flat where I extract two tabby and white kittens, prettily marked. They each fit into a hand and I am immediately in love. I have missed having animals to care for and this is a perfect present.

'They came from a friend. One girl, one boy.'

'Do they have names yet?'

'No.'

We find a corner for the litter tray and show them the kitchen where I place bowls of water and kitten food on the floor. Neither want to eat. They are so exquisitely tiny and I will have to be very careful not to step on them as I rush about doing chores. After teasing them with mice on strings, we try to settle them on a cushion. They keep escaping so Rachel gathers them onto her knee while I prepare some supper.

'This is nice,' Rachel says. 'The flat.'

'Nice … but … small. It's not the Deer Orchard.'

'You've been spoilt, Mum.'

'Yes, but it was my home for many years and at my time of life, I'm entitled to comfort.'

Rachel doesn't remind me that it was my choice to go. She turns her attention to the kittens while I cook.

I make a light tomato pasta dish for both of us and we chat about her work at an advertising agency. At present she is focused on her career and climbing ladders. She is determined to fight her way through the glass ceiling and she will probably succeed. I remember what Marianne said about the positives of being single and deliberately don't pry into her personal life. I know she dates a lot – but doesn't get involved. She says she is waiting for someone special but I worry she sets her standards too high.

'Mum, Harriet says you've been a bit of a nuisance, popping up at home while Marianne is there.'

'It's my house.'

'I know, Mum. But what do you expect Dad to do?'

'He could go and live with her in London.'

'Why should he? He's only just finished at work. And even so, he'll still be doing odd bits at the uni. He said they want to live here.'

'I thought you were on my side.'

'I am. But I want Dad to be happy. And he is. He has a chance. Don't spoil it.'

'And what about me?'

'You won't change things by being awkward.'

I ponder these words. If even Rachel is starting to side with Marianne, then perhaps I should take note. And for a moment I look at me from the outside. I've been a bit of a cow. More than a bit. Has my experience with Gianni twisted my mind?

Yet when Rachel leaves to go to the Deer Orchard, I imagine happy scenes around the fire and jealousy burns brightly. At

109

night, alone in my bed, I feel sorry for myself. And then I think of the balls of fluff curled up in the next room and an iota of joy warms my soul.

26

Christmas

Sarah

On Christmas morning, I wake not with the usual excitement, but with an unwelcome dread. All night Coll and I have lain at opposite sides of the bed; no kiss goodnight, no skin to skin, no radiating warmth diffusing from one to the other. It's as if he is here under sufferance, yet he won't reveal why. It's as if he wants me to find out by myself, too cowardly to tell me that it's over.

We lie in bed until nine and then have scrambled eggs with smoked salmon for breakfast, few words exchanged. Coll is not his usual ebullient self. Normally on Christmas morning it is like dealing with an excited child. I used to love the way that even the smallest gift was approached with joyous expectation. Last year he filled a stocking full of small goodies for me and got up in the night while I was asleep to place it at the foot of the bed.

Sometimes I find it hard to remember that only a few weeks ago he was being attentive and caring.

After breakfast, we have our present exchange of lacy underwear from Coll (for me – debatable) and a jumper from me to him.

'I bought it a couple of months ago,' he says, as if excusing why he should present me with a gift of passion, when passion with me is the last thing on his mind.

There are also presents for both of us from my sister – a handbag for me and a striking bluey-grey ombre scarf for Coll. She knows he likes his scarves. There's a pair of golden hoop earrings for me from Laura and a few small gifts from our work colleagues. It's not long before we are down to the last present, a small fancily wrapped box that has appeared tucked under the tree at the back without me noticing. Coll takes it and looks at it thoughtfully.

'What's that?' I ask.

'Oh, something for me from Felicity.'

'Felicity? You know her well enough to be exchanging gifts?' My gut reacts.

'It's a joke present. That's what she said. Nothing much.' He struggles with the red and green coloured ribbons that are tied around gold paper and hanging in festive coils. For a joke present, she's made a lot of effort with the packaging. I wonder why he's being so up front about this. Why not spare my feelings by opening it in private? Again a shiver of suspicion that he wants me to know.

'Did you give her something?'

'Not really. Nothing much. I gave her a small seal as a thank-you for selling my pictures. Not a Christmas present as such.'

'A seal? What kind of seal?'

'You know, a seal. A furry seal.'

'Why a seal?' My heart is beating a little bit faster. A seal seems somehow intimate.

'I saw it when I was out shopping one day and thought she might like it.'

I'd quite like him to give me a furry seal. Do I appear as a woman you don't give a seal? He knows I like animals; that I would have a dog if it wasn't for my job. This is more evidence she's on his mind. Apprehension mounts. I'm transfixed.

Inside the wrapping is a box and inside the box is – I don't know what …

'Oh no!' he says. 'Look at this! Isn't it great?' He smiles broadly and passes it over to me.

I examine what turns out to be a small piece of pottery: a narrow four inch oval with a hook-shape, not unlike the Cornish peninsular, at one end. It has an irregular edge and an uneven surface. It's painted different shades of green with half a dozen or so small splashes of light blue. On the back is a magnet.

'What is it?' I give him a look of bewilderment.

'You can't guess?' Coll says, taking it back and stroking the surface gently. 'It's an island. A fridge magnet island. What a brilliant idea.' And he's lost in thought with a faraway gaze.

I shake my head, still confused.

'You are so stupid sometimes, Sarah. Isn't it obvious? The island of Coll from the air.' He laughs. 'She's a clever woman. This is so subtle. She understands my humour. It's just perfect. Don't you think?' And he gives another low chuckle, opens his phone and starts sending a text.

Thoughts hammer in my brain. *A perfect present; she understands him; he gave her a seal.* It's as clear as the cool unpolluted waters of a northern lake. It's unequivocal. It frightens me.

'Does she know about me? Have you told her about us yet?'

He looks up, mid message. 'No.'

'Don't you think you should?'

'I will eventually,' he says absently.

I know what eventually means. It means when it's too late for her to run away.

'When is eventually?'

'Shhh. Let me concentrate.' Coll is preoccupied with his text message, oblivious of the effect this is having on me; on us. Christmas, ruined.

I look at the expensive jumper I gave to him, draped over the arm of a chair. It doesn't match up to the fridge magnet; to the island of Coll. It's useful, but about as lacking in humour as it's possible to be.

27

Revelation after the Turkey

Felicity

On the evening of Christmas Day, I find I am squashed around a circular table in a small beamed cottage with Chris, Rachel, Harriet and Rick. It's a far cry from the huge table in our dining room at the Deer Orchard. Also from the cosy, sensual Christmas I spent with Gianni last year before things went pear-shaped.

'You will do nothing but relax and eat,' Rick says to Chris and me, full of good cheer and wielding a wooden spoon. He looks rather dashing in a stripy butcher's apron. This is good to hear because we are exhausted after a manic lunch service and I am only too happy to put my feet up – as it were.

Rick is generally not one for chatter. I have known him for many years as a man who only speaks when there is something to say. I had thought him a traditional type, chauvinistic, inclined towards having his slippers fetched by women, so I am pleasantly surprised to find he is in charge of the cooking with Harriet acting as *sous* chef.

Over the turkey, we catch up with Rachel's life in London and her myriad of friends and acquaintances in the advertising world, all of whom live in the fast lane. I thought I was a busy type, but add a commute to and from work on the London underground and my life in Devon is a stroll in the park.

'And what about men?' Harriet asks. She's the only one who would dare.

'Oh, no one special,' Rachel says, wheeling out her stock answer. 'Although … there is a Luke I rather like, but he's a bit wild and he's got a girlfriend.'

I wonder if she will be like me and suddenly decide she wants to settle down with a more stable family-oriented type like Ted. Then I remember again what Marianne said about it being okay to be single. Perhaps I should stop fretting.

We move on to depressing world events and then local gossip – not least Olivia's crazy speed dating exploits where she appears to have met every weird fifty-something in south-east Devon.

'They probably think the same about her,' Harriet says. 'She's not exactly normal.'

Rick is of the opinion that she is heading for a disaster and it is only a matter of time before she falls for some shyster and is fleeced of her financial security.

We steer away from matters too close to home, but when the main meal is over and all but chauffeur Rachel are worse for wine, the conversation begins to flag. I pass when it comes to the Christmas pudding because I am very full and while the others are occupied with eating, I decide to give them my news. 'I've met someone,' I say, as neutrally as possible.

Rachel looks startled. 'You didn't say anything last night.'

'I'm not completely sure if there's anything worth telling. But I thought you should know, in case it develops. It looks as though things are going in that direction, albeit slowly.'

'So who is he?' Harriet asks.

'You know I'm hanging paintings in the restaurant for an artist? Well, it's him.'

'You mean the painter of our sheep picture?'

'Yes.'

The snow scene with Broadclyst church and the sheep has been very well received as a present and is already hanging on the living room wall above the fireplace.

Harriet says, 'Does this mean you will leave Dad and Marianne alone?'

'It depends if anything materialises.' I notice the eating rate has slowed.

'Thank God for that.' Harriet again.

'Will you tell Dad?' Rachel asks.

'Not yet. Only if and when there's anything to tell – so don't go spilling any beans. But I don't want you lot getting a shock like you did with Gianni.'

'What's this guy like?' Rachel says to Chris. 'Have you met him?'

'Only in passing. People like his paintings. He looks like an old rock star or an actor.'

'He's younger than me,' I say. 'And he's not scruffy. He's a teacher.'

'Oh,' Harriet says, brightening up. 'Respectable, then.'

'Always wears the same old jacket,' Chris says, stirring. 'Grey cord. Typical teacher.'

'Patches on the elbows?' Rachel asks.

Chris sniggers.

'No, actually,' I say, huffily. 'And he's asked me to go and see *Antony and Cleopatra* next week. I'm only telling you because if anyone sees us, I don't want you hearing second hand and wondering why I never said.'

'And what if Dad hears second hand?' asks Rachel. Considering she has made such a fuss about Ted and Marianne in the past, it is interesting that she is still being very protective of her dad. Or maybe the two go together.

'I'll take a chance on that.'

During the silence that follows, I become aware that Rachel has stopped eating and is looking daggers at her plate. When she exploded at Edward over the Marianne business, Harriet told me it was part jealousy and partly because she was worried about her inheritance. As far as her inheritance is concerned, she could have directed the same criticism at me when I went off with Gianni. And as things stand he has cost me quite a lot so she would have been right.

'What are you worried about, Rachel?' I ask, deciding I'd rather get things out in the open.

She looks up. 'He may be another money-grabber like Gianni.'

'I've learnt my lesson.'

Harriet says, 'All you ever think about is money, Rach.'

'It's okay you saying that when you can cosy up here with Rick. James and Kate have got their claws into the Deer Orchard, but what am I going to do for a house, especially if I don't find a partner? I live in London. Have you seen the cost of even a tiny flat there?'

'So move to a different part of the country,' Harriet says. 'Come back here.'

'Like that's going to happen. Job, friends … Get real.'

'Girls, please. It's Christmas.' I give them warning glances as I often did when they were children. 'With the cost of care, there may be very little money left in the end. You can't rely on anything nowadays. And when your father and I have sorted out our affairs, James and Kate will get no more than a quarter free of charge. The rest will remain ours and they will buy us out gradually.'

'But Dad needs his share now so he can buy a place with Marianne,' Harriet says.

'And why can't I have my quarter now so I can put a deposit on a flat?' asks Rachel.

My heart sinks. This inequitable situation between the children is hard to justify. I suppose it is similar to the landed gentry passing their estate to the eldest son while the younger children have to make their own way or marry well. I don't really approve of the law of primogeniture, although it is less abhorrent if daughters are given equal status to sons.

Rick disappears to put the kettle on. I begin to stack the pudding dishes and make a move to the kitchen. The girls follow me.

'Mum?' Rachel says.

'You know that's not possible, Rachel, unless we sell the Deer Orchard and split the proceeds. But we have all agreed that we want to keep the house in the family.'

'And if Rachel gets a quarter, so should I,' Harriet says.

'And me,' Chris says, appearing with more dishes.

What have I started? I regret mentioning Coll. 'Dad and Marianne could buy a small place up here with her money. And if they want something bigger, she should sell that flat of hers.'

'And what about Holly?' asks Harriet. 'She may be concerned if Marianne puts all her money in a property and Dad doesn't contribute a share. You are delaying deliberately. And why should she sell the flat when it's useful for both of them when they need to go to London?'

'It's a solution,' I say. 'And no matter what happens with Coll, I don't intend on having another cohabiting relationship.'

And I don't.

This seems to satisfy Rachel and while Harriet and Rick load the dishwasher and make coffee, we return to the comfy chairs in the living room. It isn't long before Chris is dozing and Rachel suggests running us home before she goes to the Deer Orchard.

At home in bed, I can't sleep. My mind is stirred by thoughts of finance and what Rachel said about owning her own property. I need to have another chat with Ted. I know he thinks I am dragging my feet, but partly it is due to indecision over the kids. We also have to consider inheritance tax issues, unpalatable though they are. If we gift any large sums or property, we have to live for seven years for them to be exempt from tax should our assets on death be outside the threshold. We may well live seven years, but it is too early to say whether we will need the money ourselves for care or for who knows what else. The law is so unfair and has not kept pace with increases in property prices.

I don't know what to do for the best. It would be so much easier if Marianne wasn't in the picture and we weren't having this stupid divorce. Ted and I could have carried on at the Deer Orchard together with James, Kate and Chris. There is room for all of us for now. Indeed, if I hadn't gone to Italy, I would still have the Retreat and Chris could have taken on the flat upstairs. If I hadn't let my hormones get the better of me, we might now be settled with this practical solution. I have been such an idiot and it's too late now.

28

Sexy

Sarah

I expect by now you're banging your head on the nearest piece of somewhere in disbelief.

'Well, I wouldn't stand for that,' I hear you say. *'Ruining an expensive holiday; calling you a liability. This woman's an idiot. Can anyone be that stupid?'*

But midlife relationships are complicated and require many factors to be taken into consideration. Some might admire my tolerance or patience. Some might call it strength rather than weakness. Coll has a difficult personality and I don't think he deliberately sets out to hurt me, he just puts himself first and I don't think he can help it. Something about his psyche seems not quite right. I can't put my finger on what it is.

And I persist because of a stubborn belief that we have enough in common to be well-suited to a partnership for the second half of our lives and that one day he will realise it and appreciate me. If I was twenty-five and thinking about starting a family, he most certainly wouldn't be a wise choice of mate, but we are well past kids and for me at least, there aren't going to be any grand-kids.

Also, as I said before, during the years between Tresco and Mrs Felicity, we've been trucking along very pleasantly. I would say, bar the odd hovering OW, we've been close and pretty settled. Future retirement together has been a distinct possibility.

There are other fish. I've heard that one many times from well-meaning friends, looking out for my best interests, hating to see me crippled by angst and upset over the OWs and the like. But remember, I did go out with guys after Pete. I wasn't a complete recluse. And none of them floated my boat in any way. Not even close. Some were nice enough, but I can do 'nice enough' on my own. I was looking for excitement; someone to challenge my introversion as Pete did. Someone to drag me away from the fire in wintertime and say let's go for a walk, or to the pictures, the theatre; someone who could make me feel like a child again. Pete did all of that and he was a good kind man who loved me. The chances of finding another Pete were small. I've heard that thrill seekers often have a difficult side. Pete didn't. Most do. Coll does. You have to take the rough with the smooth.

And Coll is incredibly sexy. When he was a young man he was gorgeous. I've seen photos from way back before I knew him, when his hair was so black it shone blue, and it was luxuriant too. No wonder he's vain. In midlife, age gives him a handsome, rugged, edge. Words do not do him justice. Even now I gaze upon his body with admiration. And often when he's asleep, and sunlight begins to force its way through the curtains, I stare at his face and think that I am lucky to have someone as desirable as this in my bed.

He has the sleeping face of a Greek statue and an expression of contentment and innocence that makes me believe that underneath he is full of goodness and kindness that he finds difficult to express; that he relishes being with me under the duvet. And much of the time, he does. I know he does, because …

Because …

Our sex drives fit well together and we have great sex. We both like to explore. When we first met, we found we had a common

119

interest in such matters that had lain undiscovered in earlier life. I'm not referring to anything too extreme, but we experimented. Mostly it was to see if we were missing out on anything, and mostly we decided we weren't. Neither of us did anything we weren't happy to try. We both knew that doing something just to please the other while feeling privately resentful was never going to work long term.

I went for some lessons in burlesque dancing. Off my own bat; no pressure from Coll. He didn't know until I presented him with a private display. They do beginners' classes at a place in Exeter. I took a bus because I didn't want anyone to recognise my car. And I wore shades and a hat. Extreme subterfuge. Imagine my fellow librarians finding out and the gossip? I didn't tell anyone. Not even Laura. I somehow can't imagine her John being adventurous in bed. He looks the *Missionary* sort. And Newcastle John would have a fit if he knew.

It's all about feigning confidence. And once I got into it, it was great fun. Coll was delighted with the result. It was money well spent. Tassels, a boa and a peek-a-boo basque come out for special treats.

We draw the line at anything involving others, though. You would think in view of the OWs, Coll might have suggested it, but he's actually quite averse. It's that puritanical streak again. And a relief to me because I couldn't have coped with a threesome.

I don't seem the type, do I? Coll used to say to me, 'Sarah, your colleagues would never believe what a siren you are.' To the outside world I am a stereotypical librarian. But they also say that the quiet ones are the worst – and in this case, it's true.

By the time Coll and I first started exploring each other's bodies, I had already amassed quite a collection of lace undies. I used to wear them to work under my modest skirts and t-shirts and floral dresses and fantasise that one day some dishy lecturer would ask me out (someone like Dr Edward) and after a few demure dates, I would invite him over for a meal and a whole load of surprises when he peeled off my clothes. But although I went out with a geographer called Maurice Mann (he was, honestly!), we didn't get beyond the dinner and drinks before I discovered that he wasn't for me.

With Coll, as soon as I knew the expense would be worthwhile, I ventured into basque territory – and a few other fancy items. One of my neighbours – a racy, glossy, plastic type called Shirley – hosted one of those lingerie parties. When the invite popped through my letterbox, I didn't want to appear stuffy. It was a midweek evening and I had nothing better to do, so I went with an open mind and had a great time.

There were all sorts of people there, young and older, mostly thirties to fifties, several clearly experienced and keen to dress up, strut and pose for the rest of us to admire. The demonstrator kept trotting out this phrase: *'high cutaway thighs for easy access.'* We laughed. Teddies were in fashion then (not the bears or the boys!) so you could see why this design feature helped. Otherwise you undid the studs or buttons and ended up with flappy bits – not the most glamorous, or practical.

Sex is one thing I know I'm good at and where my confidence is high. I don't imagine Mrs Felicity has the same repertoire. She's all glam when she's out and about, and she may be able to deliver lambs and look cool in an old sweater covered in hay, but somehow I can't imagine her dressing up for sex. It's a feeling I have. Newcastle John told me her colleagues were shocked when she ran off with the Italian. They implied that she was never much interested in talking about relationships. And Dr Edward? Noooo. But then again, as I said earlier, people would say the same about me.

29

Antony and Cleopatra

Felicity

As I busy myself getting ready to go out, I wonder what lies in store. It is odd going to the theatre with a man who isn't Ted. I have not been to see a play since before I went to Italy. And Gianni didn't like theatre. He was a restless soul who found it difficult to sit down for more than half an hour at a time. And he had enough language problems with day-to-day English, so Shakespeare was out of the question.

This trip with Coll feels like a date. Olivia says it is a date. But I am not certain. Nothing has been said to suggest more than that we are friends. If we were sixteen, I would know for sure, but now I am a free woman of middle age, the rules are unclear. Misjudging could mean a serious loss of face.

Gianni and I didn't do dates for obvious reasons. It was all behind closed doors. It started one day after a particularly combative discussion about the following week's menus when he took my hand across the table and said, 'You difficult woman, Mrs Harvey. You drive up walls.'

He was always making errors with his efforts at the language and he made me laugh. This time I couldn't stop. It was like hysteria and tears poured down my face. He joined in, laughing at me laughing at him. It broke the tension. He still had hold of my hand and suddenly he became very serious.

'You lonely with your husband away?'

'A bit.'

'Why he leave such beautiful woman? I no understand.'

'Work, Gianni. Work.'

'He work too much. He forget you.'

And he touched my cheek and I let him.

'I am getting old, Gianni.' I don't know why I said this. Perhaps a reminder to him of our age difference. I knew what he was up to.

'I think there more to you than meets eyes. I think I know what you need.'

And he leaned over and kissed me. I didn't resist. I let him take me to a place where I had never been. A place of Mediterranean passions where the olive trees dance as far as the eye can see, and smells of sun-dried tomatoes, oregano and garlic, of pasta, prosciutto and Parmigiano emanate from every kitchen on the hot summer breezes. Was it lust or love? I didn't know; I didn't care. I was swept along in a cliché of forbidden excitement and exotic sex. There was no thought or expectation of a future.

When Ted left his job in London and his midweek lodging with Marianne and Johnny, he resumed his old position at the University of Devon. But there was no going back for me. Our marriage was beyond salvation as far as I was concerned. I was aware of him making an effort and it was painful to witness. It was as if I were outside of myself watching dispassionately, disinclined to help. Only Gianni made me feel whole. He saw my unhappiness and made his move one evening after a particularly passionate lovemaking session. We were in bed naked, cuddling.

'My parents getting old and want me go back Italy to run restaurant.'

They had a small bistro in Siena.

I was alarmed. 'What will I do without you, Gianni? The Retreat needs you? It *is* you.'

'And what about you, Felicity? Do you need me?' His eyes held mine with such certainty.

'Of course.'

'Enough to come with me?'

I remember hesitating. I was shocked. 'Are you serious?'

'*Si.* We could start new life; new restaurant. Together.'

'Oh, Gianni, this is madness. You know it is.'

'I know your marriage over. I know you happy with Gianni.'

At first it seemed out of the question, but Gianni persisted and I began to listen without resistance and to hear his elaborate suggestions of what we could bring to his parents' place and what it could offer us.

As I warmed to the idea, Gianni suggested buying out his parents. 'Then we have control. We make decisions about future.' He stroked my hair. His voice was gentle and persuasive.

It seemed an attractive proposition. I never asked him about love. His love. I knew I was in love with him romantically and because of the midlife madness that comes from cyclical tedium, and a husband who no longer excited me, I said yes and set in motion a chain of events that was to break up our family irrevocably. It took a few months to sort everything out in Broadclyst and to sell the Retreat, but with Gianni's enthusiasm convincing me that we would have a perfect life together in Italy, I plunged into the unknown.

Once in Italy, for a few weeks, everything was new and blissful, but that wore off very rapidly when the papers were signed and Gianni was in control. An ex-girlfriend appeared on the scene after Christmas, ostensibly helping both of us but she was always hanging out with Gianni. Their closeness began to be a problem. It pains me to think about it. I wondered if my money had been his motivation; that he always intended a buy-out; if that was his plan from the start.

And now here I am, not even two years on, in the middle of an English winter and about to see *Antony and Cleopatra* with another man who has charm, humour and a mysterious quality that I can't quite place but which leaves me intrigued.

I drive through the dark, chilly night into Exeter and locate the street from Coll's directions and my quick glance at Google Maps before I set off. I have a satnav, but as I know many short cuts in the area, I rarely use it unless I am travelling further afield. I park the car in a nearby car park.

The theatre is in an ancient back-street building with a rickety narrow staircase that leads up to a tiny foyer with a low beamed ceiling and a bar across one end. Coll is waiting for me with a glass of wine in his hand. He says he likes my coat which is long and black. He buys me an orange juice and we order drinks for the interval. I don't drink at all when I am driving, and I wonder if it is for this reason that Coll forfeits his usual wine and orders the same. We are both guarded. Coll seems less sure of himself and his eyes constantly scan as if looking for someone. I tell him about another picture sale and ask him about his Christmas. He has already thanked me effusively by text for the fridge magnet.

'Very low key,' he says. 'I'm not religious in the traditional sense, and the commercialisation has got out of hand.'

I tell him about the awkwardness of having Marianne usurping my former position in the family home. 'But we laid on Christmas Lunch for customers and all the places were booked almost as soon as we made it known. It kept me busy until the evening when we went to Rick's.'

I wonder how he spent his day but I don't like to pry. We people who are alone don't always want to be reminded. Perhaps he was with friends. If he wants me to know, he will tell me.

'Things are looking up with Harriet and Rick,' I say. 'I told them about you.'

'Oh?' He appears surprised and frowns. 'Why would you do that?'

I get the impression he is not altogether pleased. I am too unsure of him to tell the truth. 'Your pictures. Harriet loved hers. And even Chris – who is not in the least bit artistic – said he liked your paintings.'

A squat bosomy woman with a piggy face rings a little bell a couple of times which causes people to start moving towards an opened curtain in the side wall. We join the queue.

Inside the auditorium, there is plush red velvet raked seating from, so Coll tells me, a recent refurbishment. I am pleasantly surprised as I had visions of a rustic space with hard chairs on a flat wooden floor and no hope of seeing the action if stuck behind a fidgeting giant. Our seats are to the right of middle, six rows from the front.

We settle. Anticipation grows as the lights go down and the curtains begin to open.

Ten minutes in, Coll whispers in my ear, 'Quite good, isn't it?'

I nod agreement but don't reply. I hate it when people talk in the theatre and even a few words can be a distraction to others. As it is, I immerse myself in the drama and the passion and try hard to transport myself to Egypt and to forget the Taylor–Burton epic that a stage production is always going to find difficult to match.

At the interval, with our fruit juices located and to hand, Coll quotes part of that most famous speech to me:

> *'The barge she sat in, like a burnish'd throne,*
> *Burn'd on the water: the poop was beaten gold;*
> *Purple the sails, and so perfumed that*
> *The winds were love-sick with them;'*

And then he gives me a penetrating look and says, 'You remind me of Cleopatra, Felicity: a strong woman who has a dizzying effect on men.'

I say, 'Thank you, but "dizzying" I think not.' I giggle, showing my embarrassment but enjoying the compliment. 'Once perhaps, but too old now.'

'You're not old,' he says.

'I have never told you how old I am.'

'Surely no more than fifty.'

I laugh more loudly this time. 'You flatter me. I suspect I am significantly older than you.'

'How significantly? I'm not far off fifty-three.'

'Significantly,' I say, disappointed that the gap is so large and in the wrong direction. Because it *is* the wrong direction most of the time. Gianni taught me that. 'Four years significantly.'

Coll doesn't falter, but continues to quote from the play.

> *'Age cannot wither her nor custom stale*
> *Her infinite variety ...'*

I am lost for words and am relieved when Mrs Piggy rings the bell again and we are called back for the second part.

When the play is over, we meander down the side street and to the car park, talking about the merits of the production, finding that we agree about most things.

It is quite dark, the streetlights no longer as bright as they used to be. I cannot gauge Coll's expression but he sounds buoyant. I think about what Olivia said and as we stand by my car, neither of us seemingly wanting to part, I take a chance.

'How about you come back to mine for a coffee? Then we can continue the conversation somewhere warm. Or we can find a pub?'

'Your place would be great,' he says without hesitation.

As I drive back on my own, I wonder if I have done the right thing. Most men would take it as a sign so I have to be prepared for him to have salacious expectations. I shiver at the thought.

I arrive back at the flat a few minutes before he does and have time to put on the electric fire and the kettle and to freshen my make-up and hair.

When Coll comes up, he sits in one of the easy chairs. He has not touched me or made any move to kiss me. I am a tad disappointed even though I am still unsure of what I want. I thought his decision to come here rather than a pub might suggest more intimacy and I have been thinking about what I would do if he made an approach.

'Have you considered acting?' says Coll, as I bring mugs of coffee and some leftover canapés.

127

'Never,' I say. 'But I once directed a local amateur production.'

'I usually do the artwork for school plays. I'll miss that when I retire. There's a local amateur group I may join. You could come too. They're always looking for people to direct or help behind the scenes.'

'Impossible while I have the restaurant although I may want to take more of a back seat as time goes on.'

And we chat on late into the night. He tells me more about Penny and the son in Australia with whom he is only in the barest contact. And I ask about his parents, but he says, 'Leave them for another time,' and adopts a closed look.

No man is an island, I think. But Coll seems to be one in more than name.

It is quarter past two when he gets up to leave. And I need not have worried, following my invitation, about any assumptions on his part. He treats me as a friend, nothing more. Yet this surprises me after the flirtatious comments.

Not even a kiss on the cheek.

'I'll call you,' he says. 'Very soon.'

30

Jeff

Sarah

Considering it's the school holidays, I haven't seen much of Coll. He scuttled off home after Boxing Day, mumbling about painting while he had the time. I suggested he bring his stuff over here and set up in my spare room so at least we could meet for meals.

'That wouldn't do at all, Sarah. The light is poor at the best of times. And I'd only have to take it all back again in a few days.'

Then yesterday afternoon during a phone call, he mentioned he was seeing his mate Jeff. This is bad enough, but it could be a cover for him seeing long-term work friend, Anne – or worse. I've long suspected he rings me ahead of an OW meeting, saying he'll be out with a mate so I won't phone him and discover who he's really with.

Be it Anne, Felicity or Jeff: none fills me with positive thoughts.

Jeff Kenley is one of Coll's oldest friends. They met each other way back in boarding school and despite going in different directions at university they've remained in touch, much to my consternation.

Jeff is a bad influence. He drinks, smokes, gambles, womanises and flashes the cash; cash that he often doesn't possess. Cash that he borrows, begs or (and I use my words guardedly) even steals from unsuspecting women of mature age. Steals? I don't mean 'steals' as such, but he gives sub-standard advice for hefty fees, so it might as well be stealing.

He's a financial advisor and I was very nearly one of his victims.

My suspicions about him were aroused in the early years of my knowing Coll – before we started having an intimate relationship.

'One day you'll meet Jeff,' said Coll. 'Clever, and tough as old boots. Not sure whether you'll like him though. He's a bit of a rogue.'

Coll claimed he wouldn't have survived his early years of public school without Jeff. 'He stood up for me against the bullies. Once I became Jeff's friend, they left me alone.'

I often think that it's the school bullies that are behind a lot of Coll's problems. He won't talk about it. Shuts up like a clam whenever I try to probe.

Coll feels he owes Jeff. That's how he came to introduce him to me when I was looking to invest some thirty thousand pounds from my deceased mother.

Jeff had followed no clear career path since leaving school. He dabbled in this and that, put money (seemingly his parents') into business ventures that failed and when he decided to give financial advice professionally, Coll was full of it. 'Jeff knows what he's talking about. He'll tell you what to do.'

I agreed to a meeting and it didn't go well. He came to my house and while I made tea, he wandered round the room picking up ornaments and examining signatures on a couple of paintings. Afterwards, I wished I'd had an inventory. I could swear there was a small Moorcroft vase missing. But the more I thought I remembered it being on the end of the mantelpiece, the more I thought it might have been moved during the last redecoration, six months before. I would hate to accuse and be proven wrong. I gave him the benefit of the doubt and I didn't tell Coll.

Jeff eventually sat down and arranged himself languidly in a chair while he asked about my financial details. I was reluctant to disclose. He said, 'Sarah, how can I give you advice if I don't know the bigger picture?'

I said, 'I don't need advice on the bigger picture, merely on what to do with thirty thousand pounds.'

He said, 'I wouldn't be doing my job properly if I didn't ensure that you have other options on which to draw if needs must.'

I said, 'If needs must, I have.' And I refused to say more.

This clearly didn't suit. For a few minutes, his tone was brusque and unfriendly. From the start I found him slippery, untrustworthy and not as knowledgeable about financial matters as Coll would have me believe.

He was a typical ex-public school, floppy-forelock type, with an irritating head-shake that kept his fringe poised above one eye. He said, 'Yah.' He really did. *Yah, Sarah, I know you are a private person, but if I'm going to advise you, you have to trust me.* Trust! There's a word I wouldn't put in the same sentence with

Jeff. Falseness oozed through every pore and I listened and asked questions and logged the fact that his answers didn't always make sense.

I wanted to like him. For Coll's sake I wanted to make the investment. So I kept on listening, hoping to be impressed and persuaded that my first impressions had been wrong.

At the end of two hours, he suggested I write him a cheque for the thirty thousand pounds and he would '*get the paperwork done and in the post asap*'.

The paperwork involved a supposedly legal document regarding investing on a platform set up by himself with funds from dozens of others. Basically, he was acting like a fund manager but without the backing of a larger company.

'I'm sorry,' I said, 'but I need more time to think this through. I'm not going to hand over such a large sum today.'

'There's a cooling-off period,' he said.

'What guarantee do you give me today?'

'My word.'

'How do I know you will do what you say?'

Well, that was it. He realised I'd seen through him.

'Don't you trust me?' he said, flicking his forelock. 'Coll will vouch for me.'

'As I said, I need time.'

He lost his rag, started putting on pressure, saying I had wasted his afternoon and he would be sending me a bill.

I said I was under the impression that the advice was free and that he would get a percentage of the investment if I followed through with it.

He got up to leave and said, 'Coll intimated that you were an intelligent and wise woman. I see he is mistaken. I hope he realises and doesn't become too attached to you. I couldn't bear it if he were involved with someone unsuitable.'

'Coll knows his own mind,' I said. I was tempted to retort in kind but I realised that would provoke more unpleasantness and

I couldn't wait to get him out of the house. He was a bully and a nasty, nasty man.

He did send me a bill and I refused to pay. After that, my name has been 'mud' as far as he's concerned. I haven't seen him since. And as for the Moorcroft vase, that hasn't turned up either. This saddens me because it was a wedding present from Pete's godmother and one of my most treasured possessions.

Coll won't hear any negativity. 'Jeff wouldn't deliberately deceive you.'

Yet there's a contradiction. Sometimes he admits, 'Jeff's gone too far this time.' But if I dare to offer criticism or suggest he might reconsider the friendship, I'm the one who loses.

'Do you still see that woman Sarah Bell?' Jeff apparently says to Coll at intervals. And Coll says he sees me 'now and then'. He never took my side, despite much ongoing evidence that a substantial part of my thirty thousand was likely to have disappeared.

The more I hear about Jeff's exploits, the more relieved I am that I stayed strong and resisted. Over the years, I've heard about one business venture after another going bust. He's quick to set up another in a different name. And Coll says he has unmanned addresses where mail is sent. He's the sort of person who gets chased down the road by TV reporters and cameramen for consumer shows. Except so far he's kept one step ahead. Coll says that 'no one loses out', that 'Jeff knows his finance', but I doubt it. Indeed, I wonder if Jeff is the reason that Coll is often short of funds these days. I don't ask and he doesn't say.

Not telling Jeff about us is a significant barrier to our ever getting together in a more permanent way. And it's laughable. When I told Newcastle John, he said, 'What does Coll think this fellow's going to say? It's not like a parent or a member of the family disapproving.'

'He says he'll go mad; that he's one of his oldest friends. He's very loyal.'

'Or stupid. And what about loyalty to you? If you'd gone ahead, you may have lost a significant sum.'

Jeff knows Coll has a girlfriend and he's even seen a photo – with me so much in the distance I'm unrecognisable. He even made complimentary remarks because the pose is rather 'fashion mag', sitting on a bench at the end of an avenue of trees. And as Coll won't specify who I am, Jeff refers to me as 'Charlotte'.

So, when Coll said he'd arranged to meet Jeff, my heart sank.

'Are you any further on in thinking you might tell him about me?' I asked, tentatively.

'No. In any case, he thinks I'm still seeing Charlotte. If I tell him about you, he may never speak to me again.'

'And if you don't, nor might I,' I retorted, regretting it as soon as the words slipped out.

There was silence. Then Coll said, 'Got to go,' in the way that he knows annoys me. And that was that.

31

Richard ll

Felicity

Coll calls me the following morning.

'May I see you tonight, Felicity?' he says.

I am taken aback.

He says, 'I know it's soon, but I'm making the best of being on holiday. Can you arrange cover?'

'I'll try.' It will only be for a couple of hours that I will need replacing.

Thankfully Kylie steps in. She says, 'He must like you, Mrs Harvey – two days on the trot.'

133

He arrives an hour earlier than he said. He says I remembered the time wrongly. I didn't. He said nine. It's eight. But Kylie is here and I can get ready fast. I already have my face reasonably respectable from helping with the start of service. All I need to do is to slip out of my suit and into something more casual. I decide on jeans and a jumper and loosen my hair. I think he will appreciate the Rock Chick look.

In the local pub, he seems nervous; unsettled. It is as if he has something to say, but can't think of a way to say it. I take it as a sign he may want to move our relationship forward beyond the friendliness, but that he is trying to gauge my potential response without committing himself first.

He says, 'Would you fancy *Richard ll* in a couple of weeks? It's only another local Am Dram. At the Exe Theatre.'

'Where's that?'

'On my side of the city,' Coll says.

Richard ll is one of my favourite history plays.

I am about to say yes when he adds, 'But it's a Saturday.'

'Hmm. It's our busiest night at the restaurant. Chris can manage the food, but I'm not sure if I can get cover for front of house and a waitress too.'

'No pressure,' says Coll. 'It may not be great.'

I don't want him to think I'm unenthusiastic. 'I'd like to. Love to. *Antony and Cleopatra* whetted my appetite. We did *Richard ll* at school. It would be good to be reminded, amateur or no.'

'Let me know as soon as you can. I'll get tickets on the off chance. My treat.'

We talk about our respective childhoods as only children. For me, being the only one was a reason for my mum to invite her friends round with their kids at every opportunity. For Coll, it seems he was isolated.

He says, 'My mum and dad were always into their creative projects be it music or art. I had to entertain myself pre-school.'

Perhaps that's why he seems solitary now. Rejected by a wife he once adored and often ignored by his parents. He brings out my maternal instincts. I want to give him a hug, but I don't.

'A nursery for invention and imaginary friends,' he says, referring to being an only child.

'Did you?'

'Oh, yes, a whole gang of them. We ran amok playing Cowboys and Indians. Had to take both sides. Borrowed Mum's lipstick for warpaint. And scarves for bandanas. She wasn't pleased.'

I can see him now: little Coll aged four or five, painting his face at his mother's dressing table, an artist in the making. I love the way he manages to inject humour into even the darkest of situations. I wonder if he is like some professional comedians; all life and soul in company, but a depressive on the quiet.

'Are they still alive, your parents?' I ask while he's in the mood for reminiscing about them.

'No. They died before Penny and I split. It was a difficult few years. Both struck down with different cancers one after the other.'

I tell him about my mum and her stroke. How the suddenness was both a dreadful shock and a blessing when one considers some of the alternatives. I relive the weekends of soul-destroying travelling to Surrey with Ted for house-clearance purposes.

'It had to be done,' I say. 'But going through all the drawers, the clothes, the knick-knacks, it was like journeying into the past and throwing most of it away. We didn't have time to sift through every little keepsake. Nor did we have space at the Deer Orchard for anything that wasn't beautiful or useful. And most of the valuables weren't, so we sold them.'

Coll nods and says it was the same for him. 'We tend to accumulate trivia in the mistaken belief that someone will be interested in it after we're gone. Mostly that's not the case –

unless you become famous, in which case do you really want your life picked over by biographers or collectors?'

'One of the advantages of email and texting is that much that is private will be lost in the ether.'

'A problem for jumped-up historians of the future,' Coll says.

'My mum was such a strong woman until the last couple of years. She seemed indestructible. She had no time for people who dither and complain. "Get on with it, Felicity," she used to say. I don't know if I've inherited her strength, or if it was drummed into me.'

The memories are still raw: the guilt that we lived too far away to be of much use to Mum in her declining years; the sadness that I hadn't seen her in the months before she died.

Coll gives me time to speak in a way that Ted never did and I find I am able to share with him all the grief, pain and anxieties I have bottled up for years. It is refreshing to find a man prepared to discuss emotional issues.

He says, 'Almost everyone feels guilty when someone dies. We can't be there for everybody all of the time. You cannot blame yourself. This is the way things are nowadays.'

He leans over and lays a hand on my wrist ever so lightly and his thumb brushes the back of my hand. Surely a sign of more to come. I believe he understands because he has suffered too.

But that is as far as it goes on this evening of personal revelation. Once again I am deposited back at my flat without so much as a kiss.

After the intensity of the past couple of meetings, there is a flurry of enthusiastic texting, mostly Shakespearian quotations with potentially hidden meanings for our helter-skelter developing friendship.

And then on New Year's Eve, all goes quiet. I breathe a sigh. It has been a frenetic three weeks from the moment I met him to this. I am enveloped by a cosy blanket again for the first time since Gianni. It is the blanket of confidence that comes with knowing one is attractive and liked.

I am puzzled by the fact that he hasn't made a pass at me or talked about moving beyond friendship. In some ways I'm relieved, yet I want him to want to, even though I remain doubtful for myself. Does that sound contrary? When men say women don't know what they want, in this case it is true.

The knowledge of *Richard II* in two weeks sits comfortably. I like plans. But hopefully we will see each other before that. I shall have to try to sell a few more paintings.

32

New Year

Sarah

I say, 'Happy New Year' to Coll as Big Ben clangs from the TV, and I'm about to give him a kiss when he turns his face away. I brush his cheek with my lips and wonder again what is going on. I give him a look which he doesn't acknowledge and the gulf widens between us. We drink a toast in a half-hearted fashion. It's a sham.

Yet he wants sex later – at about one in the morning when we have done with all the fireworks and Jools Holland and have made our way up to bed. It's an unusually silent and uncomfortable union; no trappings or frills. I only comply because I think it might remind him of the good times. Alas, not.

Afterwards I say, 'What's wrong?' The fatal question we women should never ask.

He sighs. 'I don't feel very well.'

'What sort of "not well"?'

'I don't know. Sick. Weird. Been like this for a couple of weeks.'

'Too much booze?' Another fatal question. Sometimes I don't think my brain is connected to my mouth. I can even rationalise at the time that it's unwise to say certain things, yet out they come as if they have minds of their own.

The silence that follows has a dark and lonely quality; a typical middle of the night quality when irrational fears manifest and grow like Japanese knotweed.

'I'm not sure about us any more, Sarah,' says Coll. 'You and me,' he adds as if it might be someone different. He's lying on his back on the bed staring at the ceiling, a gap of at least a foot between us.

'But why?' My big mouth again. My brain says *do not have heavy conversations after midnight.* Brain is wise. Tongue is not.

'I don't know. I don't know if I feel enough here.' He pats his chest top left.

'But that's no different from before – according to you.' I'm desperate to cling on; foolish, foolish woman.

'I'm confused,' he says.

'I don't understand where this is coming from,' I say. 'A month ago we were talking about getting a house. What's changed, Coll? Cold feet?' I know it's her. I want to tell him I know; to accuse. *It's Felicity, isn't it? Mrs Mayfield-Harvey of the restaurant.* Yet I can't. I wonder if he knows I know. Every sinew tightens. I prop myself up on two pillows, tugging the duvet around my shoulders.

'We're different, you and me,' Coll says.

'But different was okay before. Different can be good. You used to say we balanced each other.' I wait for him to remind me that I'm a liability.

He says, 'If you love me, Sarah, you're going to find it difficult if we decide to split up.'

If *we* decide? Like I have a choice? I think it is very arrogant of him to make this assumption. But then that's Coll. 'What makes you think I do?'

'Because you do. I know you do. You always have.'

'I see.' I can't contradict him. But I don't like him much just now. 'I did love you,' I add, trying desperately to save face.

He turns towards me. 'You've never said it before.' He sounds surprised.

'Women shouldn't say it first. In any case, you've always said I loved you so I didn't need to.' I'm being dragged towards a precipice. I don't want to fall.

'It's important,' Coll says. 'If you do.'

And I wonder why, but I don't ask because I can't bear it.

Suddenly Coll gets up to go to the bathroom. The moment of imminent danger has passed. For now.

33

While the Deer's Away

Felicity

Marianne goes back to Beckenham during the second week of January and I relax in the way that one does when difficult guests or relatives pack their bags and leave. She may be gone for some time. She has talks to give about her novel at two local libraries and several schools to visit in various parts of London regarding the sustainability project and the education pack. Ted mentions he will be joining her for at least a week to do some publicity ahead of the screening of the TV documentary that he has been involved with for the past few months. It is about sustainability and population control using St Agnes – one of the smallest Isles of Scilly – as a model. It was during the filming out there last summer that his wooing of Marianne developed some significance.

Ted has been booked to appear on *This Morning* and *The One Show* to try to attract interest. It is rather exciting: Ted the potential TV star. It is something he has wanted to do for years and this may be his big break into the medium. If things had been different and we were still together, I would have been so enthusiastic. I am still proud of him. Once he sets his mind to something, he is very committed. I am sure it will be good.

'It will be *I'm a Celebrity* this, that and t'other,' I jest, when he tells me the details. 'Chat shows, public appearances, openings of village fetes. You might even be asked to launch a boat.'

He smiles at me. It is a rare thing these days. A deep memory stirs of a young man who worshipped me.

I have dropped by to pick up veg for the next day. Without Marianne, the atmosphere at the Deer Orchard returns to the familiar and as it is Thursday and I don't have service to worry about, I am invited to stay for supper. James and Kate are an earnest pair and conversation is generally topical and stimulating. Over a seafood risotto, Kate launches into a territory that I know will make Ted squirm.

'Okay, guys,' she says. 'We're going to try for a baby and in case I do get pregnant, I want to minimise any risks to the embryo from electro-magnetic radiation. That means no wi-fi and we won't be leaving our mobiles switched on at home unless it's necessary. Good old land line communication wherever possible.'

'How inconvenient,' I say. 'What makes you think there's a risk?'

'Something Marianne said—'

'I might have known it would be something to do with her,' I snap.

'No, Mum,' says James. 'That's unfair and you of all people should support any reduction in environmental hazards. When your parents were young, no one acknowledged the dangers of smoking and who knows what effects it could have played on the health of children – including unborn ones?'

Kate says, 'In twenty years' time, there may be evidence against EMR.'

'There already is,' James says.

'I mean conclusive evidence,' Kate says. 'We can't escape it completely, especially at work, but we don't need to keep our phones on all the time when we're home. At least then I'll know we did the best we could.'

'Marianne reckons that the whole EMR business is a ticking time bomb,' James says. 'And I agree with her.'

'You would,' I say. 'What does your dad think?' I nod at Ted who is eating impassively at the other end of the table. I can tell by his face that he has zoned out at the word *baby* and is in one of his many theoretical interior worlds from which the outside bounces off like torrential rain on roof slates.

'Dad says she may be right.'

'Right about what?' Ted says, stirring.

'EMR,' James says, tossing him a glance and then continuing to talk to me. 'She's already training him to become less mobile-dependent.'

Training him? Ted?! There is a wry smile tugging at his lips.

'She says the amount of time they both spend on computers is more than enough – but of course their work virtually depends on them,' James says.

Ted says, 'No mobiles in front-trouser pockets to protect sperm.'

'Bit late for you to be worried about that,' I say. He had a vasectomy after Chris, our mistake.

'Safer for testes and prostate, just in case,' James says. 'For me, anyway, and you should tell Chris.'

'Is anywhere safe?' I muse. 'A lot of men keep their phones inside their jackets. Surely not good for the heart.'

'Possibly not,' James says.

Kate says, 'There's growing evidence of people becoming electro-sensitive. At first they were thought to be imagining it, but it appears not. And if it's true and it adversely affects some people, then the chances are we are all being affected to a greater or lesser extent – we just don't realise it.'

James says, 'When we get back from a day at uni, I can feel my body sigh with relief. I think it's more than merely because I'm home. I think unis and other computer-packed establishments are sick buildings.'

'God forbid the so-called "conclusive evidence" if it ever materialises,' I say. 'Society as we know it will collapse.'

'Indeed it will,' James says. 'And Dad's documentary will show how society could collapse on more levels than due to dangers of EMR.'

'Do you have a firm date yet for the documentary?' I address Ted.

'The last Wednesday of the month, nine o'clock, BBC4, assuming nothing gets in the way. Marianne has been into a couple Exeter schools to brief teachers about the education pack and practise for her London visits.'

'Did they go well?'

'I believe so. Just a few tweaks needed.'

James says, 'Marianne's got some interesting ideas on sustainability. You would relate to her thoughts if you'd give her a chance to talk to you without making snide remarks.'

'Would I indeed?' I am not convinced.

Kate gives James a look that says he has overstepped the mark with his terminology. 'Marianne says that we spend loads of time and energy on preserving biodiversity – plants *and* animals – because we know that lack of diversity could present a threat to the future of the planet. Yet we don't apply the same logic to ourselves. With so much geographical mobility and mass migrations, there may come a time when our species is not as diverse as it once was.'

'Hasn't it always been that way?' I say. 'We're all part Viking or Roman or Saxon or Goth. Celt … Norse … and such like.'

James says, 'Yes, but mostly Northern European. It's the mix of genes from all areas of the world and all across the world that could be dangerous in the future.'

'Like ash dieback,' says Kate.

I look at her, startled. 'What?'

'Potentially all European ash trees could be lost.'

'If we don't preserve our uniqueness, then we may be more susceptible to being wiped out by disease.' James adopts his lecturer's voice.

'So what does Marianne suggest? Forced breeding programmes?' I say sarcastically.

'We haven't got to that stage yet. But we need to be aware,' James counters.

'Being aware won't get in the way of love.' I should know this if anyone does after my mad dash to Italy, flying in the face of logic and reason.

'What about arranged marriage?' Kate says. 'You could argue that preserves the bloodline.'

'And look how much trouble it causes.' I have never approved of parents making the choice on the grounds of suitability. I suppose in this respect I am a hypocrite in view of the obstacles I've tried to put between Harriet and Rick.

'Love is a manufactured concept,' James says. 'A learned response. Not all societies feel it like we do.'

'Marianne again?' I can't help but attribute any psychobabble to her.

'She may be right. Anyway, it's not just her that says this,' James says.

'No? You mean there are others with crackpot ideas?'

James says, 'In the future we could have a situation like on Adam's Farm on *Countryfile*. A centre for rare breeds.'

'God forbid.'

'The human race may depend on it.'

'I can see becoming a lecturer hasn't quelled your tendency to wild ideas. What about hybrid vigour?'

'Hybrid vigour is all very well until a disease comes along that strikes all those of a similar type. And that's the nature of disease. Always one step ahead. We would be wise to preserve the gene pool of indigenous humans.'

'And what say you, Ted?'

He looks up. 'I think that we are hell-bent on self destruction and by the time anyone is prepared to take drastic measures, it will be too late.'

'Don't say that,' Kate says. 'We have to have hope. Think of the next generation.'

James gets up to load the dishwasher.

'There's a crumble in the oven courtesy of Chris – or fruit or yoghurt,' Kate says. 'I'm going to check the hens.'

It's good that Kate is rebuilding the hen flock. While I was away it dwindled and I sold the sheep and goats to the Molwings on the next door farm before I left.

I remember Ted saying, 'I'm not a farmer, Felicity, and I don't have the time. They'll have to go.' But he kept Meg the sheepdog; our lovely Meg. And he was heartbroken when she died. I am hoping Kate will soon reintroduce a few animals; sheep and goats at least. But that is difficult while she is working.

I put the kettle on and Ted says, 'A word, Flick, if you don't mind,' in his voice reserved for when he is displeased. I follow him through to the living room. James glances over his shoulder, mildly concerned.

'To the point,' Ted says. When was he ever anything else when he wants to have a word? 'I'm uncomfortable about you being here as soon as Marianne's back's turned.'

'I see. This is my house too. I keep my distance as far as possible when she's here. I don't have to.'

He raises an eyebrow. He knows I turn up more than I need. He says, 'I don't have a choice at present. You do.'

'James and Kate are family. I'm entitled to want to spend time with them.'

'If you feel so strongly about family, I don't know why you went to Italy.'

And nor do I. It all seems crazy now I am no longer in love with Gianni. 'Don't you see how much I regret that? I lost everything. I want to make amends.'

'Then you need to be more flexible about the house and finances. If you let James and Kate pay your share as and when …'

'Why should I? Why should you be the one to get your share in toto and me zilch?'

'It won't be "in toto" as you put it.'

'Nonetheless …'

'Flick, if you want me out, I have to have the means.'

'We have to consider the other kids too. Rachel is a bit sniffy at the idea of James effectively getting his share while she'll struggle to get on the housing ladder in London.'

'Then we need to talk it through properly. But that would be a lot easier if we could see the solicitors together instead of them negotiating on our behalf and getting nowhere.'

'Okay. But are you absolutely sure you know what you're doing?'

'For goodness sake! Not that again. Yes. How many times? Yes. Totally sure. One hundred percent.'

This wasn't the chat I had in mind when we were talking over Christmas dinner, but I am feeling defeated and agree to meet with Ted and his solicitor to discuss how we can be fair to the children.

I drive myself home and check on the kittens before going to bed. They still don't have names. Something Shakespearian would be apt but a tad pretentious.

I slump in a chair with the kittens crawling up my sleeve and trying to snuggle in the warmth of my armpit.

And I think about Ted being like a boat anchored in the middle of a millpond lake and I am on the shore, unable to swim. I've lost him. Well and truly lost him. I knew I had, but I had to try. Looks like all my eggs will have to go into the Coll basket. I shall have to unleash a serious flirtation initiative when we go to *Richard ll*. He seems to need a little encouragement.

I text him to say how much I am looking forward to it. It is a start.

34

Felicitygate

Sarah

'Did you see *Richard ll* is on at the Exe Theatre next Saturday?' I say to Coll when he graces me with his presence the weekend after New Year. 'An amateur production, but it may be worth seeing.' We had supper at mine and have walked a couple of streets to the local pub where we now sit, he with a beer and me with a half lager.

I'm uneasy. He says he's not staying overnight because he's a lot to prepare for school. It's the start of term but he never used to say things like this. I'm keen for reassurance. The reassurance doesn't come.

'Yes, but I can't make it. Sorry.' Coll is dismissive, gazing at the patterns of froth up the sides of his glass.

I'm surprised. 'Why not? We've been waiting for *Richard ll* to play locally for ages.'

'Oh, stuff. I've something else on.' His eyes roam the room.

I can tell by his vagueness that it's something he doesn't want to tell me. My intuition begins rifling through the files. I'm sure he told me he had been talking about theatre with Felicity. He said she 'loved a good Shakespeare, especially the histories.' It was all stored neatly in my memory, ready to run amok. Some would say I was overly suspicious and paranoid. Some may even say what did it matter if he took a friend to see a play? But this was a play we both loved. He should ask me first. That's the way of things. Surely?

I give him a look. He shifts his weight. He doesn't meet my eye and I detect a slight flush.

After a pause, he says, 'Do you want to see *The Taming of the Shrew* on Friday? It's being performed by an Am Dram group in Honiton.'

'That might be a bit excessive given that you're taking me to see *Richard II* on Saturday.' I'm in a provocative mood.

'I've told you, I can't.' Coll raises his voice and glares at me.

'But you haven't said why. So I'm presuming that whatever it is can be changed.' I keep my tone light and unthreatening.

'It can't.'

His mysteriousness makes me angry inside and even more determined. On the outside, I remain calm but firm. 'I'm sure it can.'

It's a game. Anyone listening wouldn't believe we'd been going out for a decade; that we talk of a future.

'God, you are so difficult,' says Coll.

'Me? Difficult?'

He's skilled in making me feel it's my fault. This is another thing that happens when love is missing for one partner and the balance of power is unequal.

A change of tone. I say, 'Are you taking someone else?'

'Drop it, Sarah. We'll go and see *Taming of the Shrew*.'

'I'd rather see *Richard II*.'

It's during a phone call the following night that I push him over the edge and elicit a confession. He'd been drinking. The conversation starts pleasantly enough, but then turns. He happens to mention two more pictures have been bought from the restaurant.

'It's great, isn't it? Felicity's overjoyed by the interest. She reckons some people have booked to eat there so they can see the paintings.'

'You can tell me more about it when we go to see *Richard ll*.'

'I've told you, I can't do *Richard ll*. I just can't. Okay? Can we leave this?' He is suddenly sharp and cross.

I take a deep breath. It's driving me mad. I would rather know the worst.

'Fiddle-faddle,' I say. 'Are you taking someone else to see *Richard ll*?'

There is a guilty pause.

'Why do you say that?'

'You know why.'

Another pause. A pause that goes on … and on … and gives me time to prepare for the worst.

'Yes.' This time his voice is quiet.

'I see. Who?'

'I can't tell you.'

'And that's supposed to be okay, is it? You might as well tell me now.'

'I can't. Just leave it.'

'You have to tell me,' I say, raising my voice. 'I know something underhand is going on. Go on. Tell me.' I grip the phone tightly, willing him not to hang up on me. I'm furious. The rage inside me builds. The jealousy erupts. If he can't tell me, then I will tell him. 'I think I know, anyway.'

'Do you?' He sounds surprised. 'Who?'

'It's Felicity, isn't it?'

'What makes you think that?' He is still quiet, treading carefully.

'You're always going on about her.'

'Am I?'

'So, is it her?'

Another long pause.

'Yes.'

Here we have it: the admission that changes everything. My heart is beating so rapidly I feel it might escape. I collect myself and try to slow my breathing.

'So what's going on?' My words come quietly, now I know it's her.

'Nothing. Nothing at all.' His voice is almost a whisper.

'But you'd like there to be something.'

Again there is hesitation and time enough for me to know that whatever he says, his thoughts are affirmative.

'Possibly.'

I can't believe I'm hearing this. It's as if all my fears are rational after all. I wanted them not to be. How I wanted them to be all down to stupid jealousy. It's a bad dream, a nightmare from which there's no waking. My world darkens; my skull seems to tighten around my brain. I begin to hyperventilate and that all too familiar knot in my stomach makes its presence known.

I say, 'Which means I'm right.'

'How did you know?'

'You go on and on about her. What is it about her that's got you spellbound?'

Another pause.

'She's different from you. So different. You know what I'm like about change. Not better … Different.' His voice is soft and wistful, slightly slurry. 'You're so sweet, Sarah … So nice. But she's different. I can't explain …'

'So what exactly is going on?'

He repeats, 'Nothing. Nothing at all. I don't know whether she feels the same about me. I really don't. She likes me. I know that. I make her laugh. She's had a tough time. Almost divorced, like me. We've a lot in common.' And now he has started, he doesn't stop and words about wonderful Felicity pour out of my

149

receiver like an excitable brook tumbling over the pebbles on a hillside. It's as if he has forgotten he's talking to me and is relieved of the opportunity to share his passion and unload his guilt.

His idea of nothing going on is not the same as mine. My stomach shuts down and bile wells up in my throat. This is serious. This is the biggest threat our relationship has faced.

When he finally stops extolling her virtues and opening his heart, I come to an obvious conclusion; a conclusion that's worse than anything I had previously imagined. I dare to say, 'Are you in love with her?'

'Maybe.'

I'm shocked. Shocked by the confession; by the honesty. I expected him to say no even if it was a lie. No attempt to spare my feelings. It's my turn to pause. This is Coll saying he's in love. Coll who claims he doesn't love me; says he has never loved anyone since Penny. The fabric of our relationship crumbles.

'Have you been out with her before?'

'Yes.'

'When?'

'Two or three times. I took her to see *Antony and Cleopatra*. It was like a thank you for all she has done for my art.'

Two or three times … Took her to see … Dates … Unquestionably dates.

'And then we went to the pub the next evening because I wanted to see her again. She said I cheer her up.'

'You make her sound like a charity case.' I know from what Newcastle John has said, and from my observations at Dick's do that she's far from helpless. 'And I presume you still haven't told her about me?'

'No.'

'Don't you think you should?'

Again the silence. And during this silence which also seems to go on forever but is only a few seconds, I come to the only possible decision.

150

And then I say the hardest thing that I have ever said. 'That's it then. You leave me no choice. I can't carry on like this. You've betrayed me.'

'I haven't. I told you, nothing has happened.'

'You've taken her out. You've two-timed me. That's cheating in my book.' My mind races. There really isn't any more prevaricating to be done. I'm not going to stand by and watch our relationship disintegrate while he woos Felicity Mayfield-Harvey. Not now I know for sure. It's time I took control. 'I can't believe this has happened. That you would risk everything we have for a nothing. For something that may not ever work out.'

'I can't help it. I know it wouldn't last more than a few months if we got together. But she's different and I can't help it.'

'That is so pathetic.'

'I can't. It's the truth. I've been dreading this. That's why I've been feeling so ill.'

It's all about him and how he feels.

He repeats, 'Nothing happened between us. We didn't do anything.'

'Love is a far bigger threat. You don't get that, do you? To a woman it's as much of a betrayal as sex.'

'It's all in my head. A fantasy.'

Pathetic.

I am determined not to relent. 'You have a few things of mine, and I of yours. And I suppose after all this time we should do this thing face to face … if you want to. And I'd like my photos back …'

Again there's a long pause. When he speaks, his voice is low and shaky, but gives nothing away as to his true feelings. 'Yes … I suppose … yes … I'll ring you tomorrow.'

And then suddenly he's gone and my world cracks and splinters into a thousand pieces. It is as if my body has been wrenched apart. All the hopes and dreams of a future shattered in one single conversation.

That night, I hardly sleep and the next day at work I'm hollow eyed and in a daze. When Laura and Newcastle John ask if anything's wrong, I tell them I had a bad night because of the neighbours and that I'm not feeling too well.

At lunchtime, I can't eat, but escape the oppressive silence of the library to take a walk in the university grounds. I walk and walk along pathways between the winter trees, my only thoughts are of Coll and what we will speak of as we say our final goodbyes. A misty drizzle wets my face and mingles with the tears I can't help but cry. A dark grey cloud hangs on the horizon, heading slowly my way with monsoon intent.

A small group of students, who are studying through the holiday, walk towards me, muffled up in beanie hats and thick long scarves, clutching folders, holding hands, arm in arm, their bouncing vitality a contrast to my leaden steps. I don't care if anyone sees me. This is what a broken heart feels like. This is what it would be like if he died, except it's worse than that, because if he died, he wouldn't have rejected me.

I feel so truly awful I believe that I might die. My world has fallen apart and every cell and fibre of my being is in agony. I go over and over our conversation, looking desperately for hope. *He didn't know if she felt the same; she didn't know how he felt. Nothing whatsoever had happened between them.*

I believe him.

But he said he was in love with her. *In* love. *In* love … He wasn't *in* love with me.

And love is such a very powerful force.

I pray that our forthcoming conversation may give me some reason to change my mind. I don't see how it can, but I can't bear the pain.

He's obsessed. Infatuated. A fantasy. He admitted it. To be rejected on a whim is what hurts most of all. He even said it wouldn't last more than a few months. Of course it wouldn't. I'm sure she doesn't know his dark side. The drinking, among other things. The OWs, the moods. If she's a tough cookie, unlike me, she won't stand for that. I can tell from seeing her at Dick's leaving do that she's not one to be messed with. But before she discovers what he's really like, they may have weeks or months of wonderment, of the type that I once had with him. I see her laughing at his jokes and Coll enraptured to an extent that he's never been with me. I'm not beautiful enough for his artistic eye. But I can't help that. Felicity takes on the guise of a bewitching goddess against whom I stand no chance. I mutter to myself. Prayers perhaps, or a madness creeping on.

'*You're so sweet, so nice,*' he said to me.

Too sweet; too nice. Nice girls don't stir the passions. I read about it in a magazine. It goes against the grain for me to be deliberately awkward. I should've started younger, learning to be awkward, but I was always inclined to chase rather than be chased. It's odd that I managed to snare a husband. Sometimes I forget I ever had one; such a long time ago. Pete. A nice man. Steady and reliable in many ways, even if he did seek adventure. We were still both so young when he died. Thinking about starting a family. Sad way to go. And there was a lot of pain. But it wasn't the same as this. Pete died loving me. I wasn't rejected. Rejection brings a different pain.

I hate myself for not being like Felicity – whatever it is that she has that is different from me. And yet it might be the reason we've lasted this long. This very thing may be the thing that would split them up – should they ever get together. I find it hard to believe that he would give up on me for something that wouldn't last; that he knows wouldn't last. And he also knows I wouldn't ever go back to him in those circumstances.

Love does strange things to people. Even people of almost fifty-three. Coll sees himself as a bit of a poet so I can believe the power of love on his soul. Artists too. That's the problem with creative types. They are volatile and inclined to follow their passions. Rationality goes out of the window. Felicity must be at

153

least a bit creative if she throws pots. Something else they have in common. I wonder if she follows her passions too.

And then I wonder why she came into our lives. Why? A newspaper advertisement. A restaurant we were unlikely ever to visit. Why?

The lights of my world go out one by one as I walk and drift through a watery haze and hope seems almost pointless, but it's all I have to keep me from collapse. Coll, bizarrely, illuminates so many corners of my life. To think of him in the past tense is impossible but I must be prepared.

To that end, I imagine our final words, our final parting and our last goodbye.

Part 2
Sarah

35

Felicitygate 2

Sarah

When Coll rings in the evening, his voice is shaky like yesterday. He speaks gently – unusually so. 'Tomorrow okay? I can come after school?'

He asks me how I am and I say, 'How do you think?' The words fracture in my throat, my mouth is desert dry and I have developed a croak. Then I say, 'Can't talk now. Cooking.' I'm not, but I don't want to say any more until we are face to face. I don't want him to hear the tears.

Another night to toss and turn; another day to wait and wonder. In the end I sleep because I'm emotionally exhausted but I wake early to imagined scenarios with unhappy endings.

I drive to work in a daze, counting the hours till I meet Coll. It's a day where I look for portents. There are magpies in the university grounds and I count them at each sighting. And I go through the motions at work while my mind struggles with possibilities and mourns the expected loss.

The clock in the library seems to stand still between my glances. It's quiet with term yet to start and a skeleton staff on duty. Dr Edward returns another book.

'I thought you'd gone,' I say.

'Gone from my office,' he says. 'This is one I found at home. Are you okay, Sarah?'

Is it that obvious? 'Tired,' I say. *Because of your blasted wife. She's ruined my life.* I wish I could tell him. I'm sure he would listen sympathetically. But I don't know him well enough for such personal disclosures.

Laura and Newcastle John are not in today and I brood with little to distract me. I don't have many of my possessions at Coll's place. I hardly ever stay there. Wash things and shampoo, a batch of photos from over the years and a cardigan for emergency layering during cold snaps. The whole lot will fit in a carrier bag. I know I told him I wanted my photos back, but in truth, I don't want him to bring them today. Fetching them will mean it really is the end; a sad exchange of the meagre evidence of our intertwined lives. Still I hope for salvage even though I can't see how it can be achieved. Not if he loves her. Not if he wants her.

Are you in love with her? … Yes … The words play over and over again and a xylophone plinks in the background like on a TV drama, a warning of sadness to come.

I drive home in a stupor and hang on to his words that nothing has happened between them; that she doesn't know his feelings and that he has no idea whether she wants a relationship or a friend. Maybe she doesn't want either. I'm sure he mentioned 'fantasy' more than once. Already I'm forgetting his exact words.

Wise people would tell me that it doesn't make any difference what she wants. The fact that he wants her should be enough for me to end our relationship for ever. Thinking otherwise is weakness. It's not as if we're married or have children with sensibilities to protect. We don't own joint property or depend on each other for financial support. There's nothing to hold us together. Nothing tangible.

Only time … such precious time.

If he brings a carrier bag, it will be a sign of his decision to let me go without a fight. I wonder if I should gather his things, equally few. Should I be prepared for the worst? I could leave a bag of his stuff by the door to demonstrate that I haven't changed my mind. I haven't. But I want him to change it for me. Yet I don't see how he can.

I decide not to be negative and to leave his stuff untouched.

I find it hard to eat, but I force myself to have some soup. I've not eaten much for two days and am functioning on adrenaline and stored reserves. Not long now. My head's a mess. I must try not to make myself ill. If he can do this to me, he's not worth it. I tell myself this, but I don't believe it. A multitude of shared pleasures dance through my thoughts and I'm lost in grief.

As the time draws near, my heart is beating fast; too fast. Such emotional stress cannot be good for people of a certain age. A broken heart. This is what it is. Broken enough to kill me. Tears are not far away. My life is about to change forever and I cannot bear the thought of never seeing him again, my darling Coll who, despite his self-centredness and pursuit of OWs, has supported me through ten years of crises; shared with me the exceptional and the mundane; laughed with me, cried with me.

And now he's lied to me by omission and he's in love with someone else. The sickness in my stomach intensifies. The darkness outside and the rain trickling down the windows add to the melancholy.

He's early. As soon as I open the door I see his drawn and worried face and the shadows beneath his eyes. He won't be looking forward to this any more than me. He hates confrontation even when he's the cause. Then I notice he's holding a carrier bag and my heart jumps and sinks as that tiny smidgen of hope flutters to the ground like a dying butterfly. A lump rises in my throat and I find it almost impossible to speak. I've hardly spoken to anyone today.

There are no smiles or hugs. Nothing of the greetings of the past twelve years. We go to my living room and sit down, he on the sofa, me on a chair opposite. He leans the bag against the leg of my dining table. I cannot bear to look at it. I try so very hard not to cry or show weakness.

He fidgets. I offer tea. He accepts. Anything to delay the talk. 'How are you?' I ask as I return with tea.

'Not good,' he says in a resigned sort of way. 'I'm so tired. I can't sleep. I've been feeling sick and faint all day.'

Much the same as me. I wonder if he's ill. 'Have you eaten?'

'Not a lot.'

'That's probably why.'

My nurturing self, my compassionate self, takes over. I offer soup.

He says, 'You really are amazing, Sarah. You should be shouting at me. Instead, you say you'll make me soup.' A thin smile.

I try to smile back. I can't.

'Shouting would achieve nothing,' I say. 'And we cannot have a proper conversation if you feel ill.'

I get up to heat some soup from the fridge and he puts on the TV. It's like old times, except it isn't. I fear what's to come. Post soup.

He eats in relative silence. We watch *News 24*. My mind is on other things.

When he's finished, I take his bowl through to the kitchen and he turns off the TV. I sit. I wait.

He launches. 'These past two days, I've never felt so terrible in my life. Not even when Penny and I split up. I haven't been able to work or paint. I have stomach pains. I can't eat. That must mean something, Sarah. All I can think about is losing you.'

I hold my breath.

'I thought I could move on and it wouldn't be a problem.' He looks at me intently, but I find it hard to meet his gaze. He hasn't looked at me like this for weeks. Not since he met Felicity. He says, 'When you said it was over, I didn't expect to feel like this. I was ready to move on. It must mean something. I think I will die without you. I don't want to lose you. I will do anything to get you back. Whatever it takes.'

My shoulders drop. A relief, perhaps. Is this the hope that I had wished for?

'I promise you nothing has happened between Felicity and me. She has done nothing. She doesn't flirt, she hasn't encouraged me. She's not like that. It's all been because of me.'

I think about the present-buying episode, when she gave him the fridge magnet. To me that constitutes flirting. It's certainly a sign. But men don't always see the subtleties that we women depend on so we don't lose face. In the early days of our friendship, Coll didn't realise that I was falling for him. I recall that Felicity sat and talked to him for ages when he dropped off paintings. Surely she knew he was interested. I would have. I did when it was me that was being wooed.

'You never told her about me,' I accuse. 'If you had, I doubt she would have spent so much time with you.'

He slouches on the edge of the chair, his elbows on his knees, his hands in two fists against his chin. 'I wanted to see where the relationship would go. I know it wasn't right, but I couldn't help it.'

'Have you not heard of "Free Will"?'

'She's so different from you. Not better; just different.'

This is becoming a mantra. I hear 'better', no matter what he says.

'She's decisive. She knows what she wants: a go-getter.'

'And I'm not. But it's the way I am and it's worked for us until now.'

'You are the nicest person in the world, Sarah. Always cheerful; looking on the bright side.'

It's a mask I wear for Coll. 'And that's a criticism?'

He rattles on, as if in a trance. 'She's had a tough time with her husband; a divorce pending. And she had unresolved issues over the death of her mother. We had things in common. That's what we talked about.'

I note the past tense. 'I had a husband once. A *dead* husband. I've been bereaved. I've had a tough time. You know I have. We had things in common too.'

'I do know.' He looks at the floor. 'But her story was fresh and new. She wanted to know about the divorce. I felt useful.'

'Useful?' It's not the most romantic of things to feel.

'And Shakespeare. She's mad about Shakespeare. But she hadn't been to a play for ages.'

'Hence *Richard ll*.'

'Yes.'

'But I like Shakespeare. We go to plays.'

'She was so enthusiastic. I enjoyed making her happy after all she's been through.'

'And you didn't think about making me unhappy? What about what you put me through?'

I listen to his lyrical prose about how Felicity made him feel; how wonderful she is; how he couldn't explain exactly, but there was something about her. Something he saw straight away that lured him in. She has become St Felicity. One thinks of rose-tinted glasses, pedestals. All of them. Classic. He looks into the far distance through my window, now streaked with racing raindrops.

He says, 'Maybe it was because she reminded me a little of Penny. She has a similar look; similar hair.'

'I can't compete with that.'

'It's not a competition.'

'It feels like it.'

'She's nothing special, really. She's fifty-six – nearly fifty-seven. Doesn't look it though. I bet she was a looker when she was younger.'

Why is he telling me this? I don't want to know. I don't believe he knows what he's saying. This isn't exactly the best way not to lose me. It's the twisting of the knife. Not deliberately, but in complete ignorance of how it might affect me.

'It wasn't her fault. It was all down to me. She didn't text me all the time. Sometimes a couple of days would pass before she would reply. She didn't phone. She did nothing to encourage me.'

So that was it, I think. She didn't chase. That in my book is encouragement. She knows how to play the game and he doesn't realise he's been deliberately trapped. Or maybe I do her a disservice. Maybe she's genuinely not interested. That's how women end up with a different guy from their first great love.

He continues, 'I know she and I could have had a good time for a few months, but it wouldn't have lasted. We're both too competitive. And I've no interest in her restaurant business or in growing vegetables. She said that was why she split up with her husband.'

'Has she got money?'

He laughs. 'I'm not after her money if that's what you think. I'm not like that. Her mum left her a small fortune, but I don't know the details. It was enough to buy the restaurant. I really don't know much about her. But we get on. She understands.'

'But *we* get on; *I* understand. I've understood for years.' I want to remind him of all the things he said in the past that makes me different from others and make us work. But I guess he must be bored by my type of understanding. Against this outpouring about the wonders of Felicity, my uniqueness leeches away. I don't feel special any more.

And he's admitting he doesn't know much about her, yet was prepared to sacrifice our relationship. What a fool. I wonder if he's mad. But then love is madness. He's romantically in love with her and love is blind. His brain has registered the negatives, but he's followed his heart.

I've always wanted him to feel that special something about me. Sometimes I thought I was close. But looking back I ruined it all by making it too easy for him. He was always too sure of me. Only now, sitting in my living room on this cold January day, only now does he doubt.

I can see his pain and it hurts me to see him in distress. That's how much I love. If we were in our thirties or even forties, the

163

thing to do would be to tell him his goose was cooked, his bed was laid and to tell him I don't want to see him any more.

But I reason that if I make him wait before at least giving him some hope, then what if something happens to him? He's a man of a certain age. Things do happen. And then what? Guilt and no going back, and self-castigation and if onlys for the rest of my days. We're at a perilous time of life. We shouldn't be hurting each other like this. I might die too. The past few days have scared me. I'm aware of a fragile heart.

I'm also scared that if I give him no hope, he might call my bluff. What if he scurries off to Felicity and says, 'How about it?' He would never need to tell her about me if he didn't choose. And yes, maybe it would only last six months and he would have regrets and come crawling back. But our relationship would be sullied forever. It could never be the same. Indeed I doubt I'd want him.

The other possibility is that he would get over 'us' in that six months and not come back at all. Right now it seems he's choosing me and I would be a fool not to leave the door ajar. It's as if for the first time in the relationship, I have power.

But what I fail to acknowledge is that he's choosing the certainty of me against the uncertainty that she would consider going out with him romantically. It isn't a fair contest and in my haste to find reparation, I overlook this fact and relinquish my power too quickly.

What is yours will come to you, say the sages. They say that I should take the risk of losing him, because if he's worth it, he will come back. But I don't listen to them and instead I throw him a rope.

'I can't promise anything,' I say to Coll. And I can't. Much depends on what he does and says next.

Coll flickers a little, like a dog hearing the rattle of a lead as someone brushes past its familiar hanging place on the back of a door. I have presented him with hope.

'What can I do?' he says, eyes pleading.

The roles have switched for the first time in our turbulent history. He has handed me power and a palliative to quell this ghastly sickness that I've been feeling for weeks. When people talk of knife edges, I now know exactly what that means.

'You can start by cancelling your date with her and *Richard ll.*'

'Yes,' he says.

But already I can see his resolve shaking as he realises that he'll have to speak to Felicity to break their arrangement. How will I know that he goes through with it?

I add, 'And you need to prove to me that you have.'

'How?'

Usually so full of ideas, Coll is floundering, his face ashen. I offer suggestions. 'By taking me to see it or coming here.'

'What if she goes anyway and sees us?'

'Is that likely?'

'Not very.'

'Well then.'

'What will I say to her?'

'Make an excuse. Like you did to me.'

There's an uncomfortable silence. I don't want to appear unreasonable or controlling, but *Richard ll* is out of the question if we are to move forward. Indeed, any socialising with Felicity is off limits. He's in love with her. I mustn't forget that hurtful admission. But he has chosen me. I mustn't forget that either.

I say, 'I know I can't ask you not to see her ever because of the paintings and I don't want you to miss out on sales, but you have to keep it businesslike; no more cosy chats.'

'She'll think it's strange.'

'She won't if you tell her about me.'

More discomfort and awkwardness in store. Coll fidgets. No doubt Felicity will wonder why he didn't say something sooner. He will be found out: as a flirt, a tease, a womaniser.

165

I tell him that it's time he was more open about our relationship and more committed in general. That I no longer want to feel I'm an option; that we need to move on, make proper plans. 'And if you can't, then you can't and I let you go.'

'I can,' he says. 'I will. I mean what I say.'

I tell him that this has hurt me badly. I say perhaps we need to go back to the beginning. No full sex for a while. I want to make it clear that there are consequences. He says he understands; that he doesn't mind waiting, however long it takes. I want to try to recapture the romance and hope that if I hold back, he will feel it too.

The minutes pass and the tension is only partially dissipated. We talk about him drinking too much and that it might be affecting his judgement. And he repeats everything that brought us to this point. Everything about the magnetism of Felicity which I don't really want to hear and the reaffirmation of nothing happening and that it was all a fantasy. I can't seem to get through to him that an emotional betrayal is to most women almost as bad as a physical one. But neither do I want him to think that it would be better to have gone further down the road and be hung for a sheep as for a lamb.

I tell him I make no promises. That both of us will have to think through what's been said.

'Of course,' he says. He thanks me for giving him a chance.

One false move, one wrong word and our reconstructed model will collapse.

When he gets up to leave, I dare to ask, 'What's in the bag?'

'Some GCSE projects. I didn't want to risk leaving them in the car. Just in case. You never know.'

'I thought it was all my stuff from your flat. I nearly packed up yours just in case so we could have had it all done and dusted today.'

He brushes a hand under his eyes. I've never seen him like this before. He reminds me of Tigger on the day his friends deliberately lost him in the fog and he was temporarily unbounced.

Days pass. Coll calls me every evening like he used to do before he met Felicity. Each time I ask him if he's cancelled the date. Each time he says, 'Not yet, but I will.' Time is running out and I worry that he isn't going to. I know he'll be wondering what to say; what excuse to make. Until he does this, I can't relax.

I keep busy at work and enrol on an evening course of life-drawing. I need to live for me and not through Coll. It's being held at the same college where I met him and the memories flood back as I'm greeted with familiar smells in the corridors.

After a week he phones to tell me he's told her. I say, 'What did you say?'

He says, 'I said I couldn't make it.'

'Was she okay with that?'

'Disappointed.'

'Well, that's too bad. Forgive me for not feeling any sympathy.'

'Would you like to go?'

'Are you sure?'

'I want to take you.'

'Okay, then. Yes.' I let out a sigh. At least he is offering proof.

We enjoy the play. Despite everything. The company comprises a group of East Devon teachers who are putting on the play because it's one of the set texts for A level. There are a lot of students in the audience. The man playing Richard is tiny and gaunt with exquisite cheekbones. He reminds me of someone I knew when I was at school, slightly camp and styled as a New Romantic like Adam Ant during his 'Prince Charming' phase.

Afterwards, we go for a drink in a nearby pub. Coll says, 'You are very important to me, Sarah. And I nearly lost you. I'm so sorry ... for everything.'

I want to believe him. But it's early days. I don't let down my guard.

36

Valentine

Sarah

You can't go back. It was foolish to try. We are fifty-something, not seventeen. Nothing remains the same after such hurt. The oak tree has been shaken and the acorns have landed where they will. Most will be eaten or stashed by squirrels and jays. If we're lucky, a few will have fallen in the wood under the open canopy, where they may germinate and turn into new saplings that may have a chance to grow. There is calm, but an uneasy calm; Felicity is ever present in my thoughts and probably in Coll's too.

On the evening of Valentine's Day, he takes me to a local fish restaurant where we eat *moules à la marinière* and chips, pretend we're in France and practise our rudimentary O level skills in the language. We laugh a lot. Coll has been attentive since *Felicitygate* and I've a renewed hope that we have a future and that it's worth hanging on to.

He says, 'I was close to losing you. And all because of a fantasy.'

'Is this a fantasy too? Us?' I say.

'No, this is real.' And he takes my hand across the table and looks into my eyes. We connect. A *frissant* of the old special magic.

The rest of the evening flows like an evening I had dreamed of but never experienced with Coll. His words are of *you* and *we* and *us* and *future*. Nothing of *I* and *her*. I begin to plan in my mind. Thoughts of moving: more space, a garden, hens.

'We'll talk,' says Coll, but he doesn't mean now.

I'm happy with the promise and I loosen up and smile more.

We go home early, getting wet in a light drizzle as we walk to the car, giggling as we weave around the puddles thinking we must look drunk. Driving back, Coll plays Love and Money's 'Shape of Things to Come' and I take the lyrics as a message of love to me; a message that he is not able to put into his own words. When we draw up outside my house, he kisses me with a new tenderness. I'm overcome by a mix of emotions, of sadness and gladness, and I let my guard down and suggest he might like to stay the night. It's only been a month, but at my age a month seems a long time. I feel the signs of hormonal uncertainty and a little voice whispers that I should make the most of what's left of desire.

'Are you sure?' says Coll.

'I am. We know where this is going. We're too old to drag it out like teenagers.'

Coll says, 'You go in, I'll be a moment,' and as I watch from the open door, from the boot of the car he produces a bunch of red roses with long stalks. Proper romantic roses.

I fill a bucket of water for them to drink as a temporary measure. We kiss again, this time with more urgency. I lead him upstairs.

It's time I let him into my heart again. And more.

Afterwards we lie close and silent, reunited and satisfied.

It's late when his phone rings. We're in bed, sleeping. I'm aware of him taking it from the bedside table and he answers it, settling back on the bed but turning away from me.

I'm so close to him that I can hear her voice, a vaguely recognisable voice that I remember overhearing in the distance at Dick Fieldbrace's leaving do. A well-spoken, educated voice that I know belongs to Felicity Mayfield-Harvey. She sounds calm and controlled. I can't help but eavesdrop and he can't escape the room without it seeming obvious. She asks how he is and he replies blandly that he's getting over another cold. This is a lie. After what happened between us and all his promises, I expect him to give her short shrift. But he doesn't.

At first he's monosyllabic to her gushing about continued picture sales. But gradually he relaxes and starts to chat about how work is going and what he's been doing regarding his latest paintings. He asks how she is and what she's been up to and then he starts to laugh at what she's saying. All the time I feel my hostility rising and I begin to sweat.

It's not so much the words that betray him, but his actions. Throughout the conversation he repeatedly lifts his arm and scratches the back of his head against the pillow. It's a 'tell'; a sure sign that he's still besotted with her. No arrangements were made, nothing, but after he hangs up, he lies on his back and stares at the ceiling.

He says, 'That was Felicity.'

'I gathered. Why was she calling you at this hour?' What I don't add is that it's Valentine's Day. I wonder if this has resonated with him as well.

He makes light of it. 'She was just asking how I am. She's sold another couple of paintings and someone's been making enquiries about whether I do commissions.'

'I wish you didn't have any communication with her,' I say, casually.

'Don't push me,' he says, rather too sharply.

I feel the threat. I've overstepped the mark. Things are not as sorted between us as I'd hoped. I fall silent. It's too late to take back what I've given him. The pleasures of the evening disappear as fast as raindrops on the sand.

37

The Shard

Sarah

After staying over on Valentine's night, Coll says he needs a week at home to sort out his flat, to prepare some stuff for school and for painting.

'But it's half term,' I say. 'I've taken a couple of days' leave. I thought we might do something.'

'It's my first chance since Christmas to have a block of time and get stuck in,' says Coll.

I can't argue with that. This will be the first weekend apart since *Felicitygate,* but I try not to read anything into it.

'I'll see you a week on Saturday,' he says. 'I'll be more relaxed when everything is sorted.'

At the weekend, I decide to visit sister Jane in Dawlish. I've only told her the barest details about *Felicitygate*. She's never been too enamoured of Coll. When I first introduced them a few years ago, he tried his usual charm offensive and Jane was unimpressed. She says she has the measure of him.

On this visit, as we sit at her pine table in the large kitchen of the type I covet, she says, 'You're looking tired, Sarah. Is that scoundrel behaving himself?'

'I'm not sure,' I say, truthfully. 'I hope so.'

'Hope is a flimsy thing,' she says, attacking a piece of cucumber as if she wishes it was Coll. 'You don't need all this stress at your time of life.'

No. I don't. I steer her onto the latest news of the children and she happily gushes about their achievements. She has a girl and a boy, fifteen and eighteen, who have suitable friends, are free from any serious angst, cause no trouble and make her life even more enviable.

Jane is lucky. Some people are. They say you make your own luck but I don't like to think this is true. If it is, I'm useless at making it. Jane is taller than me, thinner than me and naturally cleverer. I had to work hard. She breezed through without much effort. She has a natural way with people and has many friends. I have to nurture mine. Although I'm the elder by three years, she behaves like my older sister. She took on this role when she was about fourteen and acquired her first boyfriend – something I had yet to achieve.

Our mum was always singing her praises, paying her attention. I was left with scraps. I often wonder if that's how I cope with Coll. I'm used to settling for less.

Jane met her husband John the Storm at university within the first couple of weeks of arriving. A handsome chap from Exmouth. She never went through that phase of anxiously wondering if she would find anyone to love and to love her.

When I met Pete, I thanked God that perhaps life wasn't so unfair after all.

On Sunday Laura and I go to a craft market. I try to keep Coll out of my thoughts and to pretend that everything is fine, but every picture we see reminds me of him as I can hear his voice offering an appraisal.

During the following week Coll continues to call me every evening, telling me how his painting is progressing. This is good, but we don't chat for long.

My stomach is like a harbinger of doom. Even before anything concrete has occurred, my digestion slows and I'm slightly nauseous.

It's midday the following Saturday when he phones unexpectedly. Even as I pick up the receiver, I know he's calling to tell me something I don't want to hear. I'm preparing a special supper for this evening by making a *Bouillabaisse* sauce ahead of time. It's Coll's birthday early next week and I thought we'd have something a little extravagant by way of celebration. I have bought monkfish, cod, squid, prawns, mussels and clams, not to mention

172

fennel and fennel seeds which give the dish its distinctive flavour. He likes fish. He's a Piscean. I read that one should beware the Pisces male because they are prone to dithering. I did not take heed. They are also very creative and I like that.

'Guess where I am?' he says. There's excitement in his voice and a cold feeling sweeps over me. It's the feeling of dread at what's coming next. A feeling that was so familiar during *Felicitygate* but which I hoped had gone forever. On the night of Valentine's Day, it resurfaced.

I say, 'I've no idea.'

'At the top of the Shard.'

'The shard?' I echo, puzzled. 'What shard?'

'The Shard. South Bank. London.'

He waits for the words to sink in. They take a while. The Shard? London? Two hours plus on the train from Exeter? And I wait to think of a suitable response. There's something not quite right about this.

He fills the pause. 'What a building! The view is incredible. You should see the buses and trains. They're like toys on a model. It's a bit damp and misty but I can still see for miles and miles.'

There's a further beat while I register what he's telling me. Why would he choose to go on a day of inclement weather?

'But what are you doing there? You said you had things to do at home this week.'

'Oh, it was a spur of the moment thing. Fancied a trip to London.'

'I took two days off this week. We could have gone then. Gone together.'

'I was busy earlier in the week. This is my reward for hard work.'

'Had you forgotten you're supposed to be having your birthday meal here tonight?'

'I'll be back by seven.'

I wanted to ask him if he was with someone. But I was scared of the answer; scared of the lie. It seemed a huge expense to go alone. In any case, as we'd followed the progress of the building of the Shard, we'd mused that when it opened to the public, we might take a trip to London, maybe stay overnight, do the Shard and a show. A special treat.

'We talked about seeing it together,' I say.

'No point in calling you this morning, Sarah. We know you need a week's notice for most things.' A speck of criticism in his voice. 'And the weather's not too bad for the time of year. I'd finished a painting so I hopped on a train.'

He wouldn't want to go again. Not in the near future at least. I'm disappointed and can't help but sound deflated in my response.

Suddenly he says, 'Got to go.' And the call is terminated abruptly leaving me suspicious and imagining Mrs Felicity re-emerging from wherever she had slipped off to.

In the afternoon I receive another call saying he's delayed and to skip supper. He says he will see me at nine.

The *Bouillabaisse* sauce is ready and waiting, vibrant and delightful. I let it cool. I'll put it in the freezer. I make myself a fish-finger sandwich and stare at the blank screen of the TV, my mind awash with unpleasant scenarios. Afterwards, it no longer seems worth getting changed and making the effort I had planned.

When Coll arrives, half an hour later than he said, he is hyperenergised and behaving oddly. I feel as if I'm an inconvenience and that he would rather not be here. But his energy doesn't last long. We've hardly exchanged more than a few words when he's flagging in front of the TV, disinclined to talk. So much for the special birthday evening designed to help us move on. So much for him being nice and relaxed after catching up on all his chores. A new dread settles in my gut. The feeling that we had made a new start has evaporated. What next?

What, indeed.

Part 3
Felicity

38

The Cancellation

Felicity – Early January 2013

Coll did not reply to my text saying how much I was looking forward to *Richard II*, but I thought nothing of it. We were a tad intense over the holiday period and it is good to have a breather and consider where we are and what we want. I am looking forward to getting another fix of Shakespeare next weekend and find I am excited about going out with Coll again. That must count for something. A New Year and a new start. My indecisiveness about what type of relationship I want is waning and I am confident that with the right encouragement from me, Coll will take the plunge and we can see how it goes and perhaps have some fun.

Warning the children over Christmas dinner that something might be on the cards and finding it wasn't met with universal disapproval has helped to tip the balance. I have also been put in my place regarding my forlorn hope regarding Ted and my treatment of Marianne. I thought Ted was savage when he 'had a word' about the frequency of my Deer Orchard visits. Savage for him. But he had a point and I have been unfair. It can't be great having to start a new relationship with a hovering and hostile ex-wife and a batch of grown up children and partners, not all of whom approve. I call my solicitor and make an appointment. If I let Ted go in my head, it frees up space for someone else.

Weeknight bookings at Neptune have calmed down since

New Year and I suggest Chris takes a short break. He will be back for *Richard II*. Meanwhile, I take over chef duties and get Kylie in for a few days.

Then, two days before our date, Coll phones to say he can't go to the play. He says he has not been well and has a lot of catching up to do for work. I find this odd and am hacked off. Don't like being cancelled at the best of times, but especially not so close to the event and especially not after all the trouble I have gone to in arranging cover for Saturday's busy service.

There was something about his voice that didn't sound like Coll. He was not his usual buzzy self. Apologetic, but remote. I have a sneaking suspicion he might be getting cold feet about us – if there is an 'us'. If this is the case, I am glad it has not gone any further. But some things don't add up. He was so enthusiastic after *Antony and Cleopatra*. And I am sure I haven't come on too strong or overstepped the mark. If anything, the opposite. But I say to him, 'No problem,' as you do, and, 'Hope we can arrange something when you are feeling better,' by way of encouragement.

His response is non-committal.

Olivia says it is more evidence of his game-playing and I should steer clear. I say it could be genuine illness and I don't want to misjudge him.

'So why didn't he make another arrangement?' Olivia says.

She has become so smug since all this dating malarkey. All of a sudden she thinks she is an expert on men.

If Coll is playing games again, then he is a more complex character than I already thought. I decide not to waste time dwelling on him. Eventually he will be in touch regarding the paintings. No doubt all will be revealed in due course.

39

Valentine

Felicity

Another three weeks pass with no word from Coll. No texts, no visits; nothing. I wonder if he has met with some disaster; that his not feeling well turned out to be something sinister. I am mildly concerned but not attached enough to worry. It has been a tad quiet on the picture sales front since Christmas: only two small scenes of trees in blossom. I owe him a little money but not much. However, I will have to contact him at some point.

Valentine's Day is upon us. I wonder if that is why Coll has come to mind. A day of secrets; a day for lovers. Not for me any more. I am feeling sorry for myself. This time last year, Gianni and I were still apparently enjoying our new life together. There were roses and chocolates and a special giant seafood raviolo with the most exquisite and delicate oyster sauce which he said he had designed especially for me and put on the menu for one night only: *Raviolo Felicity*. The rot was yet to make itself known, although looking back there were signs to which I was blind.

And before him there was Ted and his dutiful annual bunch of quality red roses, never varying, even down to the message, 'All my love, Ted.' Never any attempt to surprise me or show imagination. I didn't fully appreciate them or him and his constancy. Sorry, Ted. I wonder if he has done the same for Marianne and if she will get bored like I did.

Three cards arrive for Chris. He is dismissive. He takes for granted that he is adored, oblivious of the girlish giggles that will have accompanied each purchase, and uninterested in following clues from addresses written in the hand of disguise.

After a busy service at the restaurant – complete with one marriage proposal via a ring in a glass of water which had the whole room clapping when the bride-to-be accepted – Chris goes out with his current girlfriend, Zoe, and says he'll be late. I am tired and retreat upstairs with a bottle of wine. I don't usually drink alone, or drink much, but after three glasses I am feeling bold and decide to phone Coll. I want to know why he has become so silent and whether I was imagining his attentions as something more than they were.

The significance of the particular day is not lost on me, but I won't say anything to him about that. I know how to be subtle. If he is as clever as he maintains, he will understand the connection. I don't send Valentine cards (not even to Ted when we were young) but even if I did, it is hardly appropriate in this case. I realise Coll, unlike Ted, is like most men and prefers to do the chasing. All he should require therefore are hints that I am receptive. It worked before. And I was getting used to the idea of a male companion at the very least. Going to the theatre with Coll was like having a legitimate escort. I enjoyed his company and believe he enjoyed mine. I am hoping he has recovered from his illness and caught up on school work. With any luck there will be another Shakespearian production on somewhere in the locality.

I get ready for bed, and once snuggled comfortably with a hot water bottle and my wine I lie back on a stack of pillows and call him from my mobile.

When I hear his voice, he sounds surprised and at first a little awkward and formal. When he copped out of *Richard II*, I put his less friendly tone down to embarrassment in having to cancel. I am confused. Is this the same person who was so keen to see me only a month ago? I wonder what I have done to push him away.

'Have I caught you at a bad time? Is it too late?' It would be too late for most people being just after eleven, but he and I did most of our texting late at night so I know he is usually up until the early hours.

'No … no.'

I ask him how he is.

'Getting over another cold. Winter. Hibernation.'

I wonder if he suffers from SAD. Perhaps that's it.

'Have you seen any more plays?' I offer an opportunity to arrange something.

'No, nothing. Quiet, really.'

This is hard work. I tell him about the couple of picture sales since Christmas, a commission enquiry and that I owe him money. When he again responds monosyllabically and without his usual enthusiasm, I add that Marianne is back in town so my visits to the Deer Orchard have once again become something to agonise over. This time his tone is sympathetic and he laughs when I refer to her as a deer.

'A dear?' he says. 'How so?'

'No. Not "a dear". Far from it. Deer as in antlers. Jumpy type.'

Then I have to explain to him about my people-as-animals thing. Gradually, he thaws and warms to the conversation and the easy repartee of before starts to creep back into the exchange.

'And what am I?' he says.

'A llama.'

'Why so?'

'Cheeky. Unpredictable.'

He laughs again. But there is no mention of him coming round or taking me out.

'I'll send you a cheque,' I say.

'There's no hurry. Wait until you've sold some more.'

And then the conversation terminates rather abruptly and I am left mildly puzzled. But it is not massively important, and I drain my glass, get up to clean my teeth and return to bed to read with a relatively untroubled mind.

40

Ted on TV

Felicity

Next day, after lunch service, I drive to the Deer Orchard on the vegetable run. I expect Marianne will be there. She has virtually moved in since her latest return from Beckenham. Ted is now properly retired from his lecturing job so they can play happy families and do things together more easily. He does odd hours of work back at the university, but this is mostly for research purposes for his next book or to give a lecture or two in areas of his expertise. No doubt his old department will be promoting his celebrity status because since the television documentary began airing at the end of last month, he's been very much in demand by the media and has made several visits to London.

My thoughts of letting him go in my head were somewhat scuppered by Coll backing off. I have also enjoyed watching him on TV. I don't tell him though. I pretend I have caught a few moments here and there, too busy to watch it all. In truth, I taped every episode of the documentary series and watched each one more than once.

You wouldn't know Ted was new to the game. He is a natural. His colleague Patrick Shrubsole is lead presenter. I call him Pompous Patrick, because he is. He reminds me of a stoat: a cute face but deadly. I can imagine him sneaking up on you from behind and burying his teeth in your neck. I met him once in London after Ted was mugged. I know from what Ted has said that he is a perfectionist and doesn't suffer fools. In my opinion Ted would do it better.

Patrick began the series by explaining the history of Scilly in the early nineteenth century when over population and drought led to mass starvation. Cut to Ted on St Agnes, with an amazing rock pile as backdrop, to explain the current sustainable working practices on the island. He has been re-modelled by the image folk who have managed to hide his facial scar with make-up. Not that it is particularly noticeable these days, but TV shows up the flaws. They have also fluffed up his hair like the wind does, but semi-permanently. I can't imagine what he thinks about that. He has always been averse to using gels. He is dressed in a pale blue shirt with jeans and has a healthy outdoor look which I once adored. *Not bad for his age.* I wonder if he will get fan mail. Patrick comes over as being knowledgeable but conceited. Ted is more down to earth.

If I am told in advance, I catch some of his publicity appearances too. Kate usually slips me the wink. She knows I am missing the excitement of sharing these moments around the TV with the whole family. On *This Morning* he adopted a languid style, explaining the concept of sustainability in simple terms and encouraging everyone to do their bit to promote the growing of free food via fruit trees and through communal cultivation of unused public plots. On *The One Show* the focus was on educating the young in horticulture, with a ridiculous *'send us a photo of your child gardening'* request and an embarrassed Ted having to read out the names of some of the best submitted. I could tell he thought it was a waste of time. I don't know how Matt Baker manages to keep a straight face. He's a great presenter, yet they expect him to front some truly banal stuff.

By contrast, On *News 24* he was grilled by Kirsty Wark about the thorny subject of population issues. Ted rates her brain power and I could tell she liked him too.

It was expected that the documentary series would have a niche audience of Serious Viewers so by Ted popping up on mainstream TV programmes, it is hoped that the word will percolate to Joe Public. The BBC plans to repeat it straight away for the benefit of those that came to it late. I will probably catch these too if work permits.

Ted and Marianne's cars are on the gravel outside the house. I spy Kate in the greenhouse and take a deep breath. It is wearisome having to deal with all this extra awkwardness. If Ted would get his own place, it would be so much easier. But of course he can't do that until the divorce is settled.

Marianne greets me and offers me tea. Today I accept because Ted is pottering back and forth and may speak to me if I behave myself. I try to show interest in what she was up to in Beckenham and while she rabbits on about the difficulties of promoting an independently published novel and how hard you have to bang on doors before anyone takes any notice, my mind wanders.

After seeming to listen politely for fifteen minutes and behaving in what I hope was a less hostile manner, there is still no sign of Ted coming in to have a chat and I take my leave.

41

Sarah

Felicity

When I return home, I am shocked to find Coll sitting in his car in the car park. He gets out as soon as I arrive. He is wrapped up against the cold weather, a fetching blue patterned scarf looped around his neck.

'Hello, stranger,' I say with the minimum amount of warmth, taking the veg box from the boot and walking straight to the back door. He is not going to get an enthusiastic welcome after his distancing. When I awoke this morning, I regretted calling him last night.

'Thanks for phoning,' he says. 'I wanted to see you. I've come straight from school.'

I shrug and he follows me.

I am slightly insulted by the sudden way in which he terminated the conversation the previous evening.

'I've come to apologise,' Coll says.

'Then you'd better come in. But I need to get rid of these first.'

I take the veg through to the restaurant kitchen, Coll hovering in the passageway, and then we go up to the flat and I throw off my coat and busy myself with the kettle. He plants himself on a chair in the living room and I call through to him, pleased that he can't see my face.

'You were a little "off" at first when I called,' I say. 'Distant. Not your usual self. What's going on?'

'I'll explain in a minute,' Coll says, adding to the mystery.

Once settled with tea, he launches. I expect an excuse about work and am unprepared.

He says, 'I have a girlfriend. I was with her when you called.'

It takes a moment or two for my mind to register this and then a ton of implications swim in a confused mass.

'You have a girlfriend?' I wonder if I misheard.

'Yes.'

'And you met her … when? Where?' I am rather hurt that his attentiveness to me should so swiftly evaporate.

'About twelve years ago. When I was going through my divorce. She attended one of my art evening classes. We discovered a common interest in theatre and exhibitions and became friends.'

'Twelve years ago?' Another surprise. 'How long has she been your girlfriend? How serious is it?'

'About ten years.'

'Ten years!' I almost shout. So he has been taking me out behind someone's back. Giving an impression that his divorce from Penny was the most significant relationship worth discussing. I feel heat rising.

185

'It's not committed,' he adds, as if this excuses everything.

'You have been going out with someone for ten years, and it is not committed? What kind of relationship is it exactly?'

'She's more committed than me.'

'I see.' I don't really. Ten years is a long time not to have some element of commitment; of expectation of exclusivity.

'She found out about us.'

This goes from bad to worse.

'She knows I've been taking you out.'

'Ah. *Richard II*. It all begins to make sense.'

Coll stares at me intently as if I am the only person who matters and the girlfriend is an inconvenience; a nuisance. 'She wanted to go. I tried to get out of it. She pushed. She was suspicious.'

'I'm not surprised.'

'I'd had a bit too much to drink and I told her.'

He's very glib. 'You fool.'

'I'm not good at hiding things.'

'You did a pretty damned good job at hiding her from me.'

I am angry. I don't like to be messed with. I had enough of it with Gianni. I realise that the person I hoped could be a good friend – possibly more – is not who I thought he was. Instead, he is another man who can't be trusted.

Coll says, 'I wanted to get to know you better, first. I like you a lot, Felicity. And you never asked.' He sounds tired and resigned.

I hear myself make a noise of incredulity. 'I liked you too and I assumed … Look, it doesn't matter. I nearly made a fool of myself again.' I glance at the clock and jump. How fast the hands have moved. 'I'm afraid I have to dash,' I say, aware that this is not the best time to terminate a meeting of such theatrical declarations. 'I have to open the restaurant for service.'

'Can't Christopher do it? Or Kylie?'

'Christopher can't be in two places at once and Kylie needs advance notice for babysitters.'

'Someone, surely?'

I get up briskly and he follows me into the hallway. 'This is my job. I have customers. I won't let them down.'

'I could wait for you.'

'Wait for me?' I am shocked. 'Wait for me?' I try a different tone hoping he realises the ridiculousness of his request. 'How long do you think service lasts on a typical evening?'

'I meant wait until you are able to chat. I could book a table. You could join me.'

'Absolutely not.'

'Okay. So when might we meet again?'

'I don't think that would be a good idea, after what you've told me.'

'I have so much more to say. To explain. There were reasons I didn't mention Sarah sooner.'

'Sarah? So that's her name.'

'Don't be angry, Felicity. I need to know what you think of me. Why you said yes when I asked you out. What you wanted from the relationship. Please say we can talk again. It's important. Very, very important.'

I am annoyed at the deception, but strangely curious to know more. I want to know what he has to say. If there really are any mitigating circumstances. And if they are not committed, maybe it is not as bad as I first thought.

'Okay,' I say. 'I'll text you.'

He seems satisfied with this and leaves. I am troubled. I know what it is like to be cheated on and I don't want to put someone else through what Gianni did to me. Coll is good company but I realise now he's not relationship material. If I was unsure before, this has confirmed it, but I still want to know more.

42

Gianni

Felicity

I wait a week before I text Coll. Sleeping on it has not changed my view – if anything it has hardened my position. I am not sure I want to discuss this girlfriend business any more. It feels wrong. There seems no point. But I see his pictures on my walls every day and I know I will have to face him sometime. Perhaps we can return our dealings to an exclusively business footing. I suggest he pops round after he finishes at school. At least that presents another limited time frame and ensures I can use the excuse of service again.

He texts back that it is half term and he can come earlier in the day. I reply that I have things to prepare and four to four-thirty is best.

In my youth, I wasn't short of admirers breaking their necks to please me, but I also dated a few rogues. Indeed, I was attracted to the type until I decided I wanted something more substantial; something that may lead to settling down. That was how I came to throw myself at Ted. Dear old faithful Ted. I find a sadness regarding Ted that wasn't there before. It has crept into my being like the damp mists of a Scottish moor. I did not appreciate him enough. It is clear to me now. For all his lack of romantic initiative and physical distance when he was absorbed with one of his archaeological projects, he never gave me cause to doubt his integrity. But I left it too late to tell him. Far too late. And I broke his trust.

Perhaps it was the wayward hormones of midlife that caused me to revert to my teenage selection process when I decamped with Gianni. And perhaps that is why I am attracted to Coll

– because he also fits the type. But it is time to engage my brain and show that I have learned something from my Italian misadventure.

When Coll arrives, I give him a penetrating look as he crosses the threshold. It is a look I used on the kids when they were young; a look that says, 'Don't mess with me'.

I lead him up to the flat.

'Why did you say you nearly made a fool of yourself again?' Coll asks before he sits down. He appears agitated and excitable.

I blink at the suddenness of his getting to the point; no gentle easing in with pleasantries. 'What?'

'When I mentioned Sarah?'

'Ah.'

'I've been thinking about it since I left you last week. Playing your words over and over. Wondering what you meant.'

He looks at me searchingly. I have secrets that may affect the way he thinks of me. I have withheld information too. The only difference is that I am free and he seems not to be. I must come clean about my history.

I make us cups of tea and then I take a deep breath and sit down. 'Bear with me. It's complicated. I've told you about Ted, but I haven't told you about Gianni.'

I hesitate in order to gauge the impact of my words. I want him to guess before I confess. I don't want him to think badly of me, yet I need him to realise that I am not the perfect women he makes me out to be.

'Gianni?' whispers Coll. 'No, you didn't mention a Gianni.'

'Ted and I split up because I went to Italy with my chef.'

Coll waits. I have never seen him so still before. A tiny muscle beside his mouth twitches. 'With as in *With*?' he asks.

I continue, 'We'd been having an affair of a sort for quite a long time – in Broadclyst – and I believed he was in love with me – as I was with him. He was ten years younger and I was a fool to think it would last long term. At the time it seemed we wanted the same things business-wise and the age difference didn't matter. He asked me to go back to Italy with him.'

'And you went?'

'I went. I helped him to buy his parents' restaurant so they could retire.'

'So you haven't been completely honest with me, either,' Coll says, a tad smugly.

'It's not the same. Gianni is history.'

'When you said "again" … Nearly made a fool of yourself "again" … Does that mean …? Would you have gone out with me?' He appears unphased about Gianni; or even uninterested, as if he refuses to listen to anything that may colour his view of me.

'I did go out with you.'

'I mean, a relationship. A proper relationship. I wasn't sure. You never hinted.'

'I wasn't sure about you either. Your signals were ambiguous. Now I understand why.'

'But would you? If I'd made a move?' He pleads for an answer that will fuel his infatuation.

'I don't want to go through it all again.'

'That's not an answer. Yes or no? Would you have gone out with me?'

'Had enough of taking chances.'

'I'm not Gianni.'

I realise I need to tell him why it matters that he has a girlfriend. 'Gianni and I had only been there six months or so when this woman kept appearing and paying him a lot of attention. She started to work in the restaurant. As time went on he flirted with her in front of me and I found it demeaning. It transpired she was an ex-girlfriend. An important ex about whom he had never spoken,' I add, pointedly. 'So when you mentioned Sarah … I don't want to get in the way.'

'But you said: "nearly made a fool of myself again". Suggesting you would,' Coll persists, looking at me intently.

'Irrelevant now.'

'I think you're wonderful, Felicity. Your determination, work ethic, love of art and theatre; excellent cook and businesswoman; potter. We could be good together.'

'You have a girlfriend.'

'You're different from her. You understand exactly what I've been through with Penny.'

This is one of the oldest tricks in the world: make someone feel indispensable and special. I can see through him, yet I am flattered. Can't help but find it good for the ego to be liked by another younger man.

'Now I know about Sarah, it makes a difference.'

'But we could be friends.' His eyes plead.

'And what would Sarah say about that?'

'She doesn't need to know.'

'Which implies she wouldn't approve.' I suspect that being friends with Coll would mean him hoping to woo me, wear me down and eventually take things further.

'Tell me more about Gianni. What happened there?'

Suddenly he is interested. I find it a relief to offload. No one knows the details.

'She was called Liliana and was someone he'd left behind when he came to England. He'd never mentioned her, so it was as much of a surprise as you mentioning Sarah. She was in her thirties and a beautiful Italian woman. She'd dumped him for someone else when she heard he was moving away.'

Gianni had wanted Liliana to wait for him. He had pleaded with her. He said that he needed to travel for a year or two to gain some experience and then he would be ready to settle. But she didn't believe him.

'It was only when he was away from her that he missed her and realised his love for her. I will never know for sure if he expected their passion to resurface when he returned. I don't think he knew beforehand that she was alone again. She started

191

coming round to the restaurant more and more, helping out at first, and then as a regular job. He wanted to get her involved with the business. It was so much easier for her to deal with the customers because of the language. The main role I had in my restaurant here – front of house – was not the most suitable for me in Italy. I began to feel pushed out.'

'I'm sure you did,' says Coll, sympathetically.

'More and more I was becoming the *sous* chef and bottle washer and she was swanning about with our clientele as if she was the Lady of the Manor. Sometimes I would hear them whispering in Italian behind closed doors; and sometimes not even hidden. He knew the limits of my language and so did she.'

'That's so rude,' says Coll. 'We have a couple of teachers in our French Department who do that in the staffroom. And in your situation it was much worse.'

'She looked at me as if she pitied me. I wasn't used to that. Never in my life. Then I caught them kissing. It was clear the way things were going and I wasn't going to hang around and fight for him. It was as if the fog had cleared. I saw him for what he was. Saw me for what I was in running off with him. A fool.'

I decide not to go into more detail. Gianni and I had many rows because he claimed to love me too. He said I was over-reacting and Liliana was useful to both of us; that she could be a friend to me as well as him. He went on and on about how much he loved me. I didn't believe him. All he wanted was my money and her love. She was young enough to have a family with him and she was sufficiently conniving to get pregnant deliberately and force a situation.

'You've had a tough time, Felicity.'

'I don't deserve sympathy.'

Yet it feels good to have someone on my side, sympathising. Since coming back, mostly I have been faced with hostility.

I look at my watch. He catches my glance and starts to rise.

'You have to go to service,' he pre-empts.

'Not for a few minutes. You came here to tell me more about Sarah.'

'Sarah is a long story. Another time.'

'I don't think we should see each other – except regarding the paintings.'

'I want to tell you about Sarah. It's not like you think it is. As I said, we're not committed.'

I hesitate for long enough for him to know he has persuaded me. He deserves at least to be heard. 'Okay.'

'Are you working tomorrow?' he asks.

'In the evening. Why?'

'Can you get cover?'

'Why?'

'Come with me to London. To see the Shard.'

I gasp, partly with excitement at such a proposition, partly at his nerve. 'Why the Shard?'

'It's only recently opened to the public. I think we would both appreciate the design.'

'I don't know if I can get cover.'

'But you could try,' persists Coll.

'I'm not sure that it would be appropriate.'

'Come with me as a friend, Felicity,' Coll says with emphasis. 'No strings. I can tell you about Sarah on the train. I need you to understand. I don't want you to think badly of me. We'll be back by evening so you won't miss the whole of service.'

Still I hesitate.

'It's a one-off never-to-be-repeated opportunity,' he says, sounding like a cruise ship tour guide. 'You're only young once. Go on. We'll have a laugh. It'll cheer you up.' He can see I'm wavering. 'Ask Kylie. Please-please. I have to tell you about Sarah. It's the tying of the loose ends. It's important.'

'Okay, I'll ask her. But this must be the last social meeting.'

'If I don't hear from you, I'll pick you up at eight.'

He starts to leave, to descend the stairs before I have a chance to change my mind.

43

The Shard

Felicity

The visit to the Shard appeals to my spontaneous nature. I can't resist. I text him before I go to bed to confirm that Kylie will step in. All this service cover is costing me a fortune but I promise myself that this is the final treat.

The day dawns chilly but fine and there is small movement of the bare and lifeless branches outside. The London forecast is similar but if anything, a couple of degrees cooler. I wrap up in my smartest chunky jumper with jeans and comfortable boots. My outer layer will be a cream padded parka jacket which I only wear for casual best because of the colour. I find myself thinking about how I may match his style and I hunt out a colourful scarf to drape and add a touch of glamour. I don't want to give him any ideas, but nor do I want to feel dowdy in his company, especially as he is four years younger than me. I pin my hair up randomly and add a clip for security. Gianni liked my hair up. He said there came a point in a woman's life when hair up was sexier than hair down. I think I came to that point several years ago, but I don't always follow the rules. The sixties girls are paving the way for a more Bohemian passage through the ageing dilemma and I like that.

'Where are you off to all tarted up?' Chris says when he comes down for breakfast.

'London. I may be back by the end of service, but if not, don't wait up. Kylie will cover.'

'London?!'

How enjoyable it is to surprise one's children with adventures. Yet I think they had their fill of this when I went off with Gianni.

Coll picks me up at eight and drives us to Exeter St David's station. I still have mixed feelings about my impulsive decision to go, but I haven't been out of the area since coming home from Italy and this trip will satisfy my wanderlust.

I am also in two minds that it will suggest to Coll that I have reconsidered and want to pursue our relationship when I don't. Irrespective of Sarah, I can't see myself in bed with this man or enjoying the intimacy of a shared existence. He is too complicated and he lies. How many other women have there been that I don't know of? In the ten years of Sarah, I doubt I am the first. It is at times like this when Ted's open-book honesty and predictability seem priceless and that I should have treasured him more.

I worry that going to the Shard is a further betrayal of Sarah. I need to find out more about their relationship. Maybe she's one of these women who doesn't mind, but given her attitude to *Richard II*, I doubt it. The journey will provide time to find out.

I raise the subject when we have settled into the rhythms of the train and the view from the window – a sea of continuous fields – becomes monotonous.

'Does Sarah know we're doing this?'

'I haven't told her.'

'Tell me the score,' I say.

'I will,' Coll says. 'Later. I don't want to spoil our day before it's begun. It's our treat. I want to forget about all my problems. I want to focus on you.'

I let it rest, but am uneasy. Ted would say I have qualms. He's fond of using the word to describe his imprecise anxieties. Instead, Coll and I talk of different Shakespearian productions we have seen and I remind him that the history plays are my favourites so I was doubly disappointed not to see *Richard II*.

He asks me how things are at home and I explain my difficulties of dealing with Marianne now she is virtually living at the Deer Orchard.

'I can't bear to see her in my lovely kitchen. I designed it. She doesn't know how lucky she is to have such a bespoke place in which to cook.'

'Do you have to visit so often?'

'I don't need to loiter. I could pick up the produce and scoot off.'

'Perhaps that's what you should do.'

Coll is probably right. He is very good at giving advice, yet I doubt he is as adept at taking it.

I discover he likes animals too and he thinks my people-as-animals thing is great. Apparently, he used to ride a lot as a child during the family's time in Ireland.

'If it were you and me, Felicity, we could move out of town and have a couple of horses.'

I let it pass without comment.

He then tells me about his childhood holidays, painting a lyrical picture of unusual delights and adventures with his mother and father in a touring caravan. But when I ask him about his schooldays, his face darkens and he changes the subject. His stories occupy me until we arrive in the city.

I haven't been to London for ages and the mass of people on Paddington station and the speed with which they move makes me glad I am based in Devon. Coll hands me a pre-paid Visitor's Oyster card, again troubling my conscience.

It is two tube trains to London Bridge and then much jostling with people on the platform and escalators as we make our way above ground. I am not used to this and find it overwhelming. It is a relief to emerge outside and I wonder at the stamina of the people who spend half a lifetime commuting. Their vacant expressions on the trains suggest resignation.

'And there it is,' says Coll.

I look up at this massive and magnificent glass structure towering above us into the sky; a new beacon on the South Bank. It is only a very short walk from where we stand and my neck hurts as I throw my head back in an effort to see the top.

Coll has already bought daytime Shard tickets via the internet. It is another sign he had this trip planned. Either he thought I would say yes, or he intended it as a surprise for Sarah. I don't like to ask because given the last-minute arrangement I suspect it is the latter. How dreadful if I have stolen Sarah's treat. It is not cheap but Coll insists he is paying.

'In that case you must let me buy lunch,' I say.

We are directed under the building to one of the lifts which glides swiftly and effortlessly to floor thirty-three where we are escorted to a second lift for the journey up to floor sixty-nine. Here there is viewing area around all four sides of the lift shafts. It has wood underfoot and, of course, floor to ceiling glass windows looking across the city and the Home Counties. I can't help but gasp. It has got the wow factor and, as we stroll from side to side, slotting into gaps as they appear between other viewing people, every sentence is prefixed with 'Oh look, there's …' such and such. It takes me a while to get my bearings.

Coll points out the London Eye, Westminster, Big Ben and the golden pinnacle of the Monument to the Great Fire. These landmarks all have modern buildings closing in on either side. Likewise St Paul's and Southwark Cathedrals.

I say, 'There is no longer the luxury of leaving space for these buildings to be properly appreciated.'

'Except there,' Coll says, nodding over to the Tower of London with grass and trees clearly visible within the outer walls.

'I wonder why they don't fill the moat with water,' I say.

'Disease, cost, Health and Safety,' says Coll. 'Someone would fall in.'

To the north, I try to pick out the buildings of UCL where Ted and I studied many years ago. The Halls of Residence, the street with the flat in which he lived and to which I moved. Coll says he spent some time in Shepherd's Bush before he met Penelope but we can't locate the street.

I am transfixed by the river and the boats and the bustle, the mass of new designer buildings that have sprung up along the Thames providing luxury waterside apartments for the wealthy. Cranes are everywhere, like magnificent Meccano.

I say to Coll that I want to take some pictures of the northern aspect. I can show Ted and the kids the bird's-eye view of where we spent our early twenties.

Coll moves off clockwise.

A few minutes later I find him again gazing out across the east with his phone to his ear but when he turns and sees me he shuts it off. I wonder who he is calling. Sarah maybe. I don't like that behaviour. It smacks of secrets and subterfuge.

We then walk up a further three flights of stairs to a second viewing platform more exposed to the elements. Coll says they have plans for a bar here, but so far there is nothing so much different from below other than when we look up we can see the shards that rise up from the top of the building and give it its name.

After taking two lifts back to ground level, we walk west along the embankment and I suggest lunch at Sea Dreamers restaurant at an expensive hotel, looking out onto the river. From the outside the hotel is nothing more than a huge stack of glass fronted rectangles but inside, so my trawl of the web suggests, there is a modern arty ambience with weird tree sculptures forming part of the wall of the reception. The creative in me would like to investigate.

'Bit pricey,' Coll says.

'I like to see what other restaurants are producing,' I say. 'Particularly trendy London ones. I checked on the net and it's an interesting lunch menu. It's not as expensive as you might think. Or if you prefer one of the chains, we passed a Wagamama.'

'As you're paying, you choose,' Coll says.

We go to Sea Dreamers and are seated with a view of St Paul's. Over lunch he asks me about my ambitions for Neptune.

'Mainly to secure its reputation as a business for Chris. I'd like to retire gradually. A separate little cottage, perhaps back in Broadclyst – if there is a truce between me and Marianne. But for that to happen, I need to reclaim my funds from Gianni, and he's stalling.'

'Do you think you'll get your money back?'

'I've decided to get my lawyer onto it.'

After lunch, we meander slowly east back along the South Bank, stopping to admire the views, popping into Shakespeare's Globe for a thirty-minute guided tour and then to the Lichtenstein retrospective in the Tate Modern where we appreciate rather than admire. Coll says, 'To do something that no one else has done and find it sells. That's the key.'

When we come out, I am flagging, the light is fading and it is cold. We ought to be getting back, but first Coll suggests a drink in a dark riverside pub called the Anchor. I can smell the history emanating from the beams and I shiver as if among ghosts. Apparently, Samuel Pepys witnessed the destruction of the Great Fire from here.

When I return from a visit to the loo, I find Coll hurriedly finishing yet another phone call.

I decide it is time to introduce Sarah into the conversation. 'Sarah. Tell me.'

He takes a few sips from his pint and wipes the froth from his mouth. 'I've told her how I feel about you.'

'And how is that, exactly?'

'I can't stop thinking about you. I think you're great. The most interesting woman I've met in a long time. Wonderful.' He pauses to gauge my reaction.

I am impassive, holding my breath. I like the flattery. How can one not at an age where passing a mirror is becoming a shock.

'I think I'm in love with you.'

Not so good. This is worse than I thought.

'Being with you today ... I haven't noticed the time ... Only you, Felicity. Only you ... We've shared life experiences. You understand me. I want to tell you everything about me; things I've never told anyone before. And I want to know all about you. Everything. You're a very special woman.'

He moves closer as if he is going to kiss me and I sit back. 'Woah,' I say.

'Is that not good?'

'It's ... surprising. It's not good for Sarah.'

'I don't love Sarah.'

'Then why are you with her?' My heart cranks up a gear. 'Are you going to split up with her?' I challenge him. 'Tell me exactly what you plan to do.'

If he is going to split up with Sarah, then perhaps – even if I don't want a full relationship – perhaps we could have more days like this. I am suddenly confused. I hear Olivia reminding me about his games. I remind myself that he falls into the category of 'Rogue'.

He says, 'I'd rather talk about you. About us.'

'You promised. It's your turn now. Sarah?'

He sits back and sighs, staring at his denimed knees. 'Sarah ... Are you sure?'

'Yes. You have to tell me the truth. How can I make judgements about how I feel if I don't know what's going on between you and her?'

'Sarah's lovely, but she's not like you. You are so different. She drives me mad with her indecision. You are strong and confident. You don't take shit.'

'And she does?'

'I've treated her badly. She's let me. I've taken advantage. I know she cares; that she loves me.'

'Are you sure you don't love her?'

'She doesn't excite me like you do.'

'I am a new interest. That might be the difference. How did you feel when you first knew her?'

Coll pauses as if struggling to remember. 'It was a long time ago.'

'But what drew you to her?'

He takes another long drink from his pint and licks his lips.

'I thought she was sexy. Not beautiful, but sexy. She didn't flaunt it, but there was something about the way she used her eyes that attracted me. And she can look good when she makes an effort.'

'Those are the cosmetic reasons, but why did you become close?'

'We got on in a way I had never clicked with anyone before. That is, until I met you. Not even Penny. I loved Penny, but we didn't exactly get on. Being a librarian, Sarah has wide-ranging knowledge. When we first met, we found we could talk about anything; everything … She's interested in art and in my art. In Shakespeare … Drama in general. We spent a lot of time going to plays.'

'So not totally different from me in that respect.'

'No.'

At this point he looks wistful. As if he is remembering a time that he has forgotten when Sarah excited him as I do.

'Do you still talk?' I say.

'Yes. There's nothing particularly wrong with the relationship. Or there wasn't until I met you. It's me that's wrong. We don't argue much.'

'Sex?'

He flushes a little. 'Yes. Fine. It was … Before you … Better than fine.'

'Then why? Why, why Coll, are you trying to ruin it by seeing me?'

'Because with her it's predictable and … and dull in comparison with what we have.'

'We don't have anything.'

'But we could have.'

'You're chasing after rainbows. There's no pot of gold. For a few weeks, perhaps. But I'm not looking for anything long term with you.'

The scope of what I am dealing with begins to dawn on me. Coll is obsessed with me and in danger of giving up on a perfectly good relationship because he wants a few thrills for as long as it lasts. I probe further.

'How did you see your relationship with Sarah in the future? What were your plans?'

'We talked of living together when we retire. Moving out of the city.'

He goes on to say that for a decade she has been his confidante and partner in the full sense of the word. His lack of commitment is something he has convinced himself of because he doesn't want to be tied down by the rules that govern such relationships. He is a man who always thinks there might be someone or something better round the corner: someone more checklist perfect than Sarah; someone to love. And in his eyes, I fit the bill.

We leave the pub and head back to London Bridge underground and take the tube back to Paddington. All the time I question him about his relationship and the more he tells me about Sarah, the more I can see that he does love her, but he doesn't recognise his feelings as love because they are not of the romantic passionate type that he seems to have for me. I try to get him to see how crazy it would be to lose Sarah on a whim.

'But you are not a whim, Felicity,' he says. 'How can true love be a whim?'

'Because it isn't true love. True love is much more akin to what you have with Sarah. Only you don't see it. You equate love with passion. But at our time of life, it needs to be based on more than that.'

I think of me and Ted and me and Gianni. I am preaching what I failed to practise myself. With knowledge of my existence, Sarah will feel at least as bad as I did when Liliana was worming her way back into Gianni's life. I feel guilty to cause her pain. Yet here I am in London with him, oh silly woman that I am.

I tell Coll what I think, but he doesn't seem to listen. He keeps saying he wants us to be friends, but I say that's impossible.

Back on the train, Exeter bound, Coll says, 'Have you enjoyed today?'

I choose my words carefully. 'It's been delightful to get away from Devon and all the family stuff.'

'Then don't let this be the last time, Felicity. Come with me to Scilly for a couple of days. We can fly from Exeter.'

Once again he has shocked me. 'Scilly? That's my husband's playground.'

'Let's make it ours.'

'No, Coll. No. You're not hearing me. This can't happen. You and me. Not even as friends. I won't do it to Sarah.' I don't mean to sound arrogant, but if he carries on seeing me, I suspect his passion in the short term will continue to grow. I continue, 'If we keep seeing each other, you won't be investing in your relationship with her and it's not fair.'

'And what if there was no Sarah? Would you go out with me properly?'

I'm not in love with him, I don't trust him and I can't offer him hope of a future. 'There *is* Sarah. We can't get away from the fact.'

'If I finish with her?'

'No. You have too much to lose.'

'But we could have some fun.'

'No.' I lie and tell him that I definitely don't want another full relationship. I don't tell him that something might have happened if there were no Sarah. We might have had a fling of some sort. But he can't know that. I don't want him finishing with her and then coming back to me with a new offer. I realise he must have no hope of changing my mind.

But even then he persists in trying to persuade me; all the way through Slough, Reading and Newbury. Then, during our passage through the expanse of Wiltshire countryside, barely visible in the dark, he falls silent and I drift into a light doze. I hope my message has got through to him.

44

Poem

Felicity

When Coll drops me off at Neptune, he pulls into the car park, and with the engine still running, he reaches into the inside pocket of his jacket and produces a folded piece of paper. We have said little since our heavy conversation on the train.

'This is for you,' he says. 'Nothing you've said can change the way I feel. I wrote it for you and I'd like you to have it.'

'What is it?'

'A poem.'

I take it from him, and in a resigned voice and with a sigh I say, 'Oh, Coll.' I thank him for it and for the trip. It's been lovely to get away from the kitchen and the family stresses. Such a shame that I shall always associate it with hearing the truth about Sarah; truth that means there can be no more such trips; no more plays or flirting or hope of something more. Again he leans towards me as if to kiss me but I turn away and hurriedly get out of the car.

'I'll call you,' he says.

'I thought I'd made my position clear.' I thought I had.

'Read the poem.'

'This can't go on.'

'Read it, please.'

And with that he is gone. Yet again leaving the door ajar.

It is after nine and the stragglers from service are leaving the restaurant. I enter from the rear door and find Kylie washing up and Chris scrubbing the work surfaces. There isn't much left for me to do and they tell me all is well.

'You are stars,' I say to both of them.

'Good day?' asks Kylie. 'I'd love to go to London but hubby panics in crowds.'

'How about we go on a Work's Outing in summer?' I say, in a fit of generosity. 'A show, perhaps? You can choose what you want to see. My treat.' I suspect Kylie's tastes are very different from mine, but it would be good for her to broaden her outlook.

'Oooh, could we really, Mrs H? That would be fab.'

'We'll do it. I promise.' I make a mental note. Perhaps we could manage an overnight stay.

Upstairs I take off my coat and boots, put the kettle on and feed the kittens. They still don't have official names but one has become Scrap and the other, Kit. I make a mug of chamomile tea and slump in a chair with Coll's poem, overcome with tiredness and a cold desolation that makes my bones ache. There is no one I can phone to share news of the trip, the Shard and of Coll's declarations. Olivia doesn't have any patience with me after leaving Ted for Gianni so she is unlikely to sympathise over the Coll affair once she knows another betrayal is at stake. I am truly alone and I begin to feel sorry for myself and wish for the times gone, for my mum and my husband and the children when they were small and needed me. I blink away the fast forming tears.

Over the years, I have been so wrapped up in family and work that I haven't cultivated proper friendships so I have few people to turn to when I have problems. I thought Coll could have been that person, but his new honesty about Sarah and the extent of his feelings for me mean he can no longer be my friend or companion. I feel cheated, but not as cheated as Sarah.

I can hardly bear to read the poem but nor can I ignore it. I unfold the paper. It is a sonnet *To Felicity* and is full of love-struck mush, likening me to a mermaid and various other mythical creatures who have used magic and sorcery to cast spells on his emotions.

Flattering though it may be, it is not me at all.

Being loved by someone I can't love back is such a waste of love. And now I know Sarah has spent a decade fighting for it, I am ashamed. I think she has made it too easy for him. Coll is a man who needs a challenge and in being a pushover, she has denied him the chase. He thrives on adulation of himself and his artwork so is constantly searching for new people to impress. If, like me, they have other things in common with him, then they will pose a threat to Sarah, especially if he keeps her a secret until he has drawn the unsuspecting woman into his web.

I cannot decide if he is ignorant of the destructive nature of his behaviour and therefore naive in emotional intelligence terms, or if he is calculating and a Casanova, a lothario, a love-rat. In either case he is deluded about the ephemeral nature of romantic love. As a chef, I liken his feelings for me to the fragility of a soufflé. They are as overblown as meringue and as brittle as millefeuilles. I can see them collapsing with the tap of a spoon, the first *contratemps*, the realisation after a few weeks or months that I am a human being with many faults and innumerable differences from him that would have made life together impossible.

I don't envy Sarah, I pity her. She is a sweet little bird caged by her desire for an unscrupulous man. If Coll didn't want her, he should have let her go in the beginning instead of accepting her love and giving her hope.

Although I have had a memorable day, I wish I hadn't gone with him to the Shard.

45

Marianne Visits

Felicity

The day after the Shard, I am still feeling sorry for myself. Age is catching up with me fast and I don't know who I am any more. I don't know how to be; whether to reinvent my style or evolve gradually. It is in one's late fifties and early sixties when attempts at being young begin to look foolish. But perhaps cutting off my hair and wearing only classics is a step too far. As I mentioned earlier, the children of the sixties have paved the way for a more eclectic decline towards the rug and bath chair, so perhaps there is still a place for colour, and skirts that skim the knees. But incontrovertible is that the window of hope and opportunity is shrinking. I am entering the swan song of midlife: a prelude to the winter of old.

At teatime there is a knock on the back door and I open it to find Marianne clutching a cardboard box brimming with carrots and leeks. She is dressed to impress – make-up and shoes with heels. I assume this is for Ted and not for me. She seems to have nailed a style to suit and I wonder if there may come a time when we share fashion secrets.

'I was expecting Kate,' I say.

'Kate is feeling sick.'

Any mention of Kate paired with sick and I hear the pitter-patter of tiny feet and the click-clack of knitting needles. Some fifty-somethings baulk at the idea of being 'Granny'. Not I. I love the baby stage. I did it four times, so long ago now it hurts. Harriet is adamant she won't, Rachel hasn't found the right man, and Chris? I think he will be in his thirties before he settles, if ever. So my hopes of being a relatively lively granny rest with Kate.

'And James is at Silverton market,' says Marianne, snapping me out of cosy dreamland.

I take the box from her before she collapses under its weight. She is not the type to heave vegetables. 'Come in, do.' She looks as if she might decline but then follows me through to the restaurant kitchen.

'And what about Ted? I suppose he doesn't want to see me if he can help it?' I put the veg in the fridge so she can take back the box.

She winces.

'Or you don't want me to see him?' I decide to confront the issues that lie between us. Since the business with Coll and Sarah, I look differently at how I have treated Marianne. I know I am no longer a threat, but Marianne doesn't know that. It is unfair to cause her unnecessary anxiety.

I persuade her to stay for a cup of tea and some leftover coffee and walnut cake. We adjourn upstairs to the flat and as her shoulders drop and she sits back in the chair, I decide to tell her about Coll, desperate to share and to have someone say *it's not you, it's him*. Once I start, it is easy. Unlike Olivia, Marianne doesn't interrupt, sigh or try to change the subject. Her expressions indicate that she is stunned by his duplicity and sad, not only for Sarah, but also, surprisingly, for me. As she listens, her body language changes from submissive to confident. At last I see her as Ted sees her: the former teacher of psychology who is skilled in analysing all sides of a relationship dilemma; someone who will listen when he wants to talk and keep quiet when he needs to work.

'What is it about him? The attraction?' Marianne asks.

'Quite good-looking for his age. Charming. Funny. Common ground of broken marriages, deceased parents, theatre, Shakespeare, art. He paints, I throw pots. He's also a poet in more ways than one. His descriptions painted pictures. Ted never does that. You are a writer so you don't need that from him. Coll's eloquence captivated me.'

'But you say you didn't fall for him?'

'Not fall, exactly. A *frisson* at the start. He intrigued me. He says there is a spark; that we bounce off each other. I think it is just him that's bouncing.'

'But something may develop in time.'

'The more I hear him talk about Sarah, the more I think he will never leave her – or not for long. He wants both of us: me to love in an idealistic way and her to provide the nitty-gritty of a relationship.'

'Sounds like a man scared of commitment. Perhaps his first wife hurt him irreparably.'

'Yes and no. He was hurt, but I believe even she wasn't the perfect woman for him either. I think his problems go further back than that. It could have been something to do with school. He was sent away and he won't talk about it.'

'Ah,' says Marianne, as if this explains everything. 'What if you had fallen for him totally? He wasn't taking your potential feelings into account at all. What a swine.' She then launches into a disclosure of confidences about her husband and a female colleague, the detail of which she tells me even Ted doesn't know.

'Is it men in general?' I ask. 'Is it biologically driven? To want cake, and more cake? Coll said he couldn't help it. As if there was a hidden force at work over which he had no control. It was only yesterday that I realised how important Sarah was. I told him to get back to her. But he is persistent.'

'He sounds obsessed.'

'He is.'

'What will you do? Will you see him again?'

'I may continue taking his paintings. But certainly nothing more. I don't trust him. He's one of those flaky men who acts on impulse and doesn't consider the consequences or other peoples' feelings. There are a lot of things I don't know about him that are probably even more difficult to deal with. I guess he presented only the positive side of himself to me.'

'I would be tempted to tell him where to go. It sounds as if he will continue to invest in you rather than Sarah if you have any contact at all.'

'That is my worry. He won't take my word that I don't want a relationship. It's as if he believes he can wear me down over time.'

'It could be that he has a narcissistic personality disorder,' says Marianne.

I hadn't thought of that. 'What are the signs?'

'Lack of empathy is one. And from what you say, he's been slow to show any. It's a disorder on a continuum so he won't necessarily display all traits or any at an extreme level. Most of us have some elements of narcissism. Indeed, in the West it can be an advantage. But disordered narcissists are vain, arrogant and exploitative. They also fantasise about success and are idealistic about love.'

'That's Coll.'

'They may consider others to be stupid and have an inflated sense of their own importance.'

I remember his disparaging comments about other teachers and how much he basked in my admiration of his work; how much he wanted me to reassure.

Marianne continues, 'They may appear ultra-confident, but are vulnerable to criticism and have a fragile self-esteem which they protect often by surrounding themselves with less successful people or those in whom it is easy to find fault.'

Now she is on her pet subject, she is in full flow. If she had wings, she would be flapping them, like a swan on a lake, ready for take-off. She sounds like she's quoting from text books or research papers – a sound I am used to when Ted goes on about archaeology or James about environmentalism.

I say, 'Perhaps that's why it's worked for so long between him and Sarah. He sees her as flawed. And it's why it wouldn't work with me.'

'Narcissists usually form relationships for personal gain,' Marianne says. 'They make excessive attempts to attract people and use their successes to justify their own worth. They often have little genuine interest in the others that they woo.'

'Coll appears to be interested in me.'

'Or it could be a strategy because you provide an outlet for his paintings.'

'He certainly does want to be the centre of attention.'

'Would it be difficult for you to back off completely?'

'No. Not now I know the score. I enjoyed flirting. Knowing I could if I wanted to. But I wasn't looking for love. I had that with Gianni. It's unlikely to come again with such intensity when you get to our age. I suppose you feel that about Ted.'

'I do. After Johnny, I never dreamed I would love and be loved again.' Marianne flushes and is quick to change the subject. 'What attracted you to Gianni?'

'He was a poet too.'

'Everything sounds poetic in Italian.'

'But he expressed himself with food and that touched my heart at a primal level.'

'And your stomach.'

We laugh. Possibly the first time we have laughed together and shared an intimacy without stress.

'Do you miss him?' she asks.

'Yes.'

'Are you still in love with him?'

'A little bit. But angry too. Furious that he went into business with me when he didn't love me in the same way. And to be

211

usurped by another woman is very demoralising.' I give a wry smile and add, 'I don't mean you, I mean Liliana.'

'You could mean me too,' says Marianne. 'Do you find it difficult – me and Edward?'

'Yes. But I gave Ted up out of choice. I don't have any right to feel usurped by you. My actions gave Ted permission to move on and it's selfish of me to want him back. I was shocked he didn't want me any more. I've been playing games; testing him. It was wrong. Childish. I'm sorry.' And I am.

Marianne raises an eyebrow at me as if saying she's fully aware it was wrong.

'So are you saying that you're not trying to get Edward back?'

'Is that what it looks like? That I want him back?'

'I get the feeling you resent me.'

'Not you, *per se*, but I find it difficult you being at our house.'

'Will it be easier when we have our own place?'

'I believe so. Hadn't really thought. But, yes.'

'You have to admit that the divorce is taking a long time.'

I squirm guiltily. 'It's financially complicated. I lost money in Italy. I was foolish.'

'I've decided to sell my flat in Beckenham. We aren't going to be making enough use of it to justify the expense. That will free up enough capital for us to buy and give James and Kate more time to buy Edward out. Or you and Edward.'

'That's a big investment for you. Are you sure?'

'I am now.'

This is an interesting development and my business brain starts whirring. If Edward and Marianne leave the Deer Orchard, perhaps I could go back to live there. James and Kate could gradually buy out Edward and me, giving us extra income as we slide into partial retirement.

'You mentioned Kate was sick. Should I read anything into this?'

'No.'

'Oh.'

'Disappointed?'

'When one's own life seems over, one looks to the next generation.'

'Oh, Felicity! Your life's not over. Look what you've achieved. And you haven't been short of suitors in recent years.'

'Suitors are too much like hard work. At least the ones I choose. No more.'

'That's what I thought when I met Edward again. I really wasn't sure if I could be bothered.'

Again we laugh.

'Marianne, I've misjudged you. What more can I say?'

'I'm glad I came,' she says. 'I nearly said no to Kate when she asked. Perhaps now we can move on.'

'I am glad too.'

It's been good to clear the air and apologise. After she leaves my depressed mood begins to lift as I imagine being back in the house and helping out with the produce. Of course, I mustn't interfere too much. It's Kate's business now. But I could be on hand on the days she is at work. We could fast track her idea for pigs, goats and sheep; grow the business more quickly to the benefit of all. And if she does have a baby, I would be able to provide support.

46

Tying Loose Ends

Felicity

Coll drops into Neptune after work the following Wednesday and we are standing in the restaurant lobby ahead of him leaving. He is distraught.

I say, 'We will not meet again. I'll put someone else's pictures on my walls when these are sold. And I'll send you a cheque. I'll know you've received it when the money leaves my account. You mustn't contact me.'

I've not invited him upstairs but have said my piece inside the front door. After the chat with Marianne and a lot of deep thought, I've decided that for Sarah's sake, I must put a stop to any hopes Coll may have of continuing friendship or anything further with me. I have been unequivocal, despite his protests.

'I could still bring paintings here. We don't have to meet,' Coll says, desperate to find a link.

'No. Because that leaves a foot in the door – which you're very fond of doing. This must be final. You'll have no trouble finding another outlet for your paintings and you must go and repair the damage with Sarah.' I am cold and decisive.

'It'll be difficult. I blame her for my not being able to have you.'

'That is monstrously unfair.'

'But it's true.'

I play Devil's advocate. 'So what's stopping you from leaving her?'

He looks at his feet. 'I would if you would … go out with me properly.'

'Despite the fact that it wouldn't last?'

'Yes.'

'It's out of the question. You have a future with Sarah. I can't offer you that.'

'You've been a breath of fresh air in my life Felicity. I'll never regret meeting you and I'll never forget you.'

I wish he hated me. 'Go and rescue your relationship, Coll. Before it's too late.'

When he leaves for the last time, I've a sense of relief and also an odd karmic feeling that I have atoned in part for some of my past wrongs with Ted. Of course there is no going back

– I accept that now – but there could be a going forward with a clearer conscience.

I wonder how much Coll will tell Sarah and if she will forgive him. And if she does tell him where to go, I suppose he will come back and try again. But I wouldn't take the risk. He's too unstable and complicated for someone at my time of life. I want peace and tranquillity in matters that are controllable. I expect Sarah does too. Is it weakness that keeps her bound to him? Or is it strength? I am not sure.

I wish I had never met Coll, yet he has given me an opportunity to show that I have learnt a lesson. And I like myself better for it. Perhaps he came into my life for this reason. But what have I done for him? For Sarah? Nothing good as things stand.

47

Windfall

Felicity

After Coll leaves for the last time, I am relieved that the door is finally shut and I throw the bolts. I shall ignore any further communication from him, if there is any. I hope that my words were final enough and that he will not try to contact me.

It is nearing the end of March and there will be much to do in the Deer Orchard garden. I have plenty to distract me and I need to speak to James and Kate about my thoughts.

I call Marianne to thank her for the chat and let her know what I have done re Coll. I can tell she approves. I invite her and Ted for a meal at the restaurant the following Tuesday, expecting it to be a quiet night. 'On the house,' I say. Ted will no doubt think I have ulterior motives but for once, I don't. I ring my solicitor and said irrespective of property and finance, I would like her to proceed with the divorce papers.

'Are you sure that's wise?' she says.

'I'm sure,' I tell her. 'We can make a start.'

If Ted is setting up with Marianne in a house paid for by her, she doesn't want the ignominy of having to explain that she is shacked up with someone else's husband. I can hear her friends telling her she is a fool and that she is risking her financial security. They won't know Ted isn't the money-grabbing type.

My focus returns to menus and the new business. I've been sidetracked and need to concentrate on earning money and not wasting it.

I have often thought that life seems to deal out good times and bad times in batches rather than a mix of the two. I hear people say, *'And as if that wasn't enough ...'* or, *'Just when you think things can't get any worse ...'* The trajectory of life is rarely a ripple; more often a mountain range of peaks and troughs. With this thought in mind, it is perhaps unsurprising that I get a call from Gianni out of the blue telling me he has a buyer for my portion of the bistro in Siena. It is a generous offer which even makes me a small profit on my original investment.

'I knew you would like,' says Gianni.

I give him details for a bank transfer and then we manage to have a short but convivial chat about our lives. He says that he and Liliana are going to get married and that she is expecting.

'I sorry it no work out for us,' he says. 'I no realise Liliana come back into my life. It was surprise. I think she go forever and you and me have future.'

He sounds sincere. I want to believe him. Since meeting Coll, Gianni's misdeeds pale into insignificance.

'No hard feels?' says Gianni.

I can't help but laugh. 'Oh, Gianni. No, not any more. No hard feels.'

Money from Gianni changes the landscape and makes my talk with James and Kate all the more purposeful.

Part 4
Changes

Part 1

Changes

48

Venice

Sarah – late May 2013

It is said that when you go to Venice for the first time, the only way to approach is by boat. We flew to Marco Polo airport and decided on the *Alilaguna* ferry service rather than the expensive but much faster water taxi.

As we wheel our cases under the covered walkway to the quay, I'm aware of glaring bright sunlight, unfamiliar heat, and excitement at what lies in store. I hope Coll will be inspired by the magic and a miracle will occur between us and launch us on a new track of togetherness.

The intervening weeks have been unremarkable. We've spent most weekends together, sharing meals, a bed, even sex. But something is clouding our happiness: something that has no distinct form, but has a presence as big as an elephant. Coll has been remote since mid February, since Valentine's Day, and my love for him is waning. On the plane, he slept and I've no idea as to his state of mind. My suspicion has continued that Felicity is somewhere lurking in the background. But I have nothing concrete with which to challenge him.

We've about twenty minutes to wait for the ferry and we spend it talking to a Frenchwoman of about thirty-five, who is travelling alone and says this is her fifth trip to Venice. Her passion is infectious and my anticipation grows. I notice how Coll comes alive as we chat to her. She has European glamour and OW potential. If we weren't on holiday and if I wasn't here,

I'm sure he'd be taking her number or asking her out for a drink. As soon as she leaves us to catch her boat, he closes up again like a Venus flytrap.

The *Alilaguna* boats are the tortoises of the lagoon – and very noisy. They have yellow hulls and are instantly recognisable. Our stop is on the blue line. A swarthy young man in a red t-shirt piles cases near the entrance, checking destinations in sharp barks. *Arsenale … San Marco … Zattere …* We step onto the boat. Passengers sit low down and close to the water. Coll chooses a window seat with me next to him, and it's his total focus on the lagoon, with no reference to me during the whole of the one-hour journey, that flags up something still being amiss and that our week might be anything but the romantic idyll I'd hoped. A small group of animated American women catch my attention. They gasp with glee at every new vista, every small island. This is how we should be – sharing the beauty – but Coll remains turned slightly away from me, stony-faced.

I mistake the first sighting of the elegant San Georgio clock tower for St Mark's Square's campanile and wax lyrical at the picturesque perfection. Coll grunts, yet I know he cannot fail to have his artistic senses stimulated, and when we round the bend and the full glory of Venice comes into view with the familiar dome of the Salute, I want him to share my excitement but am left solitary in my own little capsule of joy.

The beauty of Venice is like nowhere else on Earth. It's beyond imagination and description, a densely packed city built on logs, floating in a blue lagoon. And here we could have the perfect holiday we planned last autumn when our future was mapped and when I was enough for Coll. But now I think that he would rather be with Felicity because he fell in love with her and she is not like me. He's with me because I'm a safe bet. It's hardly flattering.

We disembark at *Arsenale* and consult the directions we've been given. Our rental accommodation is a couple of minutes from the vaporetto stop and conveniently located for travelling to all the major sights and also to the other islands. We decided to self-cater so we could justify the expense of a whole week rather than a few days in one of the hotels.

We drag our cases down a shabby narrow side street, or *calle*, and turn right down another. I notice a couple of lines of washing stretching from upstairs windows between the houses on either side. A few paces along is a squat woman waiting for us on the doorstep of our rental property. She's called Maria and is representing the owner; there to show us round and hand over the keys. She indicates that she speaks hardly any English and we say we only have a few words of Italian. Much of the communication will likely be by gesture.

The house has traditional marble floors and shuttered windows. We gather from Maria's facial contortions that it also has a temperamental cooker and I hope Coll remembers her demonstration of how to light it. She shows us the simply furnished bedroom and the stairs that lead onto a small roof terrace. We are both full of dynamism as we try to talk to her and after she leaves us and we once again fall silent, our discord seems amplified. It's mid afternoon and the shops are shut until later. We unpack and then Coll decides he will have a snooze. He doesn't invite me to join him.

He says, 'Why don't you go back to that kiosk at the boat stop and buy our three-day travel tickets?'

I'm nervous of going alone and struggling with my rudimentary words of Italian. But if I refuse he'll think I'm weak. Felicity would go. Felicity is no doubt well versed in Italian since her misadventure with the chef. Reluctantly, I set out and retrace our steps back to the waterside.

The woman in the kiosk has a sour face and the look of a prison governor. It might be due to being cooped up in a confined space and dealing with the language ineptitude of tourists. I was under the impression that most people could speak English but

221

so far this seems not to be the case. However, I manage to make her aware of my requirements and I return with two three-day tickets. I must remind Coll that they have to be fed into a machine for stamping on first use. Thankfully, I'd done my research ahead of the trip.

When Coll emerges, he's still in a weird mood but we venture out shopping together in the direction of Via Giuseppe Garibaldi which Maria indicated with widespread hands was a street housing all the food shops we would need to get started. It's two bridges away from us along the shore of the lagoon and then a left angled turn deep into the fishtail of Venice. Maria was right about the abundance of shops and stalls. What she didn't tell us was that we would have trouble getting served. In a butcher's and in the co-op, we struggle so much that Coll forgets to be awkward and we share a joke or two.

Loaded with basic essentials and with some butterflied chicken breasts and vegetables for our evening meal, we make our way slowly back, enjoying the novelty of a new destination, the lack of cars, the music of the language, the brightness of the sky and the heat of the sun.

Over supper, Coll appears more relaxed and afterwards we check the weather forecast for the next few days and plan our itinerary. We aim for two key sights or attractions per day with plenty of time factored in for mooching down lesser-known streets and for food shopping and also eating out. Then we take a walk by the lagoon to St Mark's Square, the streets thick with people ambling slowly along in both directions. My anxiety from earlier has dissipated and we enjoy the sights and sounds of the city as darkness falls and the night approaches.

On the way back we stop for a drink outside a bar on the waterfront, soaking up the balmy evening air and the surrounding chatter in many different languages. We talk of Coll's proposed escape from teaching and even the future merging of our lives. I relax a little, but am aware that Coll is drinking his wine very quickly. Given that he had two glasses with our meal, I'm slightly concerned.

'Changing the subject,' Coll says, 'I've something to tell you.'

Why do these words fill me with dread? My stomach does its usual leap into my throat and my heart flips. He sounds slightly 'loose'.

'Don't worry. It's okay,' Coll says.

But I know it won't be. I know Coll's tendency to have a few drinks before the delivery of bad news. I hold my breath.

'I've been in touch with Felicity again.' He pauses to gauge my initial response.

'About the paintings?' I say, hoping that's all it is.

'More than that.'

I'm dumbstruck.

'I had to. But it's over now. We're done.' He blurts out the words and I'm wide eyed and stunned. I know things have been far from right between us, but I didn't believe he would break my trust a second time. Not after the state he was in before. The old familiar sickness returns to my stomach. The word 'over' implies something significant.

'What? When?' I remember the phone call on Valentine's night. How his initial reservation dissolved into eagerness and those 'tells' of body-language that gave the game away.

He rubs his face as if he has an itch. 'About three months ago. There was unfinished business. I needed to know. To know if she would have a relationship with me.'

'*Three months ago?*' I whisper. 'How could you? After what happened. You promised me. You said you would die without me,' I say weakly. Despite having had a suspicion that Felicity was the reason for Coll's coolness towards me, I was not prepared for something as serious as this.

'That was before … when I thought it was a stupid fantasy.'

'What changed?'

'I didn't know then that she might have gone out with me. You may remember she called me on Valentine's night. She knew I had been distant and avoiding her. I owed her an explanation. I had to speak with her – and not in front of you. When I told her about you, she said, "I nearly made a fool of myself again." I couldn't get the words out of my head. I had to know what she meant.'

'I can't believe you would do this.' My heart is pounding. My brain is awash with indecision about what I should say. And Coll sits there calmly as if I should be pleased that he is delivering this new bombshell.

'Nothing happened. And I mean nothing. We talked. That's all.'

'How often?'

'Not often.'

'How often?' This time I speak with more force. I'm determined to establish the facts.

'Three times; maybe four. There was a lot I had to say. I wanted her to know how I felt.'

He doesn't look at me. I don't trust his answer. My imagination busily constructs their meetings and discussions and Coll bearing his soul.

'She left her husband for someone else. He was the chef at her old restaurant. She gave up everything to help him fund a bistro.'

I wonder whether to tell him that I know this. Probably best not to.

'She took her youngest son, Chris, to train with this Gianni fellow. I think I told you it's Chris who does most of the cooking at the restaurant. He's very skilled.' Again, Coll looks wistful as he reflects. I don't comment.

'And then this bloke's ex turned up on the scene and there was stuff going on behind Felicity's back. That's why she said she nearly made a fool of herself again. She knows what it's like to be hurt. She doesn't want to hurt you.' His eyes are dewy as he says this.

I consider these words carefully. Felicity doesn't want me to be hurt, yet it would seem Coll has no such compunction.

'Did you see her?'

'I had to see her about the pictures,' he says.

'Apart from the pictures.'

He hesitates. 'Yes, but not often. And we're done now. I won't be seeing her again.' His voice trails away and he looks beyond me.

'It was supposed to be business only. We agreed. Did you go *out*?' I ask.

'Once or twice.'

'Where?'

He doesn't answer. To me, the very fact of him seeing her to talk about personal things is everything. I don't know what to believe any more. There is inconsistency in his words. But would it make any difference if I pinned him down to specifics? Probably not. I remember the day he went to the Shard. I could ask him but I don't want to know.

'If I'd known that you were seeing her beyond pictures, it would have been the end for us.' I'm struggling with what this means for us now. How is it different? The betrayal happened again. Him saying it's over doesn't change that awful fact.

He says, 'I know. But I had to find out.'

I feel faint. I'm aware of a large white boat sliding into view on the lagoon.

'You don't need to worry. It's gone now,' he says.

How can he say this? *Gone … Not worry …* He makes it sound like nothing. But it's everything.

'Nothing happened,' he says again.

I know what he means by this. I think I know.

'Nothing. Not even a kiss. It wasn't like that.'

'Then what was it?'

'A fantasy in my head. She's a very decent person.'

Still she's on a pedestal of purity.

225

He continues, 'Once she found out about you …'

'When did you tell her about me?'

'As soon as I saw her again.'

'Why didn't she stop seeing you straight away?'

'I didn't tell her everything. It was gradual. I thought we could be friends.'

'How could you think that would be okay with me after you told me of your feelings?'

He ignores the question. 'As I got to know her better, I told her more about you.'

Got to know her better … That doesn't sound like a couple of meetings.

'I thought you only saw her once or twice.'

'I said we went out once or twice. We spoke more than that. The conversations were intense. I told her how you helped me after the divorce. The plans we've made. That was when she said no.'

I realise that he's saying much about her holding back and nothing about him.

'But you would have if she wanted you.'

'She didn't want me.'

'But *you* wanted her.'

'She wasn't sure that she wanted more than a friend. It may have developed. I'm pretty sure I could've won her over eventually with my humour. But even if I had, it would've been good for a few months, and then we'd have split. She knew; I knew.'

'And you'd have left me? Despite that?'

'Yes.'

He's very direct about this. When we split before – for that fleeting couple of days after *Felicitygate* – I believed he had chosen me over her and for that reason I was able to forgive and move on, love still intact.

As I dissect, replay and analyse, he prattles on. 'She didn't want to try. Once she knew about you and me and our future plans.'

But now I'm second choice. This makes a difference and I don't think he understands.

He keeps repeating that nothing happened, that she is blameless, as if that is the most important thing. What I want him to say is that he wants me more. But he doesn't. It's almost as if he wants sympathy for his broken heart.

'I'm struggling with this,' I say. 'I don't know where this leaves us.'

'We can carry on as we were,' Coll says, as if this is not in doubt.

'This changes things. I feel hurt, angry.'

'So do I.'

'You?' I'm shocked. I hadn't expected this.

'If it wasn't for you, she would have gone out with me.'

I snort.

'It will take me time to get over,' he says. 'But I will. I haven't seen her for weeks. That's a promise.'

'And what if we split? Are you trying to get me to finish with you so you can go to her and say it's over?'

'She said I had deceived her by not being straight about you. She didn't like that. She's very astute. She won't take a chance of being messed around again, and she said I was too complicated and that I wasn't being fair on you.'

'I see.' Yet again, he speaks of her not wanting him as the only reason he is still with me.

'I can't tell you everything that we said because some of it is personal to her.'

'I don't expect you to.'

'There are some things I may tell you in time. One day.'

Does he not understand the impact of these words? How cruel he is being. Letting me know that there are other things, but not being prepared to say. Letting me assume the worst. I realise he can have no understanding of the way I process information. It's all about him.

He says, 'And there are things personal to her and me.'

227

'I don't want to know everything,' I say. 'I only want to know what's relevant, like how often you met and what you did.'

'I've told you. Not often and nothing except talking.'

'If it's truly gone, I don't know why you are telling me all this.'

'I'm a bit moody at the moment. I thought it would help explain.'

I want to run away, but there's nowhere to run. I can't escape. I expect that was his plan. To relieve his conscience of the burden of the lies at a time when he knew I couldn't leave him.

That night, there's no closeness. All the pleasure of the holiday is gone, almost before it has started. I used to wonder how estranged couples could share a bed. It's easier than I thought. I don't fall asleep until the early hours. I have damp eyes.

The following morning we are woken early by bells. I feel as if I have not been to sleep at all.

We rise and dress wordlessly.

Over breakfast, Coll breaks the silence. 'We went up the Shard. Felicity and I.'

We are eating boiled eggs with toast. I wonder how many more confessions there will be. 'I thought as much,' I say. 'You knew how I wanted to go up there with you.'

'We still can.'

'It won't be the same.'

Felicity has stolen my life. She has snatched the colour print and left me with the negative. I don't suppose she meant it to be like this. It's not her fault. If it wasn't for being in Venice, I might dump him now.

Instead, we go as planned on the first of our sight-seeing expeditions.

On the vaporetto, Coll says, 'I wrote her a poem and gave it to her. Now you know everything. There's nothing more.'

He wrote her a poem. He never wrote me a poem. I'm clearly not poem-worthy. If he was looking at me, he would see the pain in my eyes. One more revelation to clear his conscience; one more stab to my heart.

'Hello?' Coll says. 'Are you in there?'

'Yes.' I can hardly speak. 'I don't know what to say.'

I am an outsider now to the passion that beats in his soul. It wasn't always so. He may have forgotten, but in the early days I was his Cleopatra, Beatrice and Juliet. Best of all, Elizabeth Bennett whom he might have passed by but for overhearing a scintillating exchange during the mid-session break at art class. It was an exchange that caused him to notice me and ask me to that exhibition where we realised that each of us had found the other half for whom we'd been searching for decades. And he says he doesn't love me, never did? It makes no sense.

Over the week, we do everything you're supposed to do in Venice. We visit the Doge's Palace, St Mark's Basilica, the Accademia, the Guggenheim Gallery, Ca' Rezzonico and various piazzas and churches. We browse in upmarket shops frequented by fashionista, and in low market tourist-tat shops and at the stalls of scarves and masks and other street merchandise. There is colourful glass of every conceivable shape and form: animals, vases, necklaces, plates and chandeliers, expensive and high quality from the neighbouring island of Murano and cheaper, gaudy, low quality imports, copying the look but not the class. The discerning can easily spot the fakes.

We buy fish from the bustling Rialto market and vegetables from a stall in Via Giuseppe Garibaldi where the *pomodori* – tomatoes – are the sweetest and most flavourful that I've ever tasted. We eat out, we eat in, we take a trip down the Grand Canal in Vaporetto Number One (much cheaper than a gondola or taxi) and we visit the islands of Murano, Burano and Torcello. We practice our rudimentary Italian skills (his, of course, are better than mine) and we learn the rules in the *mercato* grocery shops where locals shout their orders from the door and you learn to be pushy or wait forever. Even in the supermarkets the notion of queuing at the till and waiting one's turn is only barely adhered to.

At night we either stay in and cook, or eat at a local café. We take late evening strolls along the waterfront and on returning, sit on one of the concrete blocks that edge our part of the lagoon, gazing at the boats on the water as the sun sets. We talk about what we've done that day and what we will do tomorrow; about practical matters like food and money. We've almost lost the ability to laugh and when we do, it's as if Coll has forgotten some personal promise to be vile and when he remembers he becomes doubly silent; doubly remote.

We do everything you're supposed to do; everything except one. What we don't do is love. In this city of passion and beauty and immeasurable delights, there's a coolness between us that makes me think our time together will soon be over.

Despite all that, I'm enchanted by Venice and fascinated by how it functions and the engineering marvels that lie deep under the houses and under the water of the canals. I wonder about the electricity and gas supplies, the sewage system, the refuse collection and when I return home, I shall research as much as I can about the hidden workings of the city.

Coll is more enamoured by the art and his follow-up research will be of a different kind.

And there are surprises too: lots of little dogs – trotting down the streets, carried on boats, their owners always rushing somewhere with serious expressions, eyes averted from the tourist throngs.

From my Italian phrase book, I had learnt *mi scusi*, believing it would be useful to navigate through the crowds, but we discovered on the boats the locals use *permesso* when they leave their seats or require one to make way. As the days go by, I perfect my accent and become adept at buying food. But I struggle when anyone speaks back to me. When Coll sees my bemused expression, he steps in and takes over, afterwards looking at me with a smug and self-satisfied air.

Oh Venice, *La Serenissima,* now I understand the rapture

and the magic. Every morning we are woken by the haunting and romantic sound of bells and I realise that being here has brought me close to thoughts of family and loss and wasted time. I remember when we went to see *Richard ll,* I logged the quotation: *'I wasted time and now doth time waste me.'* It struck a chord and so has Venice. It's time I decided what I want to do with what is left of my little and insignificant life.

I remember that once Coll and I had a passion of a sort; a passion now ruined by a nothing, a tissue paper contact with an ordinary woman that in theory should be no match for the weighty vellum pages of our history, but in practice is managing to demolish our union. Around me are piles of rubble: bricks and mortar that were once walls. I sit in the ruins and bleed.

In my imagination every love song ever written had my name embedded in the lines and as we listened, I always heard *Sarah,* even though it never rhymed. Now all I ever hear is *Felicity,* and him thinking about her and what they were or might have been, and the pleasure from the music is replaced by unshed tears, and a hollow heart thuds joylessly, where once it beat brim full of stars.

49

James and Kate

Felicity

'I've had a thought and I want you to be completely honest,' I say.

I invited Kate and James round for supper in the restaurant followed by a private chat upstairs. I told them it was to thank them for the meals I've had at their place. We are now in my living room with cups of coffee.

'Spit it out, Mum,' James says, sprawling in an armchair.

'How would you feel if I came back to live with you? When Ted and Marianne leave.'

James and Kate exchange looks.

'Perhaps not exactly *with* you,' I elaborate. 'Not all the time. But at the Deer Orchard.'

Kate says, 'I realise we have to compromise on privacy if we are going to keep the Deer Orchard – at least in the short term. But ...' She looks at James again.

'Gianni has sent me the money he owes me – and a tad more. Some of it I want to give to Rachel so she has a decent deposit for a flat. If I were living at the Deer Orchard, you could buy Dad out as a priority.'

'That's a change of tune,' James says.

'I had a tête-a-tête with Marianne. I'm not going to be obstructive any more.'

'Good,' James says.

'If I were back home permanently, I could muck in with your plans for expanding the business and your ideas could be fast tracked while you're still working.' I am careful to make Kate feel she would still be in control.

'And I thought some of the money might be used to extend along from the office and kiln room so I could have my own domain and give you some privacy. There's enough space. Assuming Killerton permissions, and all that. I used to sleep in the office sometimes when Dad and I weren't getting on.'

'A Granny Flat,' James says.

'Less of the Granny,' I say. 'But in principle, yes.'

James and Kate exchange another glance.

'We've still got Harriet during most of the working week,' says Kate. 'And with Dad and Marianne coming and going for the past few months, we are used to a full house.'

James says, 'We will need to think about it and get back to

you. It could be a solution, but—' He has that serious look which means he has thought of problems.

I pre-empt. 'I know what you're thinking. That I'll try to take over. I promise I won't. It's your business now. I will act as a facilitator, a dogsbody. I'll do whatever you want me to do. Pigs, sheep, goats ... more hens ... more bees. All the things you've talked about wanting in the future. If I'm on site for at least part of most days, then with help from Rick we could have the place set up and earning a decent income much quicker than if you wait. And if Kate wants an on-site shop, we could start looking into that. The outbuilding by the gate would be perfect. We've never used it because it needs a new roof.'

Kate says, 'Yeah, the roadside notices are working a treat in bringing in a few customers when we're at home. We have quite a few regulars now at the weekends. But we could do so much more than a few surplus veg.'

James says, 'We could advance the plans for the cheese-making.' His eyes are now alight and eager.

I knew they couldn't resist the idea of getting their business going and I too am already excited at the prospect of such an expansion. 'Exactly. Have a chat and let me know what you think.'

50

Stake Out

Sarah

I sit in my bright blue Mini a few yards down the road from Felicity's restaurant and in sight of the car park. I'm parked outside a few shops so no one will be suspicious. Neptune is bigger than I thought and has a freshly painted white exterior. The door at the front looks as if it opens directly into a passage leading to the restaurant. There's a separate entrance at the side which I imagine gives access to the flat above. I wonder which door Coll used when he visited and whether he spent much time upstairs. I never asked him. I don't want to know. There are so many things I wish I didn't know.

We returned from Venice last Saturday, almost a week ago. Coll went straight back to his flat in order to prepare for this next half term and I haven't seen him since. I was pleased to have some space to myself. Space to think. It was claustrophobic being on holiday together with a wedge between us. He's called me most evenings, but we haven't chatted. He says he's coming over tomorrow.

Meanwhile, I've been brooding. Wondering why he chose to tell me about Felicity while we were away. I assume he told me because he wanted to be absolved. He wanted to cleanse himself from sin like at a Catholic's confession. Except he's not a Catholic. The principle is the same. Perhaps he hoped I'd give him the equivalent of three Hail Marys and an Our Father, in which case I disappointed. I didn't shout or throw things because I didn't want to ruin our time away completely, but nor did I give him the impression that it didn't matter. In truth, I didn't know what to do and I still don't. You could say I'm on an information gathering exercise.

He could've waited till after Venice. Or waited forever. It would have been more charitable of him to harbour the secret to protect me from hurt. He and Felicity could have parted and I would never have known that he had betrayed me for a second time.

I adjust my sunglasses. A young clone of Dr Edward emerges from the side door and takes two bags of rubbish to some bins under an apple tree. This must be Chris the chef; the youngest son, who went to Italy and trained with Felicity's boyfriend. I know more about Felicity's relatives than I do my own. I could write her biography.

I wait an hour and there's no more movement in or out of the premises. It's Friday and I've taken a day off work because I'm owed some holiday having worked extra days at Easter. I've been vaguely listening to Radio 4: *Desert Island Discs* and *Woman's Hour*. Some hypermanic American woman has been harping on about a self-help book she's written about abusive relationships. I wonder if she would class mine with Coll as one. She says physical abuse is clear cut, whereas verbal or mental abuse has an indistinct demarcation line between what is acceptable and what is not. She says it's normal for most of us to complain to our partners from time to time and sometimes forcefully, but she adds that there's a point at which complaint becomes aggressive and if this happens often, it constitutes abuse.

I complain to Coll about his drinking and about his pursuit of OWs – and about his involvement with Felicity. I can be forceful in my complaints too. Does this mean I'm an abuser?

She says there's a grey area surrounding restriction and control. 'Commitment usually assumes a reduction of freedoms,' she drawls. 'Say, if I expect my partner to come home to share dinner with me at least half the evenings in a week but he would rather spend another hour or two in the bar every night, is that controlling behaviour on my part if he acquiesces? And, equally, is it controlling behaviour on his part if he doesn't?' The interview throws up some interesting points. I may listen again on iPlayer when I'm less agitated.

I realise I don't know what type of car Felicity drives or what her daily schedule might be. I haven't done enough homework. I would be a useless private detective. But I do know that she opens on Friday lunchtimes and I've some idea what she looks like having seen her at Dick's leaving do.

With the sun on my face, I begin to doze and it's some minutes before an intangible something causes me to wake.

A red hatchback has appeared in the car park and a woman is heading from it to the side door, carrying a box of vegetables. I only catch sight of her retreating figure: a pile of light brown hair on top of her head; a woman in jeans; tall and quite trim. My heart rate rises as it's surely a rear-view sighting of Felicity. I should've parked closer, but I didn't want to arouse suspicion. It could be her other son's partner; the one that lives at the family home. No, the walk is a walk of a midlife woman, careful of where she steps. I've fallen over enough times to know.

Tears gather. I want to scream at her; to shout. But it isn't her fault. If what Coll says is true, she has been blameless, even selfless. He says she's thoughtful of my position. He said it looking wistfully over my shoulder as if he wished she hadn't been so. I wish she'd refused to talk to him once she knew. That would have been more thoughtful. If only she hadn't admitted to 'nearly making a fool of herself again.' How shocking to know that on one sentence, seven words, a life together can be thwarted. Not even seven words. One word. *Nearly*. Implying possibility, and hope for Coll.

I imagine her walking upstairs to an immaculate flat with modern arty decor, some of her ceramic bowls and perhaps one of Coll's paintings on her wall. If he wrote her a poem, then surely he'll have given her a painting too. How flattering to be loved. What a boost to the midlife ego. Yet if she doesn't feel the same, her gain will be nothing in comparison to my loss. She may pity him his unrequited feelings. I'm sure she pities me.

Coll said she'd lost her Italian lover in similar circumstances. It's this that gives me comfort that she understands my plight. It would be easier if there was no business connection; no paintings. Then there would be no excuse to see her beyond the personal and it would be reasonable to expect him not to contact her – and if he did, to end our relationship. I reflect on the *Woman's Hour* interview: does this make me controlling – expecting him not to see Felicity? Is this the new abuse?

Earlier in the week I told Laura the latest revelations of the whole sorry tale. We were replacing books from the trolley before the day started and the hush descended. She had wondered why I was a bit non-committal about Venice. After I explained, she said, *'I wish you'd dump the bastard but I know you won't.'* Was I that transparent? Then she suggested I come and see Felicity, *'See what the trollop has to say.'* Laura doesn't mince words.

I need to summon courage to knock on the door. Now I'm here, I want reassurance that she won't contact Coll even if his paintings sell out and her walls are bare. I know that any future contact with her will reignite whatever he's trying hard to suppress. Our future is impossible if there's any chance of their paths crossing. And again I am spiralling into the despair that erupts at the prospect of loss.

But a glance at my watch tells me it's too near to lunch. She won't have time to talk to me at least until afternoon.

Courage fails and I return home.

51

Letting Go

Felicity

I knock on the back door of the Deer Orchard and am surprised when a stranger opens it. She is about the same age as Kate, but she isn't Kate.

'I'm Felicity. Here to see Ted.'

'I'm Holly,' says the stranger. 'You'd better come in.'

Marianne's daughter. Of course. I can see the resemblance now. She has the same high cheekbones and slightly French look; longer, darker hair in a loose plait over one shoulder.

'Edward and Mum are shopping – but they won't be long. James is at work and Kate is at the dentist. I'm holding the fort. Kate said you might drop by.'

We weigh each other up. Holly is a solicitor and her presence alarms me slightly. She offers me a drink and I accept tea.

'Is this the first time you've been here?' I ask.

'Yes, it's a lovely house. Great kitchen. Super gardens.'

'How long are you staying?'

'Edward's off to Scilly soon with a group of students. I'm here to keep Mum company and to have a break.'

'He didn't tell me he was going.'

'I think it was planned a while back before he retired. Some excavation of the sunken land between Bryher and Tresco. They have to go when there are spring tides so they can access the sea bed. Exciting, don't you think?'

'Not really my thing,' I say.

We sit by the breakfast bar and she asks me how things are going at Neptune, steering me away from sensitive issues. She's very direct and appears to have good interpersonal skills.

It isn't long before Ted and Marianne return. He and I go upstairs to his office and I tell him I've been to my solicitor and asked him to proceed with the divorce petition.

I say, 'We don't have to finalise everything until the finances are sorted, but at least you know that the process is underway.'

'I'm glad,' he says.

I tell him that I will be coming back to the Deer Orchard once he and Marianne have found a place.

'James said something of the kind. Musical chairs,' he says. 'But I want you to be settled, Flick, and I think you'll be happier here than in Pinhoe.'

I thought he might object and my arguments melt away. I relax.

He says, 'Marianne was wondering if Rachel might be interested in buying her flat. It's perfectly located for commuting into London and she said she would drop the price. It would be good to keep it in the family. We could stay when we need to be in town.'

'I like Marianne,' I say. 'And Holly seems very pleasant too.'

He looks surprised.

'I mean it. I've had a sobering experience with another unreliable man and it's changed me. I don't want to be awkward or obstructive any more. I've had my life with you and lost it. It was wonderful for many years and I am grateful. We have four fantastic kids. I'm lucky. We're lucky. You have my blessing to move on. Be happy, Ted. Be happy.'

And he smiles the old familiar *Ted* smile and we exchange glances of genuine warmth. I brush away the beginnings of a tear and laugh to hide my embarrassment. 'Don't mind me,' I say. 'I'm getting sentimental in my advancing years.'

'About time,' says Ted, his eyes crinkling.

When I leave it is as if I have finally closed a book that has had a satisfying ending. Getting to this point has been a struggle but perhaps something that I owe to Coll.

52

Meeting Felicity

Sarah

I pay a second visit to Neptune, two days after the first. It's Sunday teatime. Coll has been and gone. Last night we had supper, watched telly – during which time he downed one and a half bottles of wine – spoke little and went to bed. This morning he said, 'I won't hang around Sarah, I can see you've a lot of catching up to do since the holiday.' What he meant was that he didn't want to be with me while I was being so uncommunicative. He was off by eleven. I was quite glad because it gave me another opportunity to visit Felicity.

This time I'm determined to speak to her before I've time to lose my nerve. The red car is in the car park and I turn off the road and park beside it. No more lurking in the shadows for me.

I go to the side door rather than the restaurant entrance and ring the bell. I hear footsteps coming down stairs. It's too late to run away. Felicity opens the door a smidgen, bearing an expression that suggests she thinks I want to sell her something. Her eyebrows raise and she gives a tight false smile, betraying her true feelings, no doubt practised with awkward restaurant customers. She's casually dressed and with wisps of hair escaping the clip that holds it on top of her head. Objectively, a run-of-the-mill fifty-something woman now she is no longer glammed up like she was at Dick Fieldbrace's leaving do, yet because of all the guff I have been fed by Coll, she appears luminous, like a religious icon. I feel shabby by comparison, even though I'm not. I've put on my work face especially.

'I'm Sarah,' I say.

Her brow furrows and she puts her head on one side, opening the door wider. 'Coll's Sarah?' I can tell she is surprised.

I'm comforted that this is how she thinks of me. I force a smile, but it's a struggle. I try not to sound threatening and keep my voice low. 'I'd like to have a word, if that's okay.'

'Would you like to come in?' Felicity stands back from the doorway to let me pass. She appears confident, powerful and attractive. All the virtues Coll heaped on her have been absorbed into my psyche.

I follow her down a passage and into the restaurant. We sit at one of the tables in front of the largest window which looks out across the road. I wonder if she senses danger and is positioning us to afford some protection. I don't look the type to turn, but one reads things. And a love betrayal does make one feel quite unhinged. She experienced similar so will know this.

I say, 'I don't want to worry you.'

'I'm not worried.'

I look around and there are several of Coll's paintings on the walls, but also a couple of prints in a different style, no doubt from another source. And there are shelves on which pretty ceramic bowls of various sizes glint sea-green colours in the sunlight.

We sit down opposite each other. Felicity places both arms in front of her on the table. I'm acutely aware of every move she makes; every gesture and expression that might explain her attraction for Coll.

'What can I do for you, Sarah?' She adopts a businesslike tone.

'This is a tad awkward, isn't it? I'm sorry ... about everything. I don't suppose I'm your favourite person.'

'No.' I nod an acknowledgement. 'I'm here because I want to hear your side.'

'I didn't know you existed. Not at first.'

'I know. I knew about you, though. From the beginning. And I knew you had an impact on him. He was always talking about how wonderful you were. I wanted him to tell you about me, but I know he didn't until it was too late. He's lied so much; withheld information.'

'He should have told me about you, Sarah. It was a deliberate omission. He had plenty of opportunity. I was shocked. I wouldn't have ... if I'd known.'

This is a good start.

I say, 'I want to know if there are any more shocks still to come.'

'It was all above board.'

'But love is a bigger threat to a relationship. It's all consuming. Sex is just sex to most men. I didn't understand when I was younger.'

'Love,' she mocks. 'More like infatuation.'

'It's love to him.'

'I didn't do anything to encourage him. I promise you.'

'No. You were just you. And he fell for you.'

241

'When you get to my age, you don't expect that. Especially not so fast.'

'Things have been difficult since Valentine's Day. I wasn't sure why, but I thought it might have something to do with you. We went to Venice at half term. He chose to tell me on the day we arrived.'

'That's madness. What was he thinking of?' says Felicity. 'I told him it was over long before that.'

'It should have been glorious but all the time he was distant and cold. It's no different since we've returned. His mind is elsewhere and I don't know if I should be staying with him after what he's done.'

Felicity says she is surprised I have held out this long and I can tell she is slightly scornful of my durability.

'What exactly has he told you?' she says.

'Everything, I think.'

She shakes her head. 'The fool. He tells you everything, yet he told me nothing.'

'I assume everything. Because that's what he's like. A way of offloading his guilt. He told me of the meetings—'

'There weren't many.'

'*Antony and Cleopatra.*'

'That was before I knew about you. He said he was divorced. I thought he was free.'

'The Shard; the Globe.'

'That was the day he told me how important you were. When it was too late not to go. That's when he said you had planned a future together; a future that I couldn't give him. It was a shock. I hadn't realised he and you were serious.'

'The poem.'

'Ah. I am embarrassed about that. It's ridiculous anyone writing such things about me. I'm fifty-seven. Hardly muse-material.'

'You were to him. He never wrote me a poem. Ever. Not even at the start.'

'You do believe nothing happened between us?'

'He said you talked for hours and that there was a connection. That's what he said about me when we first met. It's as if he's forgotten.'

'He hasn't forgotten. That's what he said when he told me about you. You *are* special to him.'

'Then why doesn't he show it? It's like you've stolen my life.' My voice catches.

'I'm sorry.'

'He went on and on about how you were different from me. Strong. Decisive. All the things I'm not that drive him up the wall.'

'My strength and decisiveness would eventually have caused us to clash.'

'He said that if you had wanted him, he would have left me. Even though he knew it wouldn't work long term.'

'I couldn't offer him what he wanted. When I heard what you have, I didn't feel he should lose it. I didn't care for him enough – especially after being put in the picture.'

'I don't know if we'll ever get back what we had. He loves you. He doesn't love me. He never said he did, but I thought he was in denial. Afraid of getting hurt. So I didn't believe him.'

Felicity Mayfield-Harvey. This is her. When I arrived, I hated her. Now I'm here, listening to her, I realise she is as much a victim as me.

53

Meeting Sarah

Felicity

My first thought when Sarah appeared at the door was that she may be a Jehovah's Witness. My second thought, when she mentioned her name, was that she may have evil intent. But my third thought was that she didn't look the violent type. She has big innocent eyes in a perfect heart-shaped face. She's also tiny and as I'm bigger and quite strong, I think I would have a fair chance of overpowering her if she threw a fit. I assigned her *dormouse* and decided it was okay to invite her in. But I factored in a safety net. I led her to the restaurant dining room rather than up to the flat and we are seated in front of the biggest window.

As our conversation has progressed, I have become more at ease. All she wants is reassurance that Coll has finally told her the truth and that I will stay away from him. It is a pity she can't believe him, but now I know what he is like, it is not surprising. I try to quell her fears.

'He doesn't love me,' I say. 'It's an illusion. He *thinks* he's in love in a romantic teenage way. But it's not for real. It's easy to think you're in love from a distance.'

'But whatever the truth, the fact remains that you fill his thoughts. He's obsessed.'

'I felt the same as you when I discovered Gianni – my ex – and his former girlfriend were seeing each other again. Did Coll tell you about him?'

Sarah nods.

'When Coll told me properly about you, I knew you were important. My heart sank because I realised that I was inadvertently doing to you what Liliana had done to me. I know that pain. I wouldn't wish to be the cause of it in anyone else.'

'It isn't your fault.'

'I'm terribly sorry it has come to this. But Coll could've left you. He didn't. He couldn't. That counts for something. You must hang on to that. It may not be the "in love" feeling that you would wish for, but perhaps it is a kind of love.'

'I know you are trying to make me feel better, but all I feel is I fall short and don't match up.'

Short she may be. Poor choice of words. But she's pretty and definitely looks younger than me. She hasn't a bad figure either. But I can see she is meek and mild and how easy it must be for someone like Coll to take advantage.

'I'm nothing special,' I say. 'He pictured me through rose-tinted glasses. He said I looked like his wife. You know what men are. I fit the template that sparked physical attraction. But it wouldn't have lasted. He knew that; I knew that. Yes, we like the theatre and art and have been through a lot of similar life experiences, but that's about it. He's as dismissive as Ted of my love of food production and catering. Perhaps even more so. And that's my life now.'

'And what if we do split? What would happen then?' Sarah asks.

I wonder if she is brave enough to cut the ties or if she is expecting him to finish with her and present himself to me as a free man. I wouldn't blame her for giving him the heave-ho but I don't think she's got the bottle.

'Even if he were free, now I know what I know, I wouldn't take a chance. He withheld information from me. He toyed with my feelings. He betrayed you – twice. Not forgetting he was married before. It might be a pattern. I'm a tad too old for games and for taking any more unnecessary risks.'

'I don't suppose he told you the whole caboodle of what he's really like.'

'I don't suppose he did. People don't, do they. They present their best self for as long as they can get away with it and it's only with time that the truth is uncovered.'

'Did he tell you he drinks?'

'That's interesting. No. He was always driving when we met. A glass or two of wine at most. But once or twice when we spoke on the phone, I wondered.'

'And the other women?'

'You mean other than me?' This is a revelation I hadn't expected.

'Yes, but not serious ones like you. Flirtations, you might say. Conquests.'

'Really?' This gets worse and worse. Poor Sarah. Yet I can understand why she loves him and how difficult it must be to let go after such a long time. I nearly made the same mistake. I, who think I am wise after Gianni. Ted pops up in my thoughts again. 'I spent thirty years being married to a good and faithful man. They do exist. I messed up.'

'You must think me a fool,' Sarah says.

'You have several years of investment with him where I have none. You love. You did love. I know he has good qualities too. Otherwise you wouldn't stay with him.'

'He does. He looked after me when I wasn't well a few years ago. We have fun. Or at least we used to have fun. The promise of a future together made me hang on.'

'You may love him again. It might be worth fighting for.'

'My friends think I'm a fool.'

'What do you think?'

'That they're right. That if I'd had more sense at the start, I would've seen the signs. But we all believe we can change our men; that we will be the one to cure their solitary heart. I believed I could make him fly. But you're the one that's done that.'

'He would have landed with a bump after a few months. We are both too controlling.'

'He knows that, yet he said he resents me for existing because that has meant he can't have you.'

How unfair is that? He doesn't want to leave her, but *resents* her because she *exists*? That's madness. I wonder if I should tell her what Marianne said. I take a chance.

'My husband's partner was a psychology teacher. I'm not sure if I should be saying this, but in the long run it might be helpful. She suggested Coll may be a good way along the continuum of having a narcissistic personality.'

Sarah frowns and pauses before commenting. 'That's not good, is it? But it would explain why he says he can't help it.'

'It's not the end of the world. Marianne says that it can lessen with age.'

'We had so much between us until he met you. Even without him declaring love, we'd enough in common for a midlife relationship to work.'

'You are much better suited than he and I would have been. I know that from everything he said about you. He knows it too. And I think he does love you, in his way.'

'But he would exchange all that for six months of passion.'

'Pure fantasy.'

'Knowing what he feels for you has killed my love; strangled my own feelings. I'm running on empty. The relationship has lost its sparkle.'

'Open your heart to the possibility of loving him.'

'But what if you meet again?'

'Could he not give you the reassurance that we won't?'

'He said he wouldn't contact you. And I believe him. He said you wouldn't contact him … But I wasn't sure. That's why I'm here. What if you needed more paintings?'

'I won't contact him again. When all these paintings are sold, I will send him a cheque and look for other artists. I've already found one.'

'And if they don't all sell?'

'They will. But if not, I'll post them back to him. You have my word I won't ever see him or speak to him again.'

By the time Sarah gets up to leave, I am sure I have persuaded her that I will honour my word. She takes a look at my pots and we discover that the one with a flaw that I gave to Coll was presented to her as if he had bought it. She says she loves my *Seaweed* design and buys two shallow dishes for presents for her sister and a friend at the library. I say that she can have them for nothing after all the trouble I've caused. But she won't hear of it, though she accepts a twenty percent discount.

As we walk to the door, I say, 'This midlife relationship stuff is a bit of a shit.'

And Sarah finally smiles at me with warmth. 'You've suffered too,' she says. And then she surprises me. 'I know your husband,' she says. 'We call him Dr Edward. He *is* a lovely man. We're sorry he's retired although he does keep popping in to the library.'

I knew she was a librarian, but I had no idea it was at the university.

'I saw you at Dick Fieldbrace's do,' she says. 'I nearly confronted you there, but I didn't have the courage.'

'I thought you looked familiar – but I couldn't think where. That must be it.'

And on the step we chat for a few more minutes about the university and how I once worked there in admin but it wasn't the life I craved.

'I always wanted animals and a restaurant. Sadly, Ted didn't.'

She commiserates and then says she really must leave me. She thanks me for my time. I like this woman. I can see why she has kept Coll interested for so long and why he couldn't leave her. In a different world we could have been friends. As she approaches her car in the car park, she turns and gives me a little wave.

54

Decision

Sarah

Late into the night I'm still dwelling on my conversation with Felicity. I have the reassurance I wanted. I needed to know that for her, Coll was history. I left her with gratitude and a growing confidence.

The moon casts a glow through my curtains and I'm restless, weighing up the pros and cons of my next move. Am I brave enough?

In the morning I trawl the web for information about narcissistic personality disorder. It's as she said. It's Coll with his arrogance and unreasonable expectations, his constant need for approval, his criticism of others, his vanity. Even his pursuit of the OWs can be explained by this trait. He's not as extreme a case as is possible and he does have redeeming features, but he ticks several of the boxes.

I always knew something wasn't right but to give it a name makes me shiver. *Coll with the narcissistic personality.* It's not an acceptable flaw like dyslexia or autism. I can't imagine telling friends or family, *'My boyfriend is a narcissist.'* It's surely, at least in part, a product of the environment and therefore controllable. And he has chosen not to control it. It's as if I have loved a stranger.

Have loved ... Past tense ... No, not totally past. Love is not like a tap to be turned off at will. But the water pressure is somewhat reduced. It leaves me much food for thought. As does Felicity's assurance that she wants nothing more to do with him. I believe her absolutely and it's a huge weight off my mind. It also gives me options; scope to take a risk that otherwise I would be too scared to contemplate. To have him run to her to soothe his soul would be unbearable.

I decide to adopt a new strategy. In the evening, I don't answer the phone when I know it's likely to be Coll and I ignore his follow-up text. I call him at lunchtime the following day. I can tell he's caught off guard by the switch in my behaviour. He says he will be round on Friday, taking it for granted I'll be delighted to accommodate him: an assumption I'll be available.

I say I'm meeting Laura, but Saturday will be fine.

'Oh … o-kayyyy.' He draws out the word.

Great. This has got him thinking, as intended.

'I can stay,' he says. Another assumption.

'Perhaps not this weekend. I've a lot to do.' I haven't, but this is his mantra when he wants to push me away. I hope he recognises it. He's used it many times since he met Felicity. 'The following midweek is okay though.'

He says that's fine.

'I'm thinking of getting back to painting,' I add. 'I want to use this weekend to get organised. And I'm at the hairdresser on Saturday morning.'

He sounds surprised. 'Are you all right, Sarah?'

'Not totally. But you know that. I haven't been "all right" for a while. I think we should probably have a little chat.' I know this will disturb him. He hates confrontation when he's not in control.

He raises his voice. He's cross. 'Oh God, Sarah. There's so much going on at work with exams, one of your little chats is the last thing I need.'

'Suit yourself then. We'll leave it all for another time.'

'What do you mean, "leave it all"?'

'Midweek supper. The chat.'

'Can we not have the supper without the chat?' he wheedles.

'No.'

He backtracks. 'Okay, okay. We'll talk.'

'You don't need to say a thing, you just have to listen.'

I busy myself with late spring cleaning and I have my hair reshaped in a more flattering, layered, shoulder-skimming style with added highlights.

'Bye-bye Richard lll,' I say under my breath when I see myself in the mirror.

On Saturday night I go out for a meal with Laura, and on Sunday, I visit my sister. They ask after Coll and I say I don't want to talk about him. That's a rare thing. They will wonder what's afoot.

I half expect him to cancel the midweek meal at the last minute. But he doesn't. He turns up on time. There's tension as we greet each other but he says he likes my hair.

'What's going on?' he asks. 'You're behaving oddly.'

'We'll talk after supper,' I say. He accepts only a small glass of wine, probably aware that he's most likely driving himself home later.

After vacuous chatter about our respective weeks and a few failed attempts on Coll's part that I should 'spill the beans', we near the end of the chicken and mushroom pie and I take the plunge with my well-rehearsed lines.

'I know things have been difficult since *Felicitygate*, Coll. But I believed Venice would be a time to heal for both of us. But it wasn't. Instead, you dropped your bombshell on our very first evening. Your confession made things worse, and even after that, you were remote. Distant.'

'I know.'

He swirls the wine in his glass, seeing how far up the sides he can make it go without it spilling. He's not giving my words the attention they deserve.

I continue, 'We spent all that money. We'd always wanted to go. And we did everything on the list and more. It was all we'd hoped: the art, the markets, the canals, the boats, the views. I tried my best despite everything. If anyone should have been switched off, it was me. But half the time you ignored me. You wouldn't talk to me; laugh with me. I was on edge, never sure what to say. When we did speak, you didn't want to make any plans for the future. Venice: the most romantic place in the world, but the romance was missing. It was like you wished you were there with Felicity.'

There is a long pause. Coll clears his throat. 'You're right. I'm sorry. I'll be okay soon. I'm getting there, but it takes time.'

'This thing with Felicity happened because of you. But you've been punishing me ever since as if it was my fault. You had every chance to leave me the first time. Or second time.'

Coll sighs and picks at some fluff on his needlecord jacket. 'The first time, I wasn't sure what was going on. Then, when I knew she might … that changed things. I needed to know for sure. When I told her about you, and she wouldn't because of you … I blamed you. I know it's not fair but if it wasn't for you, I could've been with her … for a while.' He's still cocky.

'Except you couldn't. She didn't want you.'

'Only when she knew about you.'

'But you said it wouldn't last. You said it was a fantasy. You've been in this mood ever since you stopped seeing her. I've made an effort but you're the one who should've made it. *You* messed up.'

He adopts a wistful expression. 'I know. It hit me badly. I fell for her … I didn't go looking.'

Still it's all about him. He shows no understanding of the amount of hurt I've experienced. 'And *I* feel like second choice.'

'Well, you shouldn't,' he says.

'And why is that?'

He doesn't answer.

'I should've finished it there and then. I can't live like this.'

Time slows and I can hear my pulse.

'What are you saying?' Coll says, leaning forward.

'That we should separate.'

'Are you dumping me?' He laughs and pulls a mocking and incredulous face as if he doesn't believe me.

'I'm giving you a chance to decide what you really want.'

At last he takes proper notice and looks me in the eye. It's the first time in ages that he's met my gaze and peered into the depths of my being.

He says, 'But I made the decision to stay with you; for us to carry on.'

'No, you didn't. Felicity made the decision.'

'Only because I said lots of stuff about you and how good we were together. Only then. Only when she realised how important you are.' There is panic in his voice. At last I've got through to him.

'That's not exactly how you told it to me before.'

'It's how it was. She knew there was something deep between you and me.'

'You're the one who should've realised how important I am. Not Felicity.'

'I do.'

'So why don't you value it, nurture it?'

'I don't know.'

'Is that the best you can do?'

'Don't you love me any more?'

Him again. The blinkers have fallen from my eyes and his selfishness is laid bare. I tell him that the problem is more about how he feels about me; that if I can't stir something in his heart that he'll admit to being a type of love then I'll always feel like a second choice, a consolation prize.

'Don't do this, Sarah. I'll try. I don't want to lose you.'

I was on a roll now. 'You treat me as a convenience. As an option. And your dalliance with Felicity has ruined what we had.'

'I can change.'

'You said that before.'

'I can.'

'I believe you can if you want to. But you have to want to.'

'I do. Let me try.'

'We went through all this once before. Your efforts didn't last five minutes. This time I want you to find out what – who – you really want. I'm letting you go, Coll. Do you hear me? I'm serious. I'm letting you go. You talk about the commitment trap and fear of being smothered. Well, now you're free.'

He moves from his chair to my side of the table and crouches beside me, taking my hands.

'I don't want to be free,' he whispers, pleading. 'I can't survive without you.'

I pull away. 'So why tell me that you'd been seeing Felicity again? Why hurt me? Why carry on like you did in Venice? Why spoil everything?' His expression is forlorn and I waver inside. But I know what happened last time when he persuaded me to let him off the hook. Felicity was right when she identified that my love had changed. Now I'm a realist and unprepared to sacrifice myself. During *Felicitygate*, the pain of losing him was worse than anything I could imagine but at least he chose me over her. This time, the pain of him choosing her is enough to weaken my hold. And I've already been through half the grieving process of loss.

Coll tries a few more times to change my mind with offers of another weekend away where he'll 'make an effort'.

'It's too late,' I say. I can see the emotion in his eyes and I have to look away for fear of giving in.

When he leaves, I give him a carrier bag with his things. 'You can return my stuff whenever,' I say. 'Text me and leave it on the back step.'

'This feels so final,' he says.

'It's up to you now. We've pussyfooted long enough.'

'*I've* pussyfooted.'

'Yes.'

'Sarah …' He touches my cheek. 'I'll make it right. I will …'

'I'm not sure that you can.' And I'm really not sure. It's about me now and I'm ready to move on. Without the same intensity of love, I've reclaimed power and choice; both denied me in the past.

On the step he hugs me. It's a proper hug of real affection; the type of hug that should have been part of our regular repertoire; a hug that I'd longed for all the time we were together. This time it's me who can't return the intensity.

He says, 'Knowing you has been the best thing in my life. The very best thing … I haven't deserved you, I know, sweet Sarah …'

I hold on tightly to my emotions, squeezing them down from the surface. My throat muscles hurt from the effort. 'Goodbye, Coll.'

Off he goes into the night, my great love. And I close the door and lean on it and feel a weight lift off me. I'm upset, but not distraught. I cry, but with relief. I've done it. I've taken charge of my life. There's no more fight left in me. No more excuses, no more agonising of whether to stay with him, no more desperate attempts to secure his love. After more than ten years, my cage door swings open and my spirit flies free.

Also by
Linda MacDonald

Meeting Lydia

"Edward Harvey. Even thinking his name made her tingle with half-remembered childlike giddiness. Edward Harvey, the only one from Brocklebank to whom she might write if she found him."

Marianne Hayward, teacher of psychology and compulsive analyser of the human condition, is in a midlife turmoil. After twenty years of happy marriage, she comes home one day to find her charming husband in the kitchen talking to the glamorous Charmaine. All her childhood insecurities resurface from a time when she was bullied at a boys' prep school. She becomes jealous and possessive and the arguments begin.

Teenage daughter Holly persuades her to join Friends Reunited which results in both fearful and nostalgic memories of prep school as Marianne wonders what has become of the bullies. But there was one boy in her class who was never horrible to her: the clever and enigmatic Edward Harvey, on whom she developed her first crush. Could the answer to all her problems lie in finding Edward again?

Meeting Lydia is a book about childhood bullying, midlife crises, obsession, jealousy and the ever-growing trend of internet relationships. It is the prequel to *A Meeting of a Different Kind* and the first part of a trilogy, the third part being *The Alone Alternative*.

A Meeting of a Different Kind

"Taryn thinks about Mr Perfect Edward Harvey and the news that he will be visiting London over the next few weeks. Marianne keeps saying he isn't the philandering type; Taryn doesn't believe a word of it. There isn't a man alive who doesn't have the potential to philander, given the right material to philander with ...'

When archaeologist Edward Harvey's wife Felicity inherits almost a million, she gives up her job, buys a restaurant and, as a devotee of Hugh Fernley-Whittingstall, starts turning their home into a small eco-farm. Edward is not happy, not least because she seems to be losing interest in him.

Taryn is a borderline manic-depressive, a scheming minx, a seductress and user of men. When her best-friend Marianne says Edward is not the philandering type, Taryn sees a challenge and concocts a devious plan to meet him at the British Museum – a meeting that will have far reaching and destructive consequences on both their lives.

Set in Broadclyst and Beckenham, with a chapter on the Isles of Scilly, *A Meeting of a Different Kind* is the stand-alone sequel to *Meeting Lydia*, continuing the story from the perspectives of two very different characters. Like its prequel, it will appeal to fans of adult fiction, especially those interested in the psychology of relationships.

The Alone Alternative

Former classmates Edward and Marianne, now 55, have lost contact and since suffered painful disruption to their home lives. When Twitter provides an opportunity for reconciliation, old passions begin to stir ... But there are obstacles in the way – not least the threat from twice-widowed Jessica, whose unstable behaviour has alarming consequences.

Set in 2012, the extraordinary weather prompts Edward and a former colleague to resurrect an idea to challenge consumerist lifestyles. The Isles of Scilly become a model for sustainability and a filming trip to the islands provides an idyllic backdrop to the unfolding romantic tensions.

The Alone Alternative explores the difficulties of starting a new relationship in midlife and is the sequel to *A Meeting of a Different Kind*. It is the third part of the Lydia series, but also stands alone as a fascinating read for both men and women.

"Authentic, stylish and sophisticated, *The Alone Alternative* engages and uplifts" – *Sharon Goodwin, Jera's Jamboree*

"...grown-up relationship fiction, written with style and intelligence ... a page-turning story populated with complex, real-life characters ..." – *Martyn Clayton, Writer*